"A very good read." **5 stars. *Amazon Reviewer***

"Another lovely romance from one of my favorite historical fiction authors." ***Blue Mood Café***

"A five star read with a delightful and unexpected epilogue!" **5 stars. *GoodReads Reviewer***

# ALSO BY ANNA CAMPBELL

Claiming the Courtesan

Untouched

Tempt the Devil

Captive of Sin

My Reckless Surrender

Midnight's Wild Passion


## The Sons of Sin Series:

Seven Nights in a Rogue's Bed

Days of Rakes and Roses

A Rake's Midnight Kiss

What a Duke Dares

A Scoundrel by Moonlight

Three Proposals and a Scandal


## The Dashing Widows Series:

The Seduction of Lord Stone

Tempting Mr. Townsend

Winning Lord West

Pursuing Lord Pascal

Charming Sir Charles

Catching Captain Nash

Lord Garson's Bride


**The Lairds Most Likely Series:**


The Laird's Willful Lass

The Laird's Christmas Kiss

The Highlander's Lost Lady

The Highlander's Defiant Captive

The Highlander's Christmas Quest

The Highlander's English Bride

The Highlander's Forbidden Mistress

The Highlander's Christmas Countess

The Highlander's Rescued Maiden

The Highlander's Christmas Lassie


**A Scandal in Mayfair Series:**


One Wicked Wish

Two Secret Sins

Three Times Tempted

Four Christmas Kisses


**Scoundrels of Mayfair Series:**


The Worst Lord in London

The Trouble with Earls

The Last Duke She'd Marry (2023)

The Duke Says I Do (2024)


**Christmas Stories:**


The Winter Wife

Her Christmas Earl

A Pirate for Christmas

Mistletoe and the Major

A Match Made in Mistletoe

The Christmas Stranger

His Christmas Cinderella (in the anthology A Grosvenor Square Christmas)

**Other Books:**

These Haunted Hearts

Stranded with the Scottish Earl

# The Trouble with Earls

Scoundrels of Mayfair Book 2

ANNA CAMPBELL

To my dear friend Claire Ravaux.

# CHAPTER ONE

*Lorimer Square, Mayfair, London, May 1817*

*C*rack!

The creak of the branch above her head warned Lady Viola Frain to jump back out of danger.

"Good heavens!" she gasped, as what looked like half an elm tree smashed down in front of her.

Half an elm tree and a complete young man, sprawled face down and unmoving amongst the chaos of leaves and twigs and splintered wood.

Viola made a note of the page that she was up to in her book before she took a cautious step closer. More of the tree might be ready to come down, although common sense told her that the branch had split because it wasn't strong enough to support the weight of the young man's body. Even with him splayed flat across the ground, she could see that he was a very tall young man. And powerfully built, with strong horseman's thighs and broad shoulders filling out his elegant dark blue coat.

He twitched and gave a heartfelt groan. At least that answered her question of whether he was alive. She slid her book into her pocket and to the sound of snapping twigs and rustling leaves, she fell to her knees beside him.

He groaned again and with difficulty rolled onto his back. Viola found herself staring into two dazed dark green eyes under level brown brows. Even someone as generally blind to male attractions as Viola noticed that he was breathtakingly handsome.

The bright spring sunshine filtering down through the leaves above revealed a face of sculpted angles. Sharp cheekbones. A straight blade of a nose with a hint of arrogance. Full lips that added earthy charm to all that chiseled purity.

"Am I dead?" His deep voice slurred, which made her fear that he'd suffered a head injury.

"I don't think so."

"You're not an angel? I feel sure you must be an angel."

She bit back the urge to laugh. The poor fellow must have a concussion. Nobody in their right mind would call her angelic. After living with her for twenty years, her family considered her nothing but a nuisance. "No, merely human."

"Delightfully human."

According to her sisters, she wasn't delightful either. "Lie still, while you get your breath back."

But it was too late. He pushed himself up until he sat opposite her. Resting his forearm on one raised knee, he surveyed her with a curiosity that she knew she didn't merit. "I'm fine."

It had been an impressive fall, but by now she guessed that he hadn't done too much damage. Apart from the possible head injury. "You must be, if you feel well enough to flirt."

That evoked a theatrical wince. Whether at her disapproving tone or because of genuine discomfort, she wasn't sure. "A judgmental angel. Although clearly I'm in heaven and not...the other place. Unless the devils down there are as pretty as peach blossom."

To her chagrin, she blushed. "You must have banged your head when you came down."

He raised an elegant hand to his forehead. All of him was elegant, she'd already noticed. If a little rumpled and dirty after his accident. He spoke with the same crisp accent that she did, and his clothing from the blue coat to the biscuit breeches and highly polished boots screamed expensive tailoring and the services of a valet.

This was the sort of fashionable, self-assured beau that she did her best to avoid. But given that he'd crashed a few inches from her toes, she couldn't abandon him yet.

Just as she took a silent moment to observe him, he was summing her up. To her regret, the haze had retreated from his eyes. Now the intent gaze made her uncomfortable. Nobody had ever devoted so much attention to her. In particular, no spectacular young men. She was used to fading into the background. Even liked it.

Viola could hardly look away. He was remarkably appealing, all long, loose limbs and ruffled tawny hair tumbling over his forehead. Wherever he went, he must set feminine hearts aflutter. Even she noticed a catch in her breath, and she was far too sensible to believe that a picturesque outer shell reflected a similar beauty of soul.

She struggled to keep her voice steady. "Perhaps you should lie down until the dizziness passes."

"I've suffered a bit of a bump, but nothing disastrous." Wry humor brightened his eyes. "They don't build elm trees like they used to."

She didn't smile. "What on earth were you doing up there?"

"That's a tale."

"I'm sure," she said dryly.

"Introductions first, I think." He rose and couldn't suppress another groan as he straightened. She'd been right about his height. From where she sat at his feet, he towered over her. "I need to reassure you that I'm here with permission. I'm not a burglar. Unless you count my desire to steal your heart."

The line was so ridiculous that she rolled her eyes. Which made him laugh. He had a nice laugh. The sort of laugh that said life provided him with a reliable supply of amusement. The sort of laugh that made one want to join in.

Viola, however, remained her usual serious self. "Does that sort of nonsense get you results?"

"You'd be surprised."

Actually, she wouldn't. This was a man who assumed with some justice that his charm would open all doors.

He extended that long-fingered hand. "May I help you out of the debris, my lady?"

She regarded his hand with suspicion. She didn't in general trust charming people, and this young man was too charming to his own good. Or hers. "I can manage, thank you."

His smile didn't falter. "I'm sure you can, but in this case you don't have to."

Which made Viola feel churlish, as well as too aware that without literally falling at her feet, this society darling would never spare her a glance.

"Thank you," she said, hearing reluctance in her voice.

He heard it, too, she knew. While he didn't comment on it, more humor quirked that sensual mouth.

She took his hand and let out a soft gasp of astonishment as heat rippled up her arm and settled in her chest, somewhere in the vicinity of her heart. Her gaze flew up to meet his and for an instant, she thought she saw her own confusion reflected in those green depths. Before she could be sure, thick brown lashes swept down to hide his reaction.

She staggered as she regained her feet. That strange sensation of her world shifting lingered. But now she came close enough to him to realize something else. Her nose wrinkled. "You've been drinking."

Perhaps his misty-eyed reaction to her wasn't due to concussion but intoxication.

He nodded without a hint of shame. "I have indeed."

"But it's only three o'clock in the afternoon."

"Time for a top-up." When he released her hand, she realized that she should have pulled free as soon as she was upright. And why was her palm tingling? Perhaps she was coming down with a chill. She'd dose herself with some elderberry syrup tonight, just in case.

He fished a battered silver flask from the inside pocket of his coat and gave it a disapproving look. "I must have landed on this. It looks like it's been through three rounds with Gentleman Jackson."

After unscrewing the top, he took a good slug of what was inside. Brandy, if Viola's nose led her right. He offered her the flask. "You?"

"No, thank you," she said, wishing she didn't sound so prim.

"As you like." With no trace of embarrassment, he recapped the flask and returned it to his pocket. "Are you going to tell me who you are? After all, you saved my life."

"Hardly." Although he could have been badly injured in the accident. The question was why he'd climbed the tree in the first place.

He ignored her unencouraging response. "Or perhaps I can guess."

The regard he directed at her was sharper than she expected, given that he'd just fallen a good twelve feet and he was under the influence of spirits. Her head swam with an echo of that strange reaction she'd felt when he took her hand.

"Lord Portdown rented this house for the season and arrived about a week ago. He has three daughters. Two have cut a dash in society, whereas the youngest sister is reputed to be a bit of a bluestocking. When I was perched in that undependable elm, a girl appeared below me carrying a book. A girl very much at home in this extravagant garden. A girl infinitely more interested in reading than the fact that Lady Juliet Frain is hosting an afternoon tea for her friends and a few lucky and eligible gentlemen."

Viola hated so much of what he said, despite most of it being true. When she arrived in London, she hadn't expected society to swoon in admiration. But even for someone as reserved as she was, it was a blow to realize that if she wasn't much interested in the beau monde, the beau monde was less interested in her. Especially when Juliet and Portia were so universally admired.

"You can't have felt too lucky, or else you wouldn't have been hiding in that tree," she pointed out with a hint of acid.

"Yes, well, there's a reason for that. But let's finish talking about you first."

"Let's not."

He ignored her, as she'd known he would. "Lady Portia is with Lady Juliet in the drawing room. Which leaves the third sister, Lady Viola. The one more interested in visiting the British Museum than Almack's."

"You're very well informed," she said through tight lips.

He shrugged. "The three Frain girls have created a splash since they arrived in Town."

"Two of them have, anyway." Juliet and Portia had been in alt since their very first ball. And for the last few days, the house had been infested with bright-eyed sprigs of society paying their respects. "I suppose you're here to add your voice to the tide of commendation."

"Watch yourself." Another of those unexpectedly sharp glances. "You sound as if the green-eyed monster has you in its grip."

"Not at all," she retorted, although while she was glad Portia and Juliet were so happy, she was getting rather sick of being the lesser Frain sister.

"And why shouldn't I call to see the young ladies who have set society on its ear? I'm as agog as the next man."

"You won't see much of Portia and Juliet from halfway up an elm tree."

"The mysterious third sister has stirred the ton's curiosity as well."

Mysterious sounded so much better than dull and standoffish, which was what her sisters called her. "And who is this clever boots who worked out my name so fast?"

He straightened and bowed with more of that striking elegance. "I'm—"

"Lord Renfrew! We feared that you'd got lost in the gardens. What a treat to find you at last!"

# CHAPTER TWO

Toby Sutton, Earl of Renfrew, only just resisted groaning in dismay when Marjorie Dimchurch's piercing soprano interrupted his encounter with this unusual and interesting girl.

Marjorie Dimwit, more like.

Struggling to hide his reluctance, he turned away from a lady as cool and refreshing as spring water to one whose determined pursuit over the last few weeks was turning him into a nervous wreck. "Miss Dimchurch," he said with a brief bow.

Marjorie minced up at the head of her usual gaggle of vapid companions. Although the other Frain girls came along as well, and at least they possessed a brain or two.

The bow reminded him that he'd lost his hat during his tumble. He looked around and realized that Lady Viola had picked it up and extended it in his direction.

"My lord?" Compared to Marjorie's affected vowels, her low voice sounded like music. He gave her a small smile – unreturned – as he accepted it.

"Goodness, Viola, what happened to the tree?" Juliet said in horror, surveying the felled branch and the chaos of twigs and leaves scattered across the once pristine lawn.

Lady Viola looked uncomfortable. She must know as well as he did that the two of them shouldn't be alone together in the far corner of the garden. But she answered promptly – and rather cleverly, he thought. But then, he'd already recognized how smart she was.

And how pretty. If in a different style from her gorgeous sisters. They were all glitter and shine, like bright sunshine. Whereas Lady Viola was more like moonlight, quiet purity and a host of intriguing secrets. Even her hair was a more subtle shade, the clear dark gold of a fine manzanilla sherry.

"Lord Renfrew was walking down the path just as the branch fell. He was very gallant and pushed me out of the way."

The small lie made it sound as if they'd only just encountered each other. It also granted him an undeserved heroic role.

"How thrilling," Marjorie sighed. "I'll have to stay close to you, my lord, in case I need rescuing, too."

Right now, he feared he was more likely to shove the henwitted harpy under a falling tree rather than away from it.

"The branch seems to have struck your face, my lord," Portia said. "There's a bruise coming up on your cheek."

"Unless Viola hit him," Juliet said, which made the others giggle.

Actually, now that he no longer focused on the fascinating Lady Viola and her unsuccessful attempts to resist his provocations, he was aware of feeling sore all over. He hadn't broken anything falling out of the tree – which was pure luck, it had been a hell of a drop. But every joint ached, and his face was stinging where it had collided with the ground.

He wasn't a vain man, but he'd dearly love a chance to look into a mirror. He couldn't be looking his best. Perhaps that explained why he'd failed to impress Lady Viola.

Perhaps he was vainer than he'd thought.

"Would you like a doctor, Lord Renfrew?" Juliet asked. "You should sit down, at least. Why not come back into the house and I'll order some tea?"

Lady Juliet was a very decided young lady, born to be a duchess. Toby however didn't like to be managed. And he definitely didn't want any bloody tea.

"Do come inside, my lord, so we can see to your comfort," Marjorie trilled. "I'll send my maid across the square to our house to fetch a special witch hazel lotion. I'm famous for my herbal remedies."

Ugh. The idea of Marjorie fluttering about him made him break out in a cold sweat. He bowed again. "I appreciate your concern, my ladies. But I'm hardly fit company after the incident. Better that I go home."

"Viola, are you unharmed?" Portia turned to check on her sister, which made Toby think more highly of her.

"A little winded, that's all," she said. He wanted to tell her that she needed to inject some more drama into her manner if she wanted to sound convincing.

"My lord, shall I send you the balm?" Marjorie batted her eyelashes at him. "It's most efficacious."

She was pretty in a banal way, although her taste for frills and furbelows did her no favors. But whenever she saw him, those limpid blue eyes turned avid with greed. She'd decided to become the next Countess of Renfrew, come what may. No matter that Toby had other ideas entirely.

"I believe my staff will attend to me, Miss Dimchurch. Otherwise, I'll call in a professional." He ignored the disappointment in Marjorie's expression and spoke to Juliet. "Thank you for your hospitality this afternoon, my lady."

If he'd known his *bête noire* was going to be here, he'd never have decided to accompany Alexander Comerford to the afternoon tea. Which would have been a pity, because then he wouldn't have made the acquaintance of the elusive youngest Frain girl. There was nothing banal about her at all. Her wide gray eyes observed the people around her, and he could almost hear her sharp brain ticking as she made sense of the various relationships.

"My pleasure, my lord," Juliet said. "Will we see you at the Plunkett ball tomorrow night?"

"Yes, I'll be there. Perhaps you'll save me a dance." Toby felt Marjorie's eyes boring into him, insisting he ask her to dance, too.

"I'd be happy to," Juliet said.

"You may be in no fit state to go out, my lord," Lady Portia said.

He laughed. "It would take a herd of elephants to do me any real damage. No puny elm tree is up to the task." He bowed to Lady Viola. "Are you also attending the Plunkett ball, my lady?"

To his surprise, she nodded. "Yes, I am."

"Perhaps you'd save me a waltz." A waltz would give him the chance to talk to her without interruption.

She looked flustered. "I..."

"Lord Renfrew saved you from a nasty crack on the head, Viola," Portia said with a hint of reproof.

"In that case, I'd be delighted, sir," Lady Viola said, looking anything but delighted. He caught

Marjorie sending her a poisonous glance, but be buggered if he was going to gratify the girl's pretensions with any special attention.

"Capital." He bowed again and put on his hat.

"You might want to ask our butler to call you a hackney, my lord," Juliet said. "Or else your appearance may alarm any acquaintances you meet in the street."

By God, he'd been right to worry. He must look like a fright. "Very kind, my lady."

He left, wishing he could have spent more time with Lady Viola before the others arrived. She was the most appealing girl that he'd encountered this season.

"Marjorie Dimchurch would give her eyeteeth to have Lord Renfrew fall at her feet, and you did it without even trying, Viola."

At Portia's laughing comment, Viola glanced up from her book and hoped to heaven that she wasn't blushing. Especially when she had nothing to blush about.

Apart from admiring a fine physique and experiencing a forbidden thrill under the observation of an intent pair of green eyes.

The three Frain girls shared the drawing room before dinner on a rare night at home. Juliet worked on her embroidery in an armchair near the fire, Portia sat at the desk, writing a letter to their aunt in Scotland, and Viola on the window seat was, as usual, reading.

Although for once, words printed on a page couldn't hold her attention. Instead of text, all she saw was the quizzical expression on a handsome young man's face, as he surveyed her from amidst a chaos of crushed leaves and splintered wood.

Lord Renfrew had called her pretty. That had surprised her, although it had been very nice. In her spectacular family, nobody noticed her. Most of the time, that was how she liked it. But something new and meltingly female made her heart leap when Lord Renfrew had looked at her as if she really was an angel.

*He'd just had a crack on the head, Viola. Not to mention that he'd been at the brandy bottle. Don't start building castles in the air.*

She bit back a sigh. Sometimes it was a trial having her feet planted so firmly on the ground.

"I'm just glad he wasn't seriously hurt when he hit the ground," she said with her characteristic equanimity. Once their visitors had gone, she'd told her sisters the truth about Lord Renfrew's accident.

"But what on earth was he doing up a tree in the first place? It seems most bizarre." With a disapproving tsk, Juliet put her sewing aside. "Is he interested in botany?"

Portia responded with a derisive snort. "From what I've heard, he's only interested in chasing lightskirts and making a splash around town as a reprobate."

"If he's such bad ton, why on earth did you invite him to tea?" Viola asked.

Her sisters were very proper, and they only associated with the most respectable gentlemen. As they both intended to make good matches this season, they needed to preserve pristine reputations. For heaven's sake, if everything went to plan, Juliet would most likely be a duchess before August.

Familiar disapproval flattened Juliet's lips. She possessed a classic blonde beauty that had already gained her a proposal from one duke and was likely to gain her another before too long. "We didn't invite him. Alexander Comerford turned up with Renfrew in tow. I think they'd been drinking."

Viola knew for a fact that Renfrew had been fuddled, but she kept that to herself.

Portia frowned. "Anyway, he's not really bad ton. If he was, Marjorie wouldn't be so determined to nab him. I've heard about numerous scrapes and escapades, and he certainly enjoys a good time, but I doubt there's any genuine vice in him. He inherited the title three years ago, after what I gather was a pretty austere childhood. The general opinion seems to be that he's blowing off steam rather than doing much genuine harm."

"That doesn't mean his behavior won't coarsen as he sinks deeper into vice," Juliet said with a sniff of disapproval.

"You're not a duchess yet," Portia said dryly. "It's too early to start looking down your nose at lesser beings, Your Grace."

The jibe left Juliet looking annoyed. Since the death of her fiancé, the Duke of Bolton, her sense of humor had deserted her. Life for Juliet had become earnest and austere. It was a pity. Especially as no amount of proper behavior would resurrect the late duke from his untimely grave. "Renfrew isn't the sort of fellow Father approves of."

"That only makes him more appealing," Portia snapped back.

"Father approves of the Duke of Granville," Juliet said stiffly, mentioning her most persistent suitor. The family – in fact, the entire beau monde – expected a proposal to eventuate before the season was over.

Portia sighed. "Granville is the dullest dog in creation."

"Don't you dare insult a good man, Portia Frain. You're just jealous."

"I am not. If you choose to marry an almighty bore, you're welcome to him."

Viola stopped paying attention. Her sisters were inclined to squabble. She didn't mind, because these days a good wrangle with her younger sister was the only time that Juliet ever showed any trace of her former vivacity.

While Viola pretended to go back to her book, her mind was busy sifting what she'd learned about Lord Renfrew. Like Portia, she'd sensed high spirits, but no wickedness. Although what did she know of rakes and roués?

He'd been charming. And interesting in a way that no other young man of her acquaintance was. He'd looked at her as if he actually saw her.

Even better, he'd asked her to dance at the Plunkett ball tomorrow night. It was absurd to get too excited about that, because no doubt he'd regret making the offer once he met her again. He was vital and dashing and clearly accustomed to the company of women much more experienced and brazen than bookish Viola Frain.

But not even that repressive voice inside her head could stifle her anticipation at the thought of Lord Renfrew taking her into his arms and whirling her around a crowded dance floor. He'd specified a waltz, too, so they'd be able to talk without having to change partners.

So far, large social events in London had proven a trial. But just this once, Viola found herself looking forward to attending a ball.

Tomorrow night couldn't come soon enough.

"What do you know about Lord Portdown's daughters?" Toby asked with manufactured nonchalance, as he raised a glass of excellent port to his lips.

He and his cousin, Leighton Anstey, Lord Shelburn, were alone in Leighton's dining room in Grosvenor Square. They'd just eaten an excellent dinner, presided over by his host's wife of a year, Kate.

Kate was an unusual creature, wealthy in her own right and the owner of several prosperous cotton mills in the Midlands. Most nights, she'd join her husband for a glass of port. But right now, she was upstairs fussing over their three-month-old son Richard, who wasn't the world's best sleeper.

Leighton burst out laughing. "Good Lord, those girls aren't your usual fodder. I'm not sure you're up to their standards, old man."

Toby resisted the urge to bristle and cast an eye around the opulent room to avoid meeting his cousin's regard. He'd delayed the factfinding that brought him to call on the Shelburns until he had Leighton to himself. Kate was clever and far too perceptive and would instantly twig to his interest in the Frain girl. With Leighton, he might have a chance of passing off his questions as idle curiosity.

Except Leighton was clever, too, and clearly knew something was up.

Toby set the crystal glass on the mahogany table and stared down into the ruby wine as if he'd never seen port before. Which was a thousand miles from the truth. It did him no credit, but he'd seen more of port, not to mention its close friends, brandy and claret and champagne, than was good for a fellow.

One of the reasons that he'd climbed that damned unreliable elm in Lord Portdown's garden this afternoon was that he'd been a little tipsy. His liquor-fuzzed mind had decided that the unconventional hiding place beat facing down a horde of well-bred young ladies and taking his leave of them like a sensible man.

But then, nobody who knew Tobias Sutton would ever call him a sensible man.

"I'm considered a catch," Toby said, surprised at the effort it took to sound like his careless self.

"Marjorie Dimchurch thinks so at least," Leighton said with another laugh.

Toby hid a shudder. She did indeed. Although he probably should thank her. If he hadn't climbed a tree half-seas-over to escape her relentless pursuit, he wouldn't have tumbled down at the lovely Lady Viola's feet.

He was covered in bruises and he had an impressive black eye. Holt, his valet had gone quite white tonight when he'd helped Toby to dress. Although to be honest that could have been lingering effects from noting Toby's appearance when his master arrived home.

"I'm glad to provide you with a modicum of amusement," he said stiffly.

The uncharacteristic tone had Leighton sobering and shooting him a searching look. "Lady Juliet, the eldest daughter, was to marry the Duke of Bolton, but the fool got himself run over by a dray at his estate two years ago. This season, the gossip is that the Duke of Granville means to offer for her. She's far too grand for a rapscallion like you."

Toby bit his lip to stifle a protest at his cousin's unflattering description. After all, he was a rapscallion. He'd worked like a devil to earn his reputation as a rattlepated scoundrel who sneered at narrow-minded morality.

When had he stopped relishing his notoriety? He had a feeling that it might have been the moment he opened dazed eyes and met a limpid gray gaze, surveying him as he sprawled amongst the remains of Lord Portdown's elm tree.

"Not her."

"Lady Portia, then? She's not so high in the instep, but I still can't see you fitting her idea of a husband."

"Who said anything about marriage?"

Leighton ignored the interruption. As his elder by six years, Leighton was used to depressing his pretensions. "She's active in charitable work. Her interests are too lofty for her to look fondly on a fribble like you."

"You're damned frank, cuz."

Leighton shrugged. "You have plenty of good qualities, although you're too lazy to make the best of them. You're no fool, when you take the time to shift your mind from mischief, and I like that you don't hold a grudge."

"Lucky for you," Toby muttered, not much liking what he heard. "At least nobody ever called me the worst lord in London."

"Yes, well, that was in the bad old days before I fell in love with a good woman." His eyes sharpened. "Actually now I think of it, Portia is a good woman. None better. Perhaps she might make you a fine wife. You'll have to clean up your act, though. She won't tolerate an idler who devotes his life to drinking and gambling and chasing shameless hussies. You'll need to show her that you've got some substance."

Actually, Toby wasn't sure that he did possess much substance. Something about Viola's assessing stare had quashed any self-deception about his wasteful lifestyle.

Leighton lifted the half-full decanter. "More port?"

Most – all – of the time, he'd say yes. But he was feeling out of sorts. Perhaps it was his cousin's assessment of his unsuitability for a decent woman. Perhaps it was the aftereffects of his fall. Perhaps it was that for once, he recognized that today he'd had more than enough to drink already. He shook his head. "No, thank you."

"Good Lord, are you sick?"

"No," he said with a hint of a snap. "But perhaps there's more to me than you give me credit for."

Leighton frowned. "Now I really am worried. You've always rather basked in your reputation for dissipation. Aren't you feeling well?"

"I'm perfectly fine," he grated out. "Although I'd be better, if every word out of your mouth wasn't a deuced insult."

He waited for Leighton to mock him anew, but his cousin sent him a rueful smile. "Sorry, old chum. You usually don't mind a bit of ribbing. If you're interested in Portia Frain, go for her. Just one small piece of advice – Lord Portdown has a mania for Shakespeare. If you want to get the girl's pater onside, you might brush up on your reading."

That was no surprise to hear. Even someone as illiterate as Toby had noted that the Frain girls' names indicated a family obsession with the Bard.

He shifted uncomfortably under Leighton's focused gaze. "I'm not going to court Lady Portia."

Although his cousin would find his sudden interest in Lady Viola more inexplicable than him setting his sights on the philanthropic Lady Portia. Before meeting Viola, he would have scoffed, too. She wasn't at all the type of girl who grabbed his attention. Not least because the pursuit of an aristocratic virgin led straight into the parson's mousetrap.

"If you say so." Leighton lifted the decanter, before putting it down without refilling his glass. Once Leighton had been as wild as Toby. Wilder. And not that long ago either. But he'd changed since marrying Kate.

Toby might want to bemoan that, but he'd never seen his cousin so happy. Leighton had become the man that he was always meant to be. Only a curmudgeon would miss the uproarious companion that he'd once been.

Silence reigned for an interval, while Toby settled his prickly temper. His cousin was right. Most of the time, he took mockery in his stride. After all, he was as aware as the next man that he was no example of rectitude.

Eventually he said, "There's another girl in the family."

"The bluestocking?" Leighton looked more surprised than ever. "Nobody's seen much of her."

"I met her this afternoon." Which was one way to describe toppling out of a tree and landing at the chit's feet, he supposed. "Portia and Juliet hosted an afternoon tea at the Lorimer Square house. I wasn't invited, but I went along with Alexander Comerford, because I didn't have anything else to do."

Which he was grimly aware summed up most of his wayward, if pleasurable life.

"Is she pretty?" Leighton paused and answered his own question. "I suppose she must be. Juliet and Portia are beauties."

"Yes, she's pretty." Which didn't do Viola justice.

Although it wasn't just her looks, but her contained calmness that had attracted his notice.

She hadn't become hysterical when he'd nearly landed on top of her. No squealing. No giggling. She hadn't even been terrifically disapproving, although she hadn't missed that he'd been drinking.

Something in his lackadaisical character hungered for more of that tranquility. It was as if he'd spent his whole twenty-seven years running from an unseen enemy, and Lady Viola Frain offered him a place of sweet refuge.

He wanted her. Of course he did. She was a lovely girl, and he was a rascal with an eye for a comely female. But the surprise was how much her ease with herself and her world made him feel at ease with himself.

Leighton remained thoughtful. "But quiet."

"Self-possessed, rather."

"Hmm." Leighton sounded unconvinced. "Perhaps you're interested, because she's a change from the saucy wenches who have taken your fancy until now."

"She is different. And I haven't said I'm interested."

"But you are."

"Maybe."

"You don't think she might...bore you?"

Actually, he was more afraid that he might bore her. Which was a new experience. Until now, he'd never lacked confidence with the opposite sex. But something about Viola Frain's discerning silver stare told him that she held him to a higher standard. "She's not...what you expect."

"Bookish. Intellectual. Missish."

He found himself smiling. "Not missish. Bookish definitely. No fool, that's for certain." He paused. "What?"

"Nothing." Leighton regarded him with an arrested expression.

"No, say it. Whatever it is." Once more, Toby shifted on his chair. "You usually don't pull your punches. You certainly haven't tonight. You don't think I'm smart enough for her, do you?"

"You're smart. I've already said that. Even if you'd rather pickle those sharp wits in brandy than pick up a book now and again. It's just that I've never heard you talk like this about a girl. You sound as if you took the time to notice more than her tits."

To Toby's chagrin, heat prickled in his cheeks. When he hadn't blushed since he was in the nursery. Despite doing plenty of things over the years that ought to make him hang his head in shame.

Worse, his eagle-eyed cousin would notice his discomfort. He waited for more digs. They weren't long in coming. "You didn't notice her bosom? I don't believe it."

Of course he had. He might have suffered a crack on the brainbox, but he wasn't dead. Very nice her breasts had been, too. Not the opulent, overflowing flesh he usually found irresistible, but plenty to fill out that modest blue bodice in a most satisfactory manner.

While he and Leighton had often discussed a mistress's abundant charms, this time for some inexplicable reason, he wasn't prepared to assure his cousin that Lady Viola had nothing to be ashamed of in that department. What the devil was wrong with him? Falling out of that tree must have done more damage than he'd realized. Perhaps when he left here, he should go home for an early night, instead of heading out in search of nefarious amusement as was his habit.

"She's a lady," he said.

Leighton looked more astonished by the second. And he'd spent most of this conversation looking astonished. "Toby, old man, I think you're a goner."

Toby's hand clenched into a fist on the polished wood. There was a knowing quality in his cousin's expression that made him dearly long to punch Leighton's lights out. "A man can admire a pretty girl."

"He can."

Toby did. Often. Even chaste, blue-blooded girls who wouldn't come to his bed without first making a trip up the aisle.

As his cousin said, he was canny. Certainly canny enough to know where he could dally without getting into trouble. But what had happened today felt different. He wasn't sure what it was, but it had stopped him in his tracks with a bump harder than dropping on his arse. "It doesn't mean anything."

"It doesn't have to."

Another awkward silence. There had been a few of those this evening, too, whereas he and his cousin had always been on the best of terms.

"I'd like a look at this girl," Leighton said at last.

"If you're going to the Plunkett ball, you'll see her."

Leighton would see her waltzing with Toby. That thought cheered him up, although perhaps concussion was to blame for his glowing memory of Lady Viola. When he met her again, maybe he'd see her as nothing so exceptional. That strange buzz – more than sexual awareness, although sexual awareness was a large part of it – he'd felt in her presence would prove a passing illusion.

He rather hoped that was the case. Otherwise, what had happened this afternoon augured a major change in a life that over the last few years had provided great enjoyment.

"I'll watch out for her. If she's turned you into a blithering idiot, she mustn't be quite the shrinking violet I've heard she is."

Toby bit back the urge to respond with a heated defense of the lady. Partly because he suspected that Leighton wanted just that.

Instead, he spoke with a composure worthy of Lady Viola Frain herself. "You'll see."

# CHAPTER THREE

oby approached the Plunkett ball with a giddy expectation that he couldn't remember feeling since he was a miserable schoolboy at Eton praying for the holidays to come. Being a dunce when your father was lauded as one of the cleverest men in England wasn't much fun.

Not that life at Brazey Castle was any picnic either. But at least there he could get outside into the stables and the woods, places where he could avoid his sire's ever-critical eye.

For once, alcohol had nothing to do with his high spirits. No, what made his heart gallop with elation tonight was the promise of seeing Viola Frain again. Even more, holding her in his arms for a waltz. Since meeting her yesterday, he'd hardly thought of anything else.

He arrived at the ball with his cousin and Kate, who despite her middle-class origins, fitted into society with surprising ease. Perhaps because she observed the ton's antics with an ironic detachment that impressed the beau monde.

In Toby's experience, an air of slight distance added to one's appeal. By God, wasn't he a victim of that himself? He'd offered Marjorie Dimwit not one hint of encouragement. Now she pursued him like a hound pursued a fox.

Lady Viola had responded to him with ironic detachment, too, when most girls strove to gain and keep his attention. Was that why he was interested? Was that what his attraction boiled down to? Bruised vanity? Lady Viola didn't want him, which made him want her? He didn't like to think that he was so shallow, but he feared he might be.

So as he surveyed the dazzling, shifting crowd that filled the ballroom, he tried to temper his anticipation. He and Lady Viola had met in extraordinary circumstances, when he'd just suffered a knock on the head. Perhaps once he saw her tonight, she wouldn't strike him as anything out of the ordinary.

His gaze slid over Alexander Comerford, here with the rest of his family. The Halstons. The Tierneys. The Colvilles.

No sign of Marjorie, thank goodness. No sign of the woman he sought either.

Had Viola changed her mind about attending the ball? A great weight of disappointment settled in his gut, way out of proportion with the situation. He began to wish that he'd joined Leighton in a brandy before they left Anstey House.

Juliet, looking as calm and collected as ever, was dancing with the Duke of Granville. Portia shared a set with Lord Edgecombe. Both girls were beautiful and very much admired, but neither sparked Toby's interest.

"Goodness me, what a crush." Kate waved her pretty silk fan with a lazy nonchalance worthy of the duchess that Juliet hoped to become. "Remind me again why we came."

"Don't pretend that you don't love it. Nobody will believe you." Affection laced Leighton's voice, as he took his wife's arm. "We came so that I can show off the loveliest woman in London."

Kate's gaze softened as it leveled on her husband. "That's the perfect answer."

Toby had never overcome his surprise to see his disreputable cousin become such a devoted husband and father. Nor was he alone in his wonder. The marriage last year of one of the kingdom's most eligible and elusive bachelors to a mill owner from Derbyshire had sent shock erupting through society. But there was no doubting the closeness that Lord and Lady Shelburn enjoyed.

"Honestly, you two are so sweet, you make my teeth hurt," he said, which made his cousins laugh.

At that moment, the crowd parted to reveal Lady Viola across the huge room, partnering Ivor Bilson. The chatter and laughter and music faded to nothing under the thunderous beat of Toby's heart. As did whatever his cousins said next.

All he was aware of was the girl. She appeared prettier now than she'd been yesterday afternoon. Yesterday afternoon, he'd thought she was the prettiest girl he'd ever seen. A pleasurable shock jarred him, as he noted how she shone, even in this glittering milieu.

He willed her to look at him, to acknowledge that they'd made a connection out of the usual. If a gaze could burn, she should feel the heat of his eyes on her skin.

Yesterday she'd worn a modest, dark blue merino gown. Today she became a stranger in spangled white sarsenet. The dress was in the first stare of fashion, and it revealed the creamy skin of her full bosom and graceful arms. Her sherry-colored hair was caught up in a mass of curls under a gold band.

Lady Viola Frain didn't look at all like a bookish hermit. She looked as good as – better than – any of the other young ladies prancing around the dance floor. Toby could almost regret that her beauty was no longer his secret.

He fought the urge to stride over and claim her. Something primitive inside him insisted that she shouldn't be holding that numbskull Bilson's hand as they danced. She shouldn't be smiling at the fellow as if she enjoyed his conversation, when everyone knew that the blockhead only ever talked about fishing and hunting. What interest could a clever woman have in fishing and hunting?

Then damn him if she didn't look up and meet Toby's eyes. All the more gratifying, her soft pink mouth curved up in a pleased smile. From the first, he'd noticed how kissable those lips were.

Warmth flooded him, and he forgot all about Ivor Bilson. He'd feared that yesterday he hadn't made a positive impression. But that smile hinted that she was glad to see him.

He found himself smiling back like he'd just won a fortune on a racehorse.

Good Lord, he hoped to hell that he didn't look like a gormless oaf. He feared that he might. And sophisticated, jaded Toby Sutton always preserved his rakish aplomb.

Well, perhaps not when he tumbled out of dashed treacherous trees in front of a lovely girl.

And it seemed not when he saw that lovely girl again across a crowded room.

To his chagrin, she turned back to Ivor Bilson, still smiling. It was odd, he and Bilson had always been boon companions. Toby had no idea why he felt a sudden impulse to knock the clodpoll on his arse.

"That's Lady Viola over there with Ivor Bilson," Kate said to Leighton. "Did you see her, Toby?"

Toby considered himself quite the Town buck, so it was an unpleasant shock to feel his cheeks heat, as if he were a bashful country bumpkin. He sent Leighton a killing glare. "You told Kate about my interest in Lady Viola?"

Leighton shrugged. "I tell Kate everything. You know that."

"Can't a man express idle curiosity about an attractive girl without the whole world pricking up its ears?" He cursed himself for opening his damned fool mouth last night.

"Apparently not." Kate's laughing hazel gaze settled on him. "Especially when the young man is for once showing an ounce of good taste. I met Lady Viola last week at the Halstons' and I was most impressed. Then I heard a strange story today at Gunther's, about you turning up in the nick of time to save her from a falling tree. You emerged from the tale as quite the hero. I was surprised you kept your exploits to yourself. You acted with credit, when I'm more used to hearing about you chasing ballet dancers or infesting some gaming hell."

Toby shifted in more discomfort, although apart from the inaccurate description of his meeting with Lady Viola, the rest of what Kate said was perfectly true. "Blasted gossiping women."

"You told me you were black and blue because you'd been at your boxing salon and you'd caught the worst of a sparring match," Leighton said.

"I lied."

"Don't be modest, cuz." Leighton's tone was mocking. "It's nice to learn that you've retained a touch of chivalry, despite all your hare-brained adventures in the stews."

Toby was well aware that neither Kate nor Leighton believed a word of the story about him turning up like Sir Galahad to rescue a maiden in distress. "You're talking a dashed load of nonsense." He frowned as he remembered something else Kate had said. "And a fellow should be allowed to sow a few wild oats without people sneering at him. You're a fine one to talk about me kicking up my heels, Kate. It's not as if you married a pattern card of respectability."

Kate, too, had dabbled in scandal, before she'd wed his cousin and made him forget what it was like to be young and rich and irresponsible in the fleshpots of London.

She bestowed an amused glance on her husband. "Oh, don't shatter my delusions, you wicked boy."

Her sarcasm made Leighton laugh and lift her gloved hand to his lips for a quick kiss before he turned to Toby. "When I finally stumbled across Kate, I had the brains to recognize the true diamond amongst all the paste. I'm wondering if perhaps you have as well."

Toby's frown deepened into a scowl. Why the devil had he asked Leighton about Viola? Except that he'd been eaten up with questions from the moment he opened his eyes to see her peering down at him. And Leighton was always up with the latest Town tattle. Toby might have called Kate a gossip, but her husband was the one who really kept current with the rumors.

"You can stow all your speculation and judgements and snickering, the two of you. A few inquiries don't mean I'm about to propose. I'm not looking for a wife. I'm perfectly happy as I am. A man can have a jolly good time with a wanton woman, I'd like to remind you. Even if she isn't eligible to become the Countess of Renfrew. Especially if she isn't eligible to become the Countess of Renfrew."

He saw that his heated response did nothing to dispel his cousins' curiosity. By God, he wasn't going to hang around to provide them with further diversion.

With a growl, he swung away to locate more congenial company. Company that thought Toby Sutton was a fine, fun fellow. Company that saw no reason for young Lord Renfrew to change his decadent ways.

Toby hadn't settled down by the time the first waltz came around. Nor had two glasses of champagne done much to restore his good humor.

Damn Kate and Leighton for making him the butt of their jokes. Although he was reluctantly aware that most of his grumpiness stemmed from the fact that Lady Viola Frain wasn't acting like a reclusive bluestocking. She'd had a partner for every set. And those partners had all been society's most sought-after bachelors. She'd also appeared willing to enjoy herself, smiling and talking and generally acting as if the world could provide no greater pleasure than the Plunkett ball. After that first quick glance in his direction, she hadn't spared Toby an ounce of attention.

He'd like to pretend that he'd been equally unaware of her, but his gaze kept turning in the direction of the slender blonde and whatever gentleman goggled enchanted into her sparkling eyes.

Toby had been so bamboozled that he'd found himself inveigled into dancing with Marjorie. At least it was a cotillion, and they'd changed partners on a regular basis. But he was wary of giving the bumptious chit any encouragement.

Now he headed toward Lady Viola, where she stood with her sisters and that stuck-up prig, the Duke of Granville. Despite all Toby's brave claims to a lack of emotional involvement in this meeting, his heart raced with anticipation. This whole night had been an interminable wait. But at last he could approach the girl whose image had haunted him since yesterday.

He watched Lady Juliet say something, before all four people turned to observe his advance. The two older Frain girls regarded him with similar unreadable expressions. He wasn't surprised. He expected downright disapproval, after he'd made such a bear's den out of their gathering yesterday.

Granville surveyed him with frosty hauteur, but that didn't mean much. He looked at everyone that way. Even the woman who gossip predicted that he'd propose to before the end of the season. Blasted hoity-toity bastard he was.

Then Toby met Lady Viola's eyes, and nothing else mattered.

If anyone had asked him, he would have said that his life offered everything he wanted. At last. His disapproving swine of a pater – he recognized the type in Granville – had held him on a leash short enough to strangle him. But these last few years, he'd done just as he bloody well liked.

Every time he swived a reckless widow or an eager actress, or he bet a thousand on the turn of a card, he addressed a loud "fuck you" to the old man resting unlamented in the family vault.

But only now as he let Lady Viola's presence seep into his soul did he recognize quite how noisy his world was. And most – all – of that noise was meaningless clamor. Whereas now, the hubbub receded and he felt at peace in a way that he never had before.

Even more bizarre, while he'd never have said peace was something he sought, it soothed him like gentle music. He'd spent the last few years doing his best to make up for the restrictions of his childhood and youth. He'd craved excitement. If he didn't find it, he created it.

When he met Viola Frain's translucent gray gaze, he admitted just what a lot of hard work it required to be such a scandalous libertine.

He hated to credit his sod of a cousin with any special insight, but Leighton was right about Lady Viola being a treasure. A diamond indeed. With a magic that Toby found impossible to resist.

He felt his lips curve in an elated smile. His heart galloped so fast that it made his head swim.

Viola looked pleased to see him, too. He tried to forget that she'd also looked pleased to see all her other partners.

"Lady Viola, I believe this is our waltz." Sounding like his usual urbane self took an almighty effort. Even then, he only remembered to bow and acknowledge the other people in the group at the last minute. "Lady Juliet, Lady Portia, Your Grace."

"Good evening, Lord Renfrew." Juliet held out her hand. "Are you recovered from your accident?"

He took her hand and bowed again. "No ill effects at all, thank you."

That wasn't entirely true. Last night going to bed, he'd been sore and stiff. The bruising on his face had faded a little, but remained noticeable. More worrying, he suspected the results of his fall included a sudden and powerful interest in the kind of virtuous young lady who had always been out of bounds.

"I'm glad," Lady Portia said. "Your Grace, Lord Renfrew saved my younger sister from a falling branch in our garden yesterday."

"Quite the knight in shining armor, Renfrew," Granville said in the superior drawl that provided an unpleasant reminder of Toby's martinet of a father. A chill slithered down his backbone at the memory.

"Just in the right place at the right time," he bit out, as he battled the urge to punch His Grace's aquiline beak.

The musicians began to scrape away at the introduction to the waltz, thank heaven. He already trod on thin ice with the Frain girls. If he assaulted Juliet's swain, he doubted that he'd ever see Viola again.

He turned to her where she stood quietly at her oldest sister's side. "Shall we, Lady Viola?"

She extended her hand and as his fingers curled around hers, his wayward heart performed a triple somersault. A blast of heat threatened to incinerate him. Good God, they were both wearing gloves. Even so, the contact left him reeling.

Through his agitation, he barely heard her murmured agreement. He was too overcome to notice whether she reacted to that incendiary touch. Which was a pity. He'd dearly love to know that he didn't weather this particular storm alone.

By the time his vision cleared, Lady Viola looked calm and cool and as if dancing with him was nothing out of the ordinary.

"You were rather short with His Grace." She regarded him curiously. "Don't you like him?"

Toby turned to face her and slid his arm around her slender waist. Another tidal wave of response.

By Jericho, what was the matter with him? No girl had ever put him in such a flap. Not even Sally Brown, the buxom dairymaid on his father's estate who had shown a confused, unhappy boy the joy he could find in a willing lover's arms.

More puzzling, Viola Frain was a girl who rank and reputation placed out of his reach, unless he intended to marry her. This dance tonight would be as far as they could go.

He'd never before kicked against the restrictions that society placed around innocent young ladies. But he kicked now. Yesterday, if for far too short an interval, he'd had Viola to himself, unobserved, uninterrupted. He wanted that again. Not just for a few minutes but for hours. Instead, propriety offered him a single waltz.

Right now, he wasted his chance, staring down at the girl as if pole-axed. If a waltz was all he had, he needed to take advantage of the opportunity. She'd said something about that damned cardboard autocrat Granville, hadn't she? "The duke?"

Around them, other couples circled in time to the music. He caught Kate's interested glance, as she glided past in Leighton's embrace. Without conscious volition, Toby's feet began to move to the melody.

Lady Viola followed straightaway, sweet as sugar. It was no surprise. He'd known even when his head was clanging after his fall that he and this lovely creature were physically compatible. Sally had had enough successors for him to recognize a woman who promised to match him.

"Yes. Most people fawn over him, but you went as stiff as a poker and almost gave him the cut direct."

Toby was in such a spin, and not because of the music, that he answered sincerely and without the usual palaver that he gave a woman when she attempted to pry beneath his rakish exterior. "The sod reminds me of my father."

She frowned and stared into his eyes, as he cursed his big mouth. Usually, he didn't care whether he impressed people or not. In fact, when it came to the high sticklers, he did his best to set them on their ears. But he wanted Lady Viola to admire him. Damn it, to like him. Bleating about his miserable childhood wasn't likely to add to his appeal.

"You didn't get along with your father?"

"No," he said shortly.

"But…but you're so charming," she said and for the first time missed a step.

Feeling happier, Toby caught her closer to save her from stumbling. Or at least so he would claim if she objected.

She didn't object, just kept watching him with an expression hinting that she found him as compelling as he found her.

"I'm glad you think so. I think you're charming, too, by the way. That's a dashed becoming gown."

"Thank you. Portia made me buy it."

"Three cheers for Lady Portia."

That made her smile. "She's a darling. Do you have brothers and sisters?"

"No, I'm an only child."

Thank heaven. He wouldn't have wished the hell of his upbringing on another soul.

She went back to looking concerned. "Perhaps that's why your father was so hard on you."

Toby's jaw hardened to rock. "I'd rather talk about your family."

"You think I'm prying. I'm sorry. I'm not very good at small talk. Juliet despairs of me."

"No, not at all." What he felt was that she threatened to expose all his shameful secrets and leave him eviscerated. That wasn't the way to win her. He spun her around in a swift turn, hoping to distract her. "Although that's not entirely true. I want to talk about you."

The surprise widening those soft gray eyes made him want to kick every single person who had ever overlooked this gorgeous creature. "I'm not very interesting."

"Yes, you are."

The twitch of her lips reminded him that he'd like to kiss her. "Well, I am if you're another bookworm. But I'm not the sort of girl dashing gentlemen want to talk to."

"Rubbish. I'm a dashing gentleman and I'm having a marvelous time." As long as they stayed far away from the subject of his father.

She studied him. "I'm glad."

Toby wasn't finished. "All the other gentlemen who danced with you were equally enthralled."

Her color rose. "Were you watching?"

"Of course I was. I think you're the prettiest girl here."

"Oh."

He dared to bring her a fraction closer. The air was thick with the scent of lilies and orchids massed in vases. And a thousand melting candles, not to mention a crowd doused in every perfume known to man. The night was warm, too, adding a hint of aristocratic perspiration to the sickly floral fug.

So it seemed unlikely that when he inhaled, he caught a hint of something fresh and light. But he would swear that he did. In this cosmopolitan crowd, Viola smelled like a spring garden. She was well named for one of the fairest flowers of all.

"I thought you were pretty yesterday, too."

"Yesterday you'd suffered an almighty bang on the head."

He laughed. Most of the girls he knew were inclined to lap up his compliments. Viola responded to his flattery with a suspicion that amused him, even as it touched him. Both Portia and Juliet drew the eye, but he was discovering that the greatest beauty was more subtle. "I'm perfectly fine tonight."

She didn't smile. "Are you sure you're all right? That was a long drop to the ground."

"I haven't seen things the same way since," he dared to say.

"You've got double vision?"

This time, his laugh was loud enough to draw attention. "No, you absurd and wonderful girl. I met you, and I haven't thought of anything else."

Instead of looking gratified, disapproval darkened her expression. "You're flirting with me."

Another delighted smile toyed with his lips. She sounded as if she accused him of murder. "Most definitely."

"You don't have to."

"No, but it's fun. Especially when right now, you look as if you're torn between kissing me and hitting me with your fan."

"You're...you're teasing me. You know I can't kiss you."

He'd managed to gain some control over himself since that startling moment when heat had engulfed him, just because she held his hand. But the mere sound of that husky voice saying "kiss" was enough to put him in a lather again.

Most uppercrust girls had a precise accent. But something about the way Viola bit off the "K" and lingered on the "S" had him imagining her under him in a bed. Where he'd do a damn sight more than just kiss her, by Jupiter.

"What?" she said, as his hand on her back coaxed her nearer. That sumptuous bosom under its covering of sparkly material shifted with every breath she took. He knew that he was a cad to pay attention, but he was a man. He couldn't help it.

"What what?"

"You look..."

"Like I want to kiss you?" Not to mention the rest. He couldn't mention the rest. She ought to slap his face for what he was thinking right now. "I do."

Toby spoke on a groan. He braced for her to tell him to behave himself, but instead her cheeks turned a beguiling pink and her until-now forthright gaze fluttered away from his.

She'd blushed before, when he'd admitted how closely he observed her. Now she was so flustered, she looked completely bewildered. Such a delicious contrast with her self-possession when they'd met.

"Lord Renfrew..."

"You're about to tell me that the idea appals you."

To his surprise – and wicked satisfaction – she shook her head. "No, I'm not. Although it should."

Excitement slammed his heart against his ribs. Urgency vibrated in his voice. "Can I take you out onto the terrace?"

"I can't kiss you in the middle of a ball. Even on the terrace."

She couldn't. He recognized that. "We could go into the garden," he said hopefully.

Viola shook her head. "No, we can't. You know we can't. And Juliet is looking daggers at us. You're holding me too tight."

He glanced across to where Juliet circled the room in the arms of that dry stick Granville. The oldest Frain sister was indeed glaring.

This time, there was no suppressing Toby's groan, but he eased his grip. "This is why I never chase girls from good families."

Viola looked ruffled, but she'd come back to herself enough to cast him a quelling glance. "Because you can't immediately get your own way?"

"Because when a fellow meets a girl he likes as much as I like you, he ought to be able to kiss her. It's deuced unnatural to expect anything else."

She didn't look overwhelmed to hear that he liked her. "But society is constructed from unnatural rules. Otherwise we'd all be living in mud huts."

"A mud hut with you would be paradise."

That made her snort. "I doubt it. And you're still too close."

"Do you really think so?"

"The ton thinks so." That lush pink mouth pursed in a way that only made the promise of kisses more irresistible.

He had no right to create a scandal. No real wish to, either. When he held Viola in his arms, he suffered the strangest urge to protect her from all harm. As a rule, he was as chivalrous as the next man. But this extended beyond a vague notion of honoring fragile womanhood to something that felt like compulsion.

As the musicians embarked on the coda to the waltz, he made himself pull back. Which was a strain when every masculine instinct urged him nearer. And nearer again.

But as Lady Viola had pointed out in that damned precise accent that shouldn't be so arousing, but somehow was, they lived in a world where a virile young man didn't fling the lady of his choice across his shoulder. He couldn't rush her behind the nearest rock to have his wicked way.

More was the pity.

They continued without speaking. Toby realized with shockingly powerful regret that their dance came to an end. While he'd very much enjoyed talking to her and even more, he'd enjoyed touching her, he'd wasted time. He should be making plans to see her again.

Then something that she'd said struck him. "Immediately?"

"What?"

"Immediately. You said I couldn't expect to get my own way immediately. Does that mean I might get my own way in the long run?"

That made her laugh. He liked it when she laughed. She seemed altogether more approachable. Approachable meant attainable.

Attainable got his vote.

"You're incorrigible, my lord."

"I live in hope." He paused. The waltz was reaching its end. "Will you come out on the terrace?"

"I won't kiss you."

"Not tonight, anyway."

"Plague take you, I'm not saying no just to put off the evil occasion."

He smiled at her. "So you will kiss me tonight?" Before she could scold him again, although her scolding struck his ears as sweeter than the most extravagant praise from anyone else he could think of, he spoke in a low, earnest voice. "Please don't leave me. Give me another few minutes."

Another hour. Hell, another year. He'd never known anyone like Lady Viola Frain. Meeting her was like opening the cover of a fascinating book. While he'd never been the slightest bit bookish, he knew that this time, the story would captivate him to the end.

She studied him. "I've promised the next dance to Alexander Comerford."

The music had stopped, and while Toby no longer whirled her around the room, he kept hold of her hand and waist. She was vividly conscious of the warmth of that contact. Around them, the other dancers dispersed as they went in search of their next partners.

"He's already danced with you once tonight."

"You have been watching."

"I told you I did."

Because she looked faintly troubled, he braced for her to abandon him, but after a second, she nodded. "Five minutes on the terrace, just to catch a breath of air. And no flirting."

With a triumphant smile, he led her toward the French doors. A clever girl like Viola would notice that he made no promises about flirting.

After all, wasn't he incorrigible?

# CHAPTER FOUR

*V*iola very deliberately didn't catch Juliet's eye, as Lord Renfrew led her outside into a lovely night. It wasn't forbidden for a girl to go out onto the terrace with a young man, as long as she didn't linger and she remained in view of other people.

But this young man had a reputation for being trouble. Not to mention that he seemed rather preoccupied with kissing.

Renfrew settled against the edge of the balustrade and drew her forward to stand beside him. They looked down into a garden turned into an oriental fantasy with a host of colored lanterns. There were people out there, wandering from shadow to shadow. Perhaps finding an unobserved moment to kiss.

Viola braced for a shudder of horror as she imagined Renfrew's lips on hers. Her one experience of the activity had convinced her that she never wanted to try something so repulsive again.

But all she felt was a surge of excitement. An excitement somehow related to the way her heart galloped and her breath caught, when he'd waltzed her around the crowded ballroom.

His grip on her arm was warm and firm in a way that even an innocent like her recognized as possessive. She should pull away. They weren't dancing anymore. He had no need to hold onto her.

Viola stayed just where she was. She liked Renfrew touching her. It was even better than losing herself in a wonderful story and having a whole afternoon ahead to finish the book.

His grip tightened. "When can I see you again?"

Startled, she tried to read his expression, but the darkness defeated her. Flaming torches lit the terrace, but the flickering illumination didn't penetrate to this corner. She should insist that they return to the ballroom. There were other people around them, but they all seemed to be couples in search of privacy. Viola was well aware that she and Renfrew stretched the bounds of propriety.

"There's a ball every night."

Something told her that expressive mouth quirked in impatience. "But you hardly ever come to balls."

"I...I can come from now on, if you like."

"Viola..." His hand slid up past the edge of her long satin glove to stroke the bare skin under her short, puffed sleeve.

She started at the contact. Despite his kid gloves, it felt like skin on skin, and that wasn't allowed. Juliet would have a fit if she saw them.

"I haven't given you permission to call me—" she began, but he continued over her, speaking in a low hum that made her foolish heart yearn.

"Viola. Viola. Viola. Your name is like music. It will play through my mind tonight, as I dance with you in my dreams."

*Goodness gracious.* "That's quite poetic."

His laugh was a soft rumble. "Isn't it? If I go riding early tomorrow morning in Hyde Park, is there any chance we might meet? I can't wait until the ball."

Could shy Viola Frain be making an assignation with a young man? And not just any young man, but a dashing fellow with a wild reputation. "You—"

"Viola, I believe Alexander Comerford is looking for you. You promised him this dance before he takes you into supper."

Sharp as scissors snipping a satin ribbon, Juliet's imperious tones cut through the enchantment enveloping Viola. She was horrified to discover that she leaned toward Renfrew. If she leaned much closer, she'd come near enough to kiss him.

With a dismayed gasp, she straightened and jerked her arm free. She waited for him to step away to preserve appearances, but he remained where he was.

Juliet hurried closer. "Viola?"

At last, Renfrew seemed to realize that he wasn't behaving as a gentleman should and he stepped back. Viola had had difficulty catching a full breath since he'd started dancing with her. Now she filled her lungs with coal-tinged London air.

"I'm coming, Juliet," Viola said without moving.

"Tomorrow," Renfrew whispered, as he bowed. He spoke more loudly for Juliet's benefit. "I hope your faintness has passed, Lady Viola."

What a convincing liar he was. A warning that she'd fallen under his spell without knowing him very well. What she did know of him should make her hesitate rather than fling herself headlong into his path.

Still, he was clever to use the heat inside as an excuse for bringing her out here. It was to her advantage to play along. "Thank you, my lord. I feel much more clearheaded now."

He gave the impression that he never nursed a thought beyond the next five seconds. But she'd recognized that he was cleverer than he liked to reveal. He'd pick up on the warning underlying her statement. Viola hoped to glory that she took her own advice.

When Juliet reached them, Viola read skepticism in her sister's expression. "If you're feeling better, it's time you went back into the ballroom."

Viola nodded, although some hitherto rebellious corner of her soul consigned Juliet to perdition for interrupting the most interesting few minutes of her life. "I'll find Alexander."

"I'll come with you," Juliet said.

Renfrew bowed, as Juliet seized her arm in a much more determined fashion than he had. "Your servant, Lady Juliet, Lady Viola."

"I don't know what you were thinking," Juliet muttered, almost dragging Viola toward her partner.

"We weren't doing anything wrong," Viola protested, unable to forget the way Renfrew had said her name. It sounded like he longed for her.

He'd said he'd dream of her.

*Grow up, Viola. A rake like him must say things like that to susceptible females a hundred times a day.*

"You were close enough for him to kiss you," Juliet hissed in outrage.

"We weren't kissing!"

Viola sounded as if the thought had never occurred to her. Lord Renfrew's bad character must be rubbing off on her. Her self-righteousness was almost as convincing as his lie about her feeling faint.

"No, and jolly lucky for you that you weren't. I know this is your first season and you like to pretend that you're above society's shallow standards, but this is the world you have to live in, Viola. Not just you. Your behavior reflects on your family."

Viola stopped in her tracks, halting Juliet's purposeful progress.

"Are you afraid that my conversation with Lord Renfrew might frighten Granville away from a proposal?" she said with a hint of uncharacteristic waspishness.

Juliet liked to rule the roost in the household and most of the time, Viola didn't kick up much of a fuss. She'd long ago discovered that if she didn't argue with her sister, she could do what she wanted unnoticed. But this evening, she hadn't broken any rules, even if she'd come close, and she didn't deserve this lecture.

She went on in a pointed tone. "If His Grace is so lily-livered, perhaps you shouldn't marry him. You'll turn into a monster, if you take on a man without the backbone to stand up to you."

"Don't talk such nonsense," Juliet snapped.

Perhaps it was lucky for future sisterly relations that Alexander Comerford appeared at the French doors just then and carted Viola off for their dance.

For Toby, an early morning assignation in Hyde Park was nothing new. He'd often arrived at sunrise to meet a lady, having gambled the night away in some tavern or gaming hell.

Last night, he'd retired at midnight. Early for him. Once he'd waltzed with Lady Viola, there had been little point in hanging about the Plunkett ball. Not to mention that Marjorie had got him in her sights by then. In the absence of another tree to climb, a quiet departure seemed the best strategy.

In general, he didn't need much sleep. He'd always been gifted with an abundance of physical energy. It was one of the things that his father, a noted scholar, had loathed about his son. As a boy, Toby couldn't sit still, prompting his unloving sire to call him a stupid yahoo.

Most days, a dawn ride helped to slough off his excess energy. Without regular vigorous exercise, he started jumping out of his skin. Later today, he'd visit his boxing salon and work off a little more of his restlessness.

A restlessness worse than usual since he'd met Lady Viola.

When he'd told her that he'd dream of her, he wasn't giving her the usual drivel that lured attractive women into his arms. After they met, he had dreamed of her. He'd dreamed of her last night, too. Hot, confused, sexual dreams that had him waking to a bed in even more disarray than usual.

Dreams that he was sure would shock innocent Lady Viola into never speaking to him again.

Now he lingered under the shade of the chestnut trees on his fine bay gelding Belvedere and observed the riders on Rotten Row. Officers in bright scarlet. Some of the more active society gentlemen who, like him, were perfectly capable of dancing the night away, then rising at first light for a punishing ride on their expensive bloodstock. The occasional lady in a severe black riding habit and high-crowned hat. More than one of those cast him a come-hither glance. He responded with a brief bow but no further encouragement.

He was interested in flirtation – but only with one lady.

One lady who so far had failed to appear.

Had he frightened her last night? In his attractions as in most things, he tended to be decisive, and decision inevitably led to action. The immediacy of his response could overwhelm the object of his interest. But he wouldn't have said that Lady Viola was too frail to handle his attentions.

At the ball, he'd have said that she was drawn to him, but not sure what to do about it. Curious, a little hesitant, but willing to see what might develop.

Or perhaps he succumbed to wishful thinking.

The fact that she hadn't yet arrived at the park told its own story. She hadn't said that she'd come. Juliet, plague take her, had intruded before Viola agreed to meet him.

Which he hated to admit was a dashed good thing. He'd been a breath away from closing the narrow gap and kissing Viola. At a ton event. Under society's eyes. With no thought to her good name.

If he'd kissed her, there would have been an almighty scandal. Ending in a trip down the aisle to make Lady Viola Frain his countess.

Toby waited for the usual chill in his gut at the thought of a wedding, but to his astonishment, there was nothing.

The prospect of marriage had always daunted him. Why enter another cage, when he'd already spent his childhood trapped with his father's disappointment and anger? In adulthood, he was careful to avoid raising expectations. He refused ever again to take the blame for being the man he was.

A wife had a right to expect care and loyalty and respect – and a spouse who behaved to her credit in public. Ugh! Not to mention the possibility of children. Double ugh! According to his father, Toby was incapable of caring for a potted plant, let alone another vulnerable human being.

That supreme tranquility he experienced in Lady Viola's company promised salvation. But marriage? That was a major step. Especially when he'd only met the lady twice.

And it looked like this morning wasn't going to make it three times.

Hope had turned the day to gold when he'd sprung from his bed. But as he lingered under the trees, hope shrank to the size of an old, dried-up walnut. She wasn't coming. More troubling, the disappointment was devastating.

Toby was just about to head off and take Bel for an extended gallop outside the city, when he caught a glimpse of a lady and a groom in the distance.

A slender lady in a dark riding habit on a prancing roan that he could already see was a peach. Toby loved horses. He always had, although that love had given his father another whip to beat him with. As punishment for some minor infraction, his father had sold Toby's first pony. Forbidding his son to ride was a more effective way to enforce discipline than violence.

These days, Toby owned one of the best stables in the country.

At the sight of Viola, his heart swelled, until it threatened to burst free from his chest. By George, he needed to regain some control before he met her, or he'd frighten her back to Lorimer Square. But as he urged Bel into a fast canter, he bit back a whoop of triumph.

Viola hadn't got to bed until after three and it was now only seven. She'd barely slept, too excited at the prospect of meeting Lord Renfrew again. Her sisters were so spectacular that most of the time, she was a mere afterthought. Young men dismissed her as bookish and quiet and, if she was honest, as dull as ditch water. She remained astonished that the dissipated Lord Renfrew was interested in her.

But last night, he'd danced with her and he'd said he wanted to kiss her. Nor had she mistaken the regret in his striking features when Juliet did her mother-hen act.

Now Viola looked up to see Renfrew riding toward her. He looked remarkably handsome, sitting in the saddle as if he'd been born on horseback. Her heart had never before stirred at the sight of a man, but Lord Renfrew made her thrill.

As he reined his mount in before her and removed his stylish hat to perform an elegant bow, her groom fell back. Soames hovered far enough away to allow her a little private conversation, but not so far that he couldn't intervene if Lord Renfrew tested propriety.

Viola sat up straight on her mare, Juno. She was bewildered to discover that for once in her uneventful life, she wanted a young man to break the rules and sweep her into his arms. How had this happened so fast? Less than forty-eight hours ago, Lord Renfrew had been a stranger. Now when he smiled, she felt like he gilded the world with sunlight.

"Lady Viola, how lovely to meet you here."

She bent her head in acknowledgement. "Good morning, my lord."

He cast a glance at Soames, who did his best to imitate a block of wood as he stared into the distance. A deaf block of wood.

The groom had known Viola since she was a toddler. He'd put her on her first pony. He must have guessed that something significant was going on when she asked him to saddle her horse at this hour.

"May I ride with you a little way?" Renfrew asked. "I so enjoyed our conversation last night at the ball. I'd love to continue it."

"I enjoyed our conversation, too." Viola had never cast a man a flirtatious glance in her life. But the look she sent him under her lashes was worthy of Juliet or Portia. "I'd be delighted if you joined me."

He set his hat back on his ruffled tawny head and maneuvered that superb horse until he rode at Viola's side. "So shall we talk about kissing?" he murmured, as Soames lagged further behind.

She laughed, surprised that the suggestion was enthralling rather than shocking. Was Renfrew corrupting her? She couldn't help thinking of his hands on her. Perhaps her lifelong chastity resulted from lack of opportunity rather than inherent virtue.

"Perhaps not wise," she managed to force out past a constricted throat.

"No, perhaps not. Anyway, I'd rather give you a practical class in the art. Talking about it just gets me stirred up for nothing." He paused. "I suppose you've never been kissed."

She frowned, as her breath caught to think that she, humble Viola Frain, put this experienced man in a lather. "Isn't it too early in the morning for this?"

He shrugged, as she told herself to settle down. That was more difficult than it should be, when he looked so magnificent on a horse. All long-limbed strength and easy control. That was what he'd been like as a dance partner, too. When he'd whirled her around the floor, it had been like flying. For the first time, she'd understood why her sisters got into such a flutter at the prospect of a ball.

"At least it is when we have a chaperone."

"My lord, perhaps we should change the subject." Viola tried to sound firm, the way Juliet did when quashing some suitor's pretensions. But her voice emerged quivery and breathless. She sounded as if Lord Renfrew's mere presence sent her into a spin.

Plague take him, it did. A man with half his experience must know that he stirred up a delicious if terrifying giddiness inside her. This agitation translated to Juno, who curvetted and snorted until Viola brought her under control.

Renfrew studied her from below the brim of his hat, his eyes the rich dark green of a river pool under overhanging willows. "Do you like London?"

That made her laugh. "Now you're trying too hard to be polite."

He had an engaging smile. Like his laugh, it invited the world to share his amusement. "I really want to know, not to mention it saves me from stealing you away for a kiss behind that oak tree."

Viola cast a worried glance at a tree that she'd ridden past most days and found entirely inoffensive. "You wouldn't."

"I'd like to."

So, heaven forgive her, would she. It turned out that wickedness indeed lurked in her soul. "Yes, I do."

He looked startled, then remarkably lascivious. "Really?"

She laughed again. Most of the time, she was inclined to be serious, but Renfrew made her giggle like a tipsy dairymaid. That made him devilish appealing, beyond the power of those startling good looks. "You misunderstand me. You asked if I like London. I do."

"Why?"

She guided Juno into a copse. At this hour, the park was busier than it was when she rode in the middle of the morning. Many of the people who descended on London for the season were country folk at heart. They missed the chance to get outside for a long walk or a good gallop. Hyde Park was the best opportunity for clearing away the mental cobwebs of late nights and heavy drinking and too much rich food.

Viola had noticed a few heads turning in her direction. One of the things that she didn't like about London was being under constant observation. The neighbors at home in Wiltshire enjoyed a good gossip, but nothing had prepared her for Mayfair's rumor mill.

"I like the museums and the shops and the history." Now she was alone with his lordship on a narrow path, with only Soames to keep an eye on her. Soames trusted her. Which right now seemed unjustified. "I like all the interesting people I've met."

Renfrew raised his eyebrows. "Like me?"

Definitely like him, but she'd relaxed enough to tease. "I heard Coleridge speak. The other day, I met Mr. Turner at the Royal Academy. And Papa invited some actors from the Theatre Royal to do a private reading of *Antony and Cleopatra* last week. Papa is mad about Shakespeare."

"You don't say."

The flat response aroused a wry smile. "Our names rather give it away, don't they?"

"Just a little." The horses were ambling now, choosing their own pace and direction, while the riders sank deeper into conversation. Lord Renfrew moved within touching distance. His leg in tan breeches and a polished black leather boot was mere inches from her skirts.

She'd never been so aware of anyone's physical presence. The world was full of male humans, but this was the first time that the difference between her soft femininity and a man's muscled vigor struck her as cause for celebration.

So much happened under the surface of this encounter that it became an effort to concentrate on what they were discussing. What had he said last? That was it. Lord Renfrew had asked about Papa.

Because Viola was very fond of her eccentric father, warmth infused her tone. "Papa considers it the abiding misfortune of his life that he was born to wealth and privilege, and a duty to inherit a distinguished title."

"Instead of treading the boards?"

"He would have made a marvelous actor."

"People line up to hear him speak in parliament. Not me, of course. I'm too busy setting society on its ear."

"Politics give him some small outlet for his talents. And we grew up doing amateur theatricals."

"It sounds like fun."

Something in his voice troubled her, before she remembered the hints of a difficult relationship with his father. With a desperation as disturbing as the unfamiliar inner tumult, she hoped that one day he'd trust her enough to explain. It puzzled her that a man of such natural warmth looked so cold when he spoke of his parent.

"It is." She kept her tone light. Something told her that if she pushed before he was ready, this promising new friendship would smash on the rocks of her curiosity. "At Christmas, I gave a memorable Laertes to Papa's Hamlet."

"You play male roles?"

"With three girls in the family and no sons, it's inevitable."

A glint in Lord Renfrew's eyes told her that he found the idea titillating. "In breeches?"

She blushed, although it hadn't felt so outrageous at the time. Perhaps because in the family, the thought of Viola arousing anybody to lascivious thoughts would have sparked hilarity. "Yes. Juliet and Portia fight over the decent female roles. I'm left with the second-string males."

"Your father always takes the lead?"

"Always. His Richard III would give you shivers."

"I fear I'm not a great one for Shakespeare. All those deuced words." Renfrew sighed. "Why the devil did the fellow have to be so blasted longwinded? I sat through *Romeo and Juliet* last week. Why the nincompoop hero didn't just steal his darling away after the ball, I don't know. Asking for trouble, mucking about for another couple of hours, then giving up the ghost just before the chit woke up."

Juliet gave a horrified snort. "Never say that to Papa. He'll ban you from the house."

Renfrew eased his mount closer. "That would be a pity."

"So you're game to call on us, after your mishap with the elm?"

He touched her hand where it held the reins. With them both wearing gloves, the surge of heat was unexpected. Except that every time he touched her, she tingled with response. "I'm willing to defy all dangers to reach your side, my lady. Even homicidal elm trees."

Viola laughed, but abruptly stopped when Soames coughed behind her. Horrified, she jerked away from Renfrew and directed Juno to the far side of the path.

This had happened last night when she'd come so perilously close to kissing him. Everything except Renfrew and the powerful attraction that he exerted receded from her awareness. She met laughing green eyes and a rueful expression that she didn't quite trust.

"Perhaps it's time to return to Lorimer Square, my lady," Soames said in a neutral voice.

Viola wasn't a natural rebel. Why should she be, when she got to do most things she wanted, simply by avoiding notice?

But now a spirit of defiance stirred. Why on earth couldn't she talk to someone she found so fascinating? Why should she retreat in shame, just because he was male and she was female?

She wasn't a fool. She wouldn't do anything rash. But if she wanted to hold Lord Renfrew's hand, what harm was there in that?

Renfrew swept off his hat again and directed another bow at her. "Are you going to the Tierney ball tonight?"

"Yes. Are you?"

"Yes." He sent her a meaningful glance. "Will you save me another waltz?"

"I'd love to," she said, and blushed at her eagerness.

"Capital. See you this evening." He turned his horse toward a side path. "Good morning, Lady Viola."

"Good morning, my lord."

As the earl rode away, Soames trotted up to her, all pretense of neutrality abandoned. "Lady Juliet will have my guts for garters when she finds out that you came out here to rendezvous with that young rascal. He's got a reputation with the ladies that I hesitate to mention to a sweet girl like you."

Viola glanced at the man who knew her so well. "Then perhaps it might be better if Lady Juliet doesn't find out."

His mouth flattened. "You think she won't hear about what you've been up to before she sits down for lunch? If you do, you need your head checked. Someone is probably chewing her ear about your tricks right now." He clicked his tongue in disapproval. "You've never been no trouble before, my lady. Don't tell me you're going to kick over the traces at this stage of your life."

"In that case, I won't tell you," she said shortly and urged Juno into a canter ahead of him.

# CHAPTER FIVE

Luckily, when Viola returned home, Papa had bustled in from their estate in Wiltshire and was busy turning the house into the usual chaos. Also as usual, he and Juliet were at loggerheads. The two of them faced off across the spacious marble hallway, surrounded by all Papa's luggage.

Viola's appearance caused her father to turn to her as if he was drowning and a ship sailed along to pluck him from the waves. "Viola, my dear, tell your sister that it will be no trouble to build an amphitheater in the back garden. I've been reading the Greeks, and I want to present the *Oresteia* next year in an authentic production."

She was happy to see him, and not just because his arrival saved her from having to explain this morning's excursion to Juliet. "Welcome back, Papa. Is all well at home?"

As Viola went up to greet him, she caught Juliet's mulish expression. He let her kiss his cheek, but she knew his attention had shifted away from her. "Yes, yes, yes. But what about my theater?"

"The house isn't ours, Papa. The lease doesn't allow us to destroy the garden, however authentic your theater might be." Juliet's tone turned coaxing. "We could build a theater at Afton Park. No question who owns the ground there. No nasty lawsuits to deal with. And plenty of room if you decide to expand."

Her father stared at her as if she'd suggested drinking inferior claret as a way of economizing. "But, my dear, nobody who came would have the taste to appreciate my production. The neighbors are a blundering band of Philistines, who only care for foxhunting. My innovations require a discerning audience. Otherwise I'm casting my pearls before swine."

"Hardly fair to our neighbors, Papa," Juliet protested. "You've always said you like local society."

Viola's father struck a pose worthy of King Lear. The sight was familiar. Papa often identified with the misused king. After all, Lear also had three daughters who drove him to distraction. "Not when it comes to matters artistic. London is where the connoisseurs will acclaim me."

Juliet sighed, looking harried and weary. Viola felt a pang of sympathy for her sister. Juliet was old before her time, and not entirely through her own fault. For heaven's sake, she was only twenty-six. But since Mamma's death, the responsibility for their eccentric father and her two younger sisters had descended on her. The death of her betrothed had only added to the strain.

"Papa, perhaps you should speak to Mr. Kean about it." Viola hoped that the mention of Edmund Kean, her father's idol, would distract him. "An actor of genius may have some suggestions to offer."

"Topping idea, Viola." Tragic King Lear transformed into a plump English aristocrat, who looked much more cheerful. "I'll go straight to my club and ascertain where he is."

"Then you should visit Cambridge and Oxford and discuss your thoughts with the dons there."

Out of the corner of her eye, Viola saw Juliet suck in a relieved breath. If they could keep Papa mired in the consultation stages of his plan, the lease on the Lorimer Square house would end before building could start. The Caldecotts' flowerbeds would be safe.

They'd been lucky to find the property. Last season, Lord Deerforth had taken an extended lease, but the scandals that had engulfed the Ridley family meant that they'd vacated the house early.

"But I've read—" Papa began.

"I'm sure they'd love to hear your insights," Viola said. "After all, a man with your acting gifts will introduce them to a whole range of new concepts. Frankly, I believe it's your duty."

Her father was nodding. "My thoughts will revolutionize scholarship."

"Just so, Papa," Juliet said. "Perhaps you should call on the British Museum, too. If you're going to do this, you need to do it right."

Caught up in the potential of his ideas, Lord Portdown muttered to himself as he ascended the stairs. Viola tried to slip away after him, but she wasn't so lucky when it came to making her escape.

"Viola, can you spare me a word?" Juliet said in the tone that hinted she meant to exert her authority as elder sister and custodian of the family honor.

"I'd like to wash, Juliet. I smell of the stables."

Juliet didn't relent. Viola hadn't thought that she would. Juliet never shirked her duty. She and Granville would make a perfect pair. Together they'd reform the country. Whether the country wanted to be reformed or not. "That won't worry me."

Sighing, Viola trudged back down the stairs and trailed Juliet into the morning room. It was a beautiful, late spring day. Through the French doors, the dewy garden looked magical. Viola couldn't help thinking of her first encounter with Renfrew, out amongst all that burgeoning greenery. Since their meeting, spring seemed to have arrived in her life. She felt more alive than ever before.

Juliet took a seat behind the desk near the windows. "Please sit down."

Viola's lips tightened, as she sank into the chair in front of the desk. "Why do I feel like I've been called into the headmistress's office?"

Juliet didn't smile. "What is Lord Renfrew to you?"

There was a question. One, even at this early stage, that she wasn't sure she wanted to answer. "We met when he fell out of the tree. We danced last night. Neither of those things seem to merit a scolding."

Juliet looked sterner. "On the terrace, he looked like he was about to kiss you."

"We were in a public place. Nothing happened that either his lordship or I need to apologize for." Viola cursed that her fair skin colored so easily. "He kept me company while I caught a breath of air. The flowers in the ballroom were so overpowering, I had a headache."

"He held you too close in the dance."

"He meant no harm."

"I think he did. I think he does." Juliet's delicate jaw hardened. "And the pity of it is that if anyone suffers because of his recklessness, it won't be him. It will be you. The world is much kinder to brash young men than it is to girls who test the bounds of propriety."

"I'm not a fool, Juliet," Viola snapped, resenting her sister's patronizing tone.

"I wouldn't have said so. In fact, you've always been very circumspect in your behavior. Portia's generosity of nature sometimes sparks difficulties because she leaps before she looks, but you haven't caused me any trouble at all." Juliet's eyes narrowed on Viola in a way that made her feel her older sister saw every forbidden longing in her heart. "Until now."

"I haven't done anything wrong."

"Let's keep it that way. What did you do this morning?"

"You know what I did." Impatience sharpened Viola's voice. "I took Juno to Hyde Park for some exercise. I'm sitting in front of you in a riding habit, for pity's sake."

"Don't play games with me, Viola Frain. Your usual practice of operating under the cover of compliance, before going on your own merry way, isn't good enough here. There's too much at stake."

Viola was surprised that Juliet was aware of her tricks, although she shouldn't be. Juliet was a clever woman. "Like you becoming a duchess?"

Juliet frowned. "You always speak as if what I want doesn't matter."

Viola thought the boot was on the other foot, but she didn't say so. "You don't need to worry."

"Don't I? Three days ago, the idea that I'd have to remind you of what constitutes acceptable behavior wouldn't have occurred to me. Since then, I've caught you alone in the garden with a young man of tarnished reputation. I've seen you make a public spectacle of yourself at a ball. And you've sneaked out of the house to meet this young man for a tryst."

"It wasn't a tryst," Viola said, aware that when Juliet put it like that, her recent activities didn't sound quite so innocent.

"Yes, it was. He asked you to be there and you went." Juliet sighed again. "The strangest thing about all this is that he's the sort of high-living wastrel who you usually wouldn't give the time of day. He's handsome, I grant you, but I wouldn't have thought you shallow enough to fall for good looks alone."

Viola's cheeks felt like they were on fire. Partly because Juliet was right.

Renfrew's attractions had bewitched her. Juliet wasn't the only one who found that mystifying. A single glimpse of those chiseled features had her heart doing acrobatics. When he touched her, she went up in flame.

He hadn't kissed her yet – and she was well aware just how that thought would damn her in Juliet's eyes. But the thought of his lips on hers made her stomach clench with wicked anticipation. "He's nicer than you think he is."

"No, he's not. He's a womanizer and a cad, and he likes to drink and gamble more than any decent man should. He has no idea of anything beyond where to look for his next pleasure. I fear that right now, he's turned his attentions from the demimonde where they belong to an innocent girl of good family. If he wants to ruin someone, let him ruin Marjorie Dimchurch. She already promises to spark a scandal because she's so mad for him. You deserve better."

The defiant spirit that had stirred in recent days screamed denial to everything Juliet said, however sensible it might sound here in the family home, away from Renfrew's powerful influence.

Because he *was* nice. And he made her feel pretty and charming and interesting in a way that she never did in this family.

Viola spoke through stiff lips. "Juliet, I don't know what you want me to say."

Juliet cut the air with one hand. "I want you to say that you'll go back to being my shy, bookish sister."

Hurt pierced Viola like a knife, although the remark held no spite. "You believe I'm too tedious to hold his interest."

Juliet looked hunted, which did nothing to contradict Viola's impression. "He has a taste for flashy women. You're not flashy."

"I'm not as pretty as you or Portia, I know that. But I'm not a total fright."

"You're not a fright at all." Juliet had the grace to look abashed. "You're very pretty."

"Thank you," Viola responded with bitter irony. Her sister still sounded patronizing.

"But you're much quieter and more serious than his other women."

"Meaning he couldn't possibly find me attractive?"

Juliet was wise enough not to take up that challenge. At least directly. "Meaning I don't want you hurt. I love you, Viola. You know I do. I realize that you think I'm worried about the family reputation – and I am. Not just because of Granville. But most of all, I don't want to see my lovely youngest sister disgraced and heartbroken because she tumbled headlong for a rake's lying flattery."

Viola wanted to resent Juliet's interference, but she knew her sister was worried about her. Not to mention that Juliet was six years older than she was and more worldly wise.

But her instincts insisted that Renfrew wasn't the man that her sister described. Or at least he wasn't when he was with Viola. "I'll be careful," she said quietly. "But I've enjoyed meeting Lord Renfrew. I look forward to getting to know him better."

Juliet's expression didn't soften. "I don't approve."

"So do you forbid me to speak to him?"

"I'm not sure I have that power, although I'm in a position to give you a strong warning that you're embarking on a course that places your reputation in jeopardy."

"You could tell Papa, and he could send me home."

"He could. But I don't think he'd welcome any involvement in the matter." Juliet gave an unamused snort. "We both know that the only things likely to attract his interest are written in blank verse."

It was true. Juliet was the stable center of this family, not Lord Portdown.

Viola's pique faded, as she recognized yet again that Juliet took on responsibilities too onerous for a young woman. So she responded in a gentler tone. "I like Lord Renfrew. I like him more than any gentleman I've ever met."

"Viola..." Juliet's dismay was obvious.

Viola made an apologetic gesture. "I know I've just met him. I know it's too early to think of him as a suitor—"

"He's a rake. He makes every woman he meets feel like she's special. That's what rakes do." Juliet shook her head, as if the idea of such a libertine choosing reticent Viola Frain as his wife beggared imagination. "You're too innocent to see the truth."

"I'm innocent, but I'm not brainless," she retorted. "A few dances with him won't turn me into a scarlet woman in society's eyes. Apart from that, I'll be careful."

Juliet looked dissatisfied, and her tone was dark as she replied. "Very well. I've spoken my piece. We'll leave it there. But you mark my words. You'll have trouble with Lord Renfrew before you're finished with him."

# CHAPTER SIX

When Viola attended the Tierney ball that night, she did her best to forget Juliet's dire warnings. But trying so hard not to think about something meant that she ended up thinking about it all the time anyway.

The unwelcome truth was that on the surface, Juliet's misgivings made a lot of sense. After all, nobody in their right mind would think to match Lord Portdown's youngest daughter with the louche and disreputable Lord Renfrew. She and his lordship were opposites in every way, not least because he had a reputation as a Lothario and she was a complete novice when it came to relations between men and women.

To counter that, all she had to offer was that she'd never met anyone who seemed to understand her the way Renfrew did. He might be a stranger, but he didn't feel like a stranger.

It was a feeble defense when if she was wrong about him, she risked not just her own future, but her sisters' as well.

"Viola, I'm so glad you came. I wasn't sure you would." Elizabeth Tierney, lovely, blonde, rich, accounted a diamond of the first water, descended upon Viola and took her hands to kiss her on the cheek.

Viola liked Elizabeth. She was open and friendly and didn't play spiteful games like Marjorie Dimwit – Dimchurch! – and her coterie.

"I wouldn't have missed your ball for the world," she said, meaning it, although perhaps more for Renfrew's sake than for Elizabeth's.

This was Elizabeth's second season. Gossip was that she'd turned down half a dozen proposals last year and had already received more proposals than that this season.

Elizabeth leaned in and spoke *sotto voce*. "What's this I hear about you and Renfrew?"

Oh, dear, Viola was blushing again, and her answer sounded unconvincing in her ears as she replied. "He saved me from a falling branch."

Elizabeth's silvery laugh attracted curious glances. "And since then, you've danced with him and met him in Hyde Park. I'm impressed. I'd feared that you might end up with a dusty old antiquarian, not one of the wildest men in London."

"We've only just met," Viola said, not surprised but displeased to learn that her every interaction with his lordship was common knowledge.

"I'd love to hear more, but I've given this waltz to Alexander Comerford."

"You're the center of attention tonight."

Elizabeth wasn't listening. Instead, she stared over Viola's shoulder with an arrested expression. "Well, well."

Again without surprise, Viola turned to find two handsome gentlemen bearing down on them. One was Elizabeth's partner. The other was the man she'd dreamed about for the last two nights.

Lord Renfrew looked magnificent in a perfectly tailored dark blue coat and biscuit pantaloons. The snowy white froth of his neckcloth set off the pure line of his jaw to perfection.

"Elizabeth, this is our dance," Alexander said with a charming smile. "Come and give me all the latest tattle."

Viola feared that the latest tattle included the strange pairing of Lord Renfrew and Lady Viola Frain. Which didn't stop her smiling at Renfrew. Despite everything, the sight of him filled her with pleasure.

She curtsied. "My lord."

His lips twitched at the formality, as he performed one of his graceful bows. She read genuine warmth in his gaze as it settled on her. "My lady."

At that instant, she decided that Juliet was wrong. Whatever her unexpected bond with this unruly young man might be, it was real. Was it friendship? Attraction? Curiosity?

On her part, the affinity included all three elements, plus some extra spice that she couldn't yet identify. Who knew what the result of their meeting would be? But she refused to pass up this chance to know Renfrew, just because he was notorious for kicking up his heels.

He took her extended hand. Gloves had never before struck her as instruments of torture, but just once, she longed to feel his touch on her skin without the decorous intervention of thin kidskin. He'd held her hand when he helped her up after his fall. Then the zing of reaction had astonished her, whereas now it was familiar, if still disturbing.

"You were kind enough to agree to waltz with me," he said.

"I'd be delighted." A sidelong glance revealed Alexander and Elizabeth observing her with unconcealed interest. Past their immediate circle, other gazes focused on them with varying degrees of curiosity and disapproval.

Viola had never before caused a stir in society. She decided that she didn't much like it. In a fit of self-consciousness, she jerked her hand free of Lord Renfrew's.

"Ignore them." With a determined air, Renfrew took her arm and steered her toward the dance floor. "They don't matter."

"But they do," she said equally quietly. "Wishing they don't doesn't change reality."

"Just dance with me and forget all the wagging tongues. I've missed you."

Startled, she let herself meet his eyes. They were bright with approval and what looked like concern. She felt care in the way he took her hand and slid his arm around her waist.

Juliet would tell her this compatibility was all in her imagination. Plague take her straitlaced sister. "You saw me this morning."

A huff of self-mocking amusement escaped him. "That was years ago."

Her awkwardness dissolved, and her smile became more natural, as they began to move to the lilting music. "You're impossible."

"Without question. Will you come riding again tomorrow?"

"Yes," she said, before prudence could stop her.

"Capital." He tightened his grip on her waist and performed a dizzying turn that had her seeing stars. Although she feared that the stars had nothing to do with the dance and everything to do with her partner.

"And will you walk on the terrace again with me tonight?"

"For five minutes. But you need to keep your distance better than you did last time. I've already had a lecture from Juliet on causing talk."

Groaning, he briefly closed his eyes. "It's devilish hard to be good when the provocation is irresistible."

Arrested, she stumbled. Her heart raced so fast that she could hardly see. "My lord..."

Renfrew easily rescued her from falling before he spoke, as if what he said didn't change her world forever. "You know I want you."

"You...you talked about kissing, but I assumed you did that with every lady you meet."

He cast her a direct look. "I talk about kissing with *some* of the ladies I meet. When I talk about kissing you, I'm expressing a stronger than usual preference."

Viola knew that she was blushing again. "But you might say that to every lady you meet, too." She caught his disgruntled reaction. "The ladies you invite to kiss you anyway."

"You don't take me seriously. My bad reputation begins to rankle."

He kept spinning her in graceful circles. About them, a hundred couples revolved in the dance. Last night when they'd waltzed, Viola felt as if she and Lord Renfrew inhabited a private bubble. It was the same now. Whenever she was with him, she sensed that a whole universe of communication flowed beneath their actual words.

She didn't smile. "I'd like to kiss you, too."

Heat flared in his eyes. "Viola—"

"But you know we can't."

"I know we can't here." He frowned. "Have you been kissed before?"

"My horrid cousin Terence kissed me last year. I planted him such a facer, he ended up sitting in the lily beds."

"The swine."

Lord Renfrew looked outraged. And jealous, which made that strange, inchoate emotion inside Viola swell until she had difficulty speaking.

She licked dry lips and made herself go on. "He's always bothering the maids. Because he's scared of Juliet and Portia, he wouldn't dare to annoy them. He thought I might be an easier target. Now he's afraid of me, too."

"I'm wondering if I should be afraid of you." Humor sparked in Renfrew's eyes, although the heat lingered. "You and your good right hook."

Her laugh set a few heads tilting in their direction. Juliet was dancing with Ivor Bilson, and she was doing her best not to glare at Viola. Portia however regarded her with open curiosity, as she circled the room in Granville's arms.

"You've been warned."

"I have. Did you enjoy it?"

"Punching Terence?" She didn't bother to hide her satisfaction. "I most certainly did. He's a nasty little sneak."

"No, you absurd creature, the kiss."

"Not at all. It was wet and cold and slobbery." She shuddered. "Ick."

Renfrew laughed. "I'm glad."

Startled, she only just saved herself from stumbling again. "You are?"

"It means that when I kiss you, you'll discover what it's like if it's done properly."

"Improperly, rather," she responded in a dry tone, wondering at his certainty that the occasion would arise. "Why is it that we always end up talking about kissing? The subject never crops up with anyone else."

"That's easy to answer." His smile broadened. Her wayward heart gave a little shimmer at the way he eyed her, as if she was a chocolate éclair and he was a connoisseur of French pastries. "We talk about kissing all the time because we're caught up in a powerful attraction."

Before she could express her confusion, he swung her around until she was giddy. With a few deft turns, they were out on the terrace.

While the Tierney ballroom wasn't as fuggy as Lady Plunkett's, the evening was warm and the terrace was crowded with people seeking some fresh air. Or as fresh as air in London ever got.

"Damn all these people. I want you to myself," Toby muttered with audible frustration. "Will you come down into the garden?"

The Tierneys lived on Lorimer Square, just as Viola did, where the houses all had larger than usual gardens. Like Lady Plunkett, Lady Tierney had adorned her garden with colored lamps that created a pretty pattern from above. Viola saw couples moving along the gravel paths. The picture was romantic and enticing – and forbidden to a debutante wishing to avoid unfavorable notice.

"You know I won't."

He groaned and tightened his clasp on her arm. "Even if I promise to behave?"

"Even if you swear on a stack of Bibles." She sighed. "I'm sorry I'm so much trouble."

More lanterns lit the terrace, so she had no difficulty reading his rueful amusement. The expression was astonishingly attractive. For a flaring instant, she wondered if it would really be too bad to take a stroll in the garden.

He shook his head in mock despair. "This is why I've always refrained from pursuing girls from good families."

Her wayward heart leaped in a most unsettling way. "Are you pursuing me?"

She waited for another teasing response, but the laughter faded from his features. The gaze that he leveled on her was hot enough to sear her skin. "I am."

She stared up into his eyes, rapt in what she saw there. Desire and intent and determination. Just now, he didn't look like a light-hearted wastrel, who wandered through life without a care. He looked like a man who had found what he wanted and meant to get it.

All the moisture dried from Viola's mouth, and she had trouble swallowing. Then she realized that Renfrew had backed her against the balustrade and into the shadows.

"My lord..." she said in a reedy voice, as she fought the impulse to close the narrowing gap between them. He was close enough for her to catch his scent. Something fresh and healthy and deliciously male. Plus a hint of sandalwood soap.

He loomed even nearer. "Call me Toby."

Viola leaned forward, as he drew her the way a magnet drew iron filings. What on earth was this power that he exerted over her? "Toby..."

She heard melting surrender in her voice. He must hear it, too.

He bent toward her with unmistakable intent. "Yes?"

*Yes. Yes. Yes.*

Her heart galloped like a bolting horse, and she gulped for air. She kept forgetting to breathe.

Elizabeth and Lily Bilson were outside as well. Their heads lowered in conversation, they passed in front of the French doors. Viola woke up to where she was and what she was about to do.

"You're standing too close." Her voice was shaky. "I think you should take me back into the ballroom."

It broke her heart to say the words. But while she was near to lost in the attraction surging between her and this infernally appealing young man, she couldn't forget what she owed her family and her good name.

Kissing Lord Renfrew in full view of the ton wouldn't benefit anyone.

Well, it would answer her aching curiosity about how Toby's lips would feel upon hers, but that didn't count against the cost of her recklessness.

"By George, Lady Viola, I'm sorry. I really meant to behave myself." To her surprise, he stepped back straightaway. The sudden snapping of tension made her slump against the balustrade. He raked one hand through his thick tawny hair, leaving it beguilingly untidy. "The moment I'm with you, I forget all my good intentions. Feel free to punch me like you punched Terence."

For once, he sounded as befuddled as she was. She realized that despite his sensual experience, he was all at sea, too. That helped her gather her composure and straighten. She'd been doing a good imitation of a wilting tulip.

"That would be as scandalous as a kiss." To her relief, she no longer sounded ready to collapse.

Toby's laugh almost sounded normal. "I suppose you're right."

"Anyway, I have no desire to hit you."

"If you knew what was going through my mind, you might summon up the urge."

This time, she laughed. "Perhaps in that case, it's good that I don't know."

He sighed. "I'll take you inside." The orchestra played the introduction to a quadrille. "I feel like I've wasted our chance to talk. When I swear talking was all I intended. There's so much I want to know about you."

"There's a lot I'd like to know about you, too," she said with a hint of shyness that struck her as absurd when he'd come within a breath of kissing her.

"Unless you'd like to give me this dance?"

Even as she shook her head, she couldn't stifle a thrill at the hope that she heard in his question. "Ivor Bilson asked me when I arrived at the ball."

Toby sighed again, with a theatrical exaggeration that made her smile. "Why do you have to be so popular? I really feel that I was led up the garden path when people told me Lord Portdown's youngest daughter was a timid recluse."

"It's reflected glory from Juliet and Portia."

She expected him to laugh at that, but he sent her a thoughtful glance. "You shouldn't put yourself down, Viola. I'm not the only man who's noticed how pretty and sweet and altogether delectable you are."

"Oh," she said, nonplussed to receive such praise. "That's a very nice thing to say."

"It's the truth, damn it. Although my iniquitous plans would be easier to accomplish if nobody else realized how charming you are."

Her heart fluttered in her chest like a bird trying to escape from a net. "You...you shouldn't say things like that unless you mean them."

"Of course I bloody well mean them," he said with some force. "I—"

"Lady Viola, I believe this is our dance."

Viola, who was generally an even-tempered creature, cursed Ivor Bilson's arrival with a savagery that appalled her. Something told her that she and

Toby were about to move beyond social niceties and talk about important things at last.

It was more of an effort than it should have been to plaster a smile on her face and speak as if partnering the good-natured if vacuous young man constituted the height of pleasure. "I'm glad to join you, Mr. Bilson."

But she wasn't glad. And as she left the terrace on Ivor Bilson's arm, her heart yearned to stay with Toby, who remained behind in the shadows.

# CHAPTER SEVEN

"May I fetch you a glass of lemonade or champagne, my lady?" Ivor asked, as he led Viola off the dance floor at the end of the quadrille.

"Yes, please," she said, trying to locate Toby amongst the crowd. He was so tall that she should be able to catch a glimpse of that unmistakable tawny head.

"Capital." Ivor left her to seek out the refreshment table. She liked Ivor. He was kind and easy company, despite making no pretense to being a clever man.

At last, she caught sight of Toby on the other side of the room. He was talking to his cousin, Lord Shelburn. As if sensing her attention, he turned his head and sent her a smile hinting they shared an intimacy that they really didn't. She reminded herself that she'd only known him a couple of days. She'd be a fool to imagine that he was anything other than an attractive stranger.

Ivor returned to her side, excusing himself as he passed close to Marjorie Dimchurch. Viola didn't see what happened next, but Ivor stumbled and the contents of two glasses of cold lemonade cascaded down the front of her azure taffeta gown.

Far too late, she lurched out of the way. "Oh, no!"

Sticky, sugary liquid left a great dark patch from her neck to her hem and dripped into a puddle on the polished parquet floor.

"Lady Viola, heavens above, my apologies," Ivor exclaimed, finding his balance. He clutched both empty glasses in one hand, while he fished in his pocket for his handkerchief. "I don't know what happened. I'm such a bungler."

But Viola had caught the satisfied smile on Marjorie's face. The girl must have deliberately tripped Ivor and jarred his elbow. "It doesn't matter," she said in a flat voice.

"Let me..." Ivor began to scrub at her dress, which made Marjorie and her cronies snicker.

Blushing, Viola snatched the handkerchief away and did her best to soak up the mess. But a small square of linen was no match for an ocean of lemonade. Her skin itched at the sensation of a hundred eyes arrowing in on her with curiosity and amusement and sympathy.

Two footmen glided up. One took the glasses from Ivor. The other kneeled to mop up the pool on the floor with a towel.

"Let me help you, Lady Viola." To her surprise, Marjorie adopted a concerned expression. She came up and took her arm. "If we go to the retiring room, you'll be out of the public gaze. We can send a maid for water and towels to repair the damage to your dress."

"I'd rather just go home, thank you," Viola said in a wary voice, as she tried and failed to shake Marjorie off. A *tête-à-tête* with the nasty little cat was the last thing that she wanted.

"I'm sure we can fix this. Then you can come back to enjoy the ball."

"Yes, go with Miss Dimchurch," Ivor said, clearly having no idea that his stumble wasn't an accident. "It would be a pity if my dashed oafishness spoiled your evening."

Viola's lips tightened, but it seemed that she'd have to make another scene to escape Marjorie. "Thank you." She hoped that she didn't sound as unenthusiastic about the girl's company as she felt.

"I'm so frightfully sorry, Lady Viola," Ivor said again.

"You have nothing to apologize for, Mr. Bilson." Viola meant it.

With an insistent grip, Marjorie hauled Viola down the corridor to the retiring room. For once, the cohorts remained behind, which was a relief. Marjorie was the sort of girl who always traveled at the head of a gang of vocal supporters.

When they reached the retiring room, Marjorie turned to the maid in attendance. "Go outside and stand at the door. Nobody else is to come in. This lady and I wish to be private for a few minutes."

The abrasive tone had the maid blanching and performing a shaky curtsy. "Very good, my lady."

Viola's stomach clenched, as she braced for trouble. Was Marjorie planning a physical attack? If she was, she'd discover the punishing right hook that had felled Terence. Viola might have a reputation for quietness, but she refused to let this conniving witch bully her.

"Sit down," Marjorie said with an authority that Viola felt that she had no right to claim. Viola noted that the girl made no attempt to clean up the lemonade stain.

"I'd rather stand," she said shortly. "Please say whatever you feel you must, then go away. It's cold hanging around in wet clothes."

Viola's bluntness took Marjorie aback. She must have expected Lord Portdown's youngest daughter to be a wilting violet. The girl's jaw squared in a way that did no favors to her blonde prettiness. She'd be an attractive girl, if it wasn't for a hardness around her eyes and mouth. "Very well. Stop your embarrassing pursuit of Lord Renfrew. He's mine."

Viola felt no surprise. What else could this be about? Society might joke about Marjorie's single-minded attempts to become the next Countess of Renfrew. It didn't seem half so amusing when Viola was trapped in a room alone with someone who glared at her with unconcealed hatred.

She had enough experience of bullies to know that any display of weakness was fatal. She leveled her shoulders and raised her chin. "I don't believe that you can own anyone. If Lord Renfrew wishes to marry you, he's perfectly capable of coming to that conclusion on his own. If he doesn't wish to marry you, no amount of scheming on your part will convince him otherwise."

Temper flared in Marjorie's pale blue eyes. "We're perfect together, as he'd see if you weren't so busy distracting him. Stay away from him. Or it will be the worse for you, you little bitch."

"Charming." Sarcasm dripped from Viola's tone.

"I'm just giving you a friendly warning that you're making an enemy."

"Are you threatening to throw more lemonade over me?" Viola asked in a steady voice.

Marjorie didn't bother denying her part in the scuffle. "Lemonade will be the least of it."

Viola shifted forward, hoping Marjorie would fall back and let her pass. "I won't listen to any more stupid threats."

Marjorie didn't shift. Viola fought not to let the other girl's confidence daunt her.

"I'm not finished. I want your promise that you won't encourage Lord Renfrew further, and that you'll step aside and let matters between him and me reach their proper end."

"Even if I fell off a cliff tomorrow..." Viola hoped that she wasn't tempting fate by saying that. There was a glint in Marjorie's eyes that indicated violence awaited, if she didn't get her own way. "...there's no guarantee Renfrew will choose a life of domestic bliss with you."

"I'll make sure he does." The complacency in Marjorie's tone made Viola wonder whether Toby had the slightest chance against her. God help him if he wed this harridan. He'd live in misery for the rest of his days.

"Do your best," Viola said shortly, losing what little patience she had with the girl. "I'm not staying here to argue."

Marjorie didn't shift. "Do I have your word that you'll stay away from Renfrew?"

"No, you do not," Viola snapped.

Marjorie's fists closed at her sides. "I won't let you go until I get it."

Viola wondered if she might have to fight her way out of the room. It seemed ludicrous that only yards away from a room packed with blue bloods and powerbrokers, she prepared for a brawl with a woman who held the same exalted rank as she did.

"What in heaven's name is going on here?" The door behind Marjorie slammed open and to Viola's relief, Juliet appeared. She'd never in her entire life been so grateful for her sister's authoritative manner.

As Marjorie glanced back, the tautness leached from her body. "Lady Juliet…"

Juliet pulled the door shut behind her to preserve their privacy. "Viola, you've been gone an age, and that poor girl outside was almost too terrified to let me in."

"Miss Dimchurch was just leaving," Viola said shakily. Now that she was no longer alone with Marjorie, this disagreeable scene left her quaking.

"I was helping Lady Viola with her wet dress," Marjorie said.

"I can take over from here." Juliet cast a speaking look around the room. Their surroundings offered no evidence of Marjorie's claim. No towels. No bowls of water. "I believe it's time you rejoined the party, Miss Dimchurch."

"As you wish," Marjorie curtsied to Juliet, who was unstoppable in her *grande dame* mode. The girl wasn't finished with Viola, though. She shot her a pointed look. "I trust you'll remember what we discussed, Lady Viola. It would be to your advantage to take me seriously."

Viola didn't reply. Now that Juliet had arrived, her fright receded, and with it, her artificial show of strength. She felt like someone had punched her in the stomach.

As Marjorie flounced out, Viola sank onto a padded stool. "I'm so glad you came. Things were getting unpleasant." Her voice was wobbly, as it hadn't been when she faced down Marjorie.

"I suppose the vulgar cow wanted to warn you away from Lord Renfrew. I told you that association would cause trouble."

Viola was so grateful to Juliet for rescuing her that she didn't mind the scolding. "She's determined to have him, whatever his thoughts on the matter. She's half-mad with the idea."

"Yes, well, I hope you told her to get back into her box."

"I did, but I don't think she was listening."

"I assume that she has something to do with the marks on your gown."

"Yes. She tripped up poor Ivor when he was bringing me a glass of lemonade." She plucked unhappily at the sticky mess. "I should go home."

"Let me see if I can clean you up. It would be a pity if you retreated with your tail between your legs, just because that harpy played a trick on you." Juliet opened the door. "Please fetch a bowl of warm water and some towels, and be quick about it."

The maid must have been hovering outside, because Viola heard a murmur of instant obedience.

"I suspect my dress is beyond saving," she said when Juliet returned.

"Nonsense."

So it proved. By the time Juliet performed her magic, Viola looked almost as good as she had when she arrived at the ball. Drying herself out in front of the fire in the small hearth even meant that she ended up only a little damp instead of soaked.

"Are you coming out now?"

So far, they'd been left alone, for which Viola was grateful. She didn't feel up to dealing with a flood of feminine curiosity. She didn't feel up to dealing with any curiosity at all.

"I might sit quietly in here for five minutes. Miss Dimchurch was rather...overwhelming."

"I should have come sooner, but most of the time you can handle yourself. Look how you dealt with Terence."

Startled, Viola glanced up at her sister. "You know about that?"

"Odious little toad deserved it, although it's a pity the daylilies were his innocent victims."

A huff of amusement escaped Viola, before her voice lowered into sincerity. "Thanks, sis. Things were about to get really horrible."

"I'll always come to your rescue, Viola. Don't you know that?"

"I do. But I often wonder what it cost you to give up your girlhood to keep watch over Portia and me."

"Someone had to. Papa is..."

"Papa," Viola said, her tone full of wry affection. But however much she loved her father, she wasn't blind to the price that his daughters and particularly his oldest daughter had paid for his refusal to take responsibility.

"Stay here and dry off properly, then come back to the ballroom when you're ready."

To Viola's surprise – and relief – she had privacy to steel herself for a return to the crowd. When she left the retiring room, she tipped the maid, who had almost had as bad a time with Marjorie as she had.

She made her way down the corridor. It took her a second to realize that everyone must have gone through to supper. There was no music, and the conversation and laughter created a distant hum instead of a hubbub in the next room.

Before she made it back to the ballroom, a door opened on her right. A hand reached out to drag her into a small side room leading out onto the terrace. "Are you all right?"

Without surprise, she met Toby's worried eyes. "Yes, I'm fine. Although I can't say I'm eager for another conversation with Marjorie Dimchurch."

"Now you know how I feel." He gave a grunt of amusement. "Next time you hear her coming, climb a tree like I did."

She couldn't help bursting into laughter, before she realized that she should be more discreet. If anyone found her alone with Toby, there would be the devil to pay. "So that's why you were in the elm."

"It seemed the best way to avoid her."

"You couldn't just go out the back gate like a normal person?"

"She's a blasted female Napoleon. She deploys those silly widgeons who follow in her wake like an army. They'd blocked off my escape. My only choice was to go up."

"And come down."

"Falling at your feet was the best thing that ever happened to me."

Another extravagant compliment. Except she was starting to believe him. "I'll agree that it's made life more interesting."

He kept hold of her arm. She couldn't summon up the will to pull away, although every rule insisted that she did.

"It has at that." His lopsided smile was so charming that Viola actually felt her heart flop over onto its side like an adoring puppy when its master came home. "Do you know this is the first time we've been alone since the day we met?"

She did. Partly because the excitement that she always felt in his presence was headier than ever. It turned her blood to rushing flame and seethed in her stomach like a restless ocean. "Yes."

"With everyone at supper, we could sneak out into the garden."

"That wouldn't be sensible," she said, knowing that if she heard the regret in her answer, so would Toby.

He stared into her eyes as if he searched her soul. She told herself to look away before he discovered too many of her secrets. Most of all, the secret that she liked him far too much for her own good. But that steady green gaze held her captive.

"So you won't come?"

It would be foolhardy to say yes. If Juliet found out, she'd hit the roof. Right now, and more than usual, Viola was in charity with her sister.

But on the other hand, the idea of spending a few unobserved minutes with Toby offered the prospect of heaven. "We'd have to be careful."

He must realize that she hovered on the verge of consenting, because his eyes glittered with satisfaction. "Let's go."

Viola was nervous, but her encounter with Marjorie had left her rattled and queasy. Now she wanted to do something purely for her own pleasure.

"Yes, let's go."

# CHAPTER EIGHT

oby's grip on Viola's arm firmed, and he swept her through the French doors. Triumph blared inside him, as powerful as a hundred trumpets.

During supper, the terrace was deserted, apart from a few couples. But like Viola and him, they were more interested in privacy than checking to see who else might slip down into the garden for an unremarked encounter.

Beside him, Viola was quick and light-footed. He'd noticed her grace the first time that they danced together. Now she didn't hang back, but darted across the marble floor and skipped down the stairs to the gravel path. He supposed that she tried to avoid notice, but he preferred to think that she was as eager to be alone with him as he was desperate to be alone with her.

He *was* desperate. It was a bit of a surprise how desperate. Right now, his heart was racing and anticipation turned the dark night to fire. In his time, he'd wanted plenty of women. Women from whom he could expect more than a mere kiss.

Because he was so keen to touch Viola, he soon swung her off the path and into a secluded arbor. He stopped near the tinkling fountain in the center. Blind Cupid poised on a scallop shell and aimed his arrow straight at Toby. Some superstitious urge made him step out of the direct line of fire, although he feared that it might already be too late to save himself.

Now Viola became the target. For some reason, that idea didn't make him nearly so uncomfortable.

"You knew this was here." She was breathless. More excitement? Or was it just that he'd made her run?

"I did." They both kept their voices low. The splashing water covered their conversation. He used the excuse of wanting to hear her to move closer.

"Some previous naughtiness?"

"A gentleman never tells." He'd had Lady Plunkett in this grove, one sunny afternoon last June. The encounter had been torrid, but as he stared down at Viola in the light of the half moon, he had difficulty remembering any other woman except this one.

"That's a relief."

"Does that mean that you're going to let me kiss you?"

The cold white moonlight and the flickering shadows transformed her into a creature of enchanting mystery. Her gloating smile made his blood surge. "I hope you are."

Satisfaction vibrated in his low laugh. "Right answer."

His hands shook with the force of his hunger, as he drew his gloves off and shoved them into his pocket. "I love..." He paused and swallowed. "I love that you don't play games."

Dear God, he'd come close to stumbling there. He didn't want Viola getting any false ideas about his emotions.

The light was bright enough for him to see her eyes flash up to inspect his features. "Your voice just cracked."

He swallowed again to relax a throat as taut as a drumhead, and heat tinged his cheeks. Out of all the pretty girls in the world, only this one could make him blush.

Usually when he set out to lure a lady, he spouted all sorts of nonsense. With Viola, he had a feeling that only the truth would do. "It's mad. But I'm as nervous as a grouse on a Scottish moor in August."

She laughed. "I can't imagine why."

He cupped her delicate jaw. Her skin was soft and smooth and beguilingly warm. Her breath changed as he touched her.

His fingers flexed in a caress. "Can't you?"

"You've done plenty of kissing."

"Indeed I have."

"You should know your way around, then."

"One would hope so."

"Whereas I'm new to the activity."

"Apart from Cousin Terence."

She grimaced. "Don't remind me. At least I don't want to hit you."

"That's good to hear."

"So why would you be nervous?"

He sucked in a lungful of air. The night was tinged with green growing things and a hint of the Thames. And most delicious of all, the sweet perfume of Viola Frain. "I've kissed other women, but I've never kissed you."

Her faint sigh expressed pleasure, and she lifted a gloved hand to press his palm closer against her face. "I doubt that I'm built any differently."

He didn't think she was. Which made it more of a puzzle that this encounter should seem so out of the ordinary. But it did seem special. While he wasn't sure why, he couldn't deny that it was so.

Toby leaned in, until he hovered a breath away. His voice was lower than a whisper. "Perhaps I should make sure."

"Yes, please."

It was Viola, not Toby, who closed the infinitesimal gap between them.

Toby's lips were softer than Viola expected. Terence's lips had been hard and wet, a bit like a clammy stone.

Then all memories of that horrid assault dissolved in a glowing wash of magic, as Toby's mouth moved under hers. Such pleasurable pressure.

"Oh," she said against his lips, then "oh" again when he shifted his hand from her face to gather her close into that tall, impressively muscled body.

He radiated the most alluring warmth. Her arms curled around his neck. Velvety darkness enveloped her, as she gave herself up to the kiss. Her knees dissolved to water, and her heart pounded so hard that she feared she might swoon with the sheer thrill of it all.

He gave a growl of approval, as she fitted herself to him as if created to rest in his arms. The pressure against her lips deepened, until the blood rushed through her veins with dizzying speed. She pressed nearer in silent encouragement.

When Toby lifted his head, a wordless complaint escaped her. A wordless complaint that faded beneath another kiss. He began to tease her with fleeting brushes of his lips, creating a heady mixture of delight and torment.

That first kiss had left Viola poised on the edge of flying. Now she hung suspended between earth and heaven, unsure whether she was about to soar or fall back to the ground with a bump.

"Toby..." she protested, when she failed yet again to capture those dancing lips. "Kiss me properly."

"Are...you...sure?" A quick kiss punctuated each word.

"No," she stammered, shifting her hands to his shoulders.

Toby responded with a faint laugh. This time when he kissed her, he lingered. Viola lost all grip on prosaic reality, as the ground beneath her feet disappeared. Unprecedented pleasure made her part her lips on a gasp. When his tongue fluttered against her lips before slipping through, she went rigid with shock.

He was *tasting* her.

As he pulled back, she raised heavy eyelids. The world around her was no longer the same. Her life was divided into before she'd kissed Toby Sutton and after she'd kissed Toby Sutton. The revelation proved even more alarming than that bizarre moment when his tongue invaded her mouth.

The moon had gone behind a cloud, making the copse as black as a cave. The darkness felt intimate rather than intimidating.

"What did you do that for?" Her voice was shaky. *She* was shaky.

Toby's arms around her waist kept her upright. She reveled in his easy strength. Her knees hadn't yet returned to their reliable selves. She hooked her fingers over his shoulders. She'd never before noticed how nice a man's broad shoulders could be. Not to mention how useful they were, when a girl felt like her legs were about to collapse.

"Did it disgust you?"

It should have. If anyone had told her that a young man would lick her mouth, she'd be horrified.

But in practice? In practice, when the young man was Toby, she'd been startled, but not repulsed. She might even say that the act had been…intriguing. "No."

That evoked a soft huff of amusement. "You don't sound very sure."

"I'm not. I wasn't prepared for—"

"How frightening it is to kiss a man?"

Viola shook her head, although she wasn't sure that he'd see. "I'm not frightened."

"You're not?" He sounded pleased.

"No. But…" She licked lips that tasted of Toby. "I was unprepared for the intimacy. 'Kiss' sounds like such a simple word. Yet when you place your mouth on mine, I feel…"

His grip tightened around her. "Yes?"

"You'll laugh at me."

"Never."

Humor warmed his ironic response. She didn't mind. Not when Toby listened to her the way nobody else ever had. It was a remarkably powerful sensation. Almost as powerful as those tantalizing kisses.

"When you kiss my lips, it's as if you lay claim to my whole body."

Toby sucked in an unsteady breath. "Viola…"

He hauled her closer than before, and there was no more teasing. Instead, his mouth was hot and demanding, and when his tongue traced the seam of her lips, she opened, helpless to resist.

This time, while the flicker of his tongue was no surprise, its effect was more overwhelming. Searing heat shuddered through her. Everything ignited into a new and glorious universe, bright with flame.

Her stomach clenched, and her legs wobbled. Despite her innocence, she recognized the thrumming ache inside her as desire. When Toby lifted his head, she was trembling and disoriented, and astounded at the intoxicating pleasure that he'd summoned.

"Kiss me back," he growled in a voice so low that it set her bones vibrating.

"Kiss you back?" she echoed.

"Do what I do."

"You mean—"

Before she could put it into words, he caught her chin with one hand and tilted her face up. More radiant heat. More masculine demand. But this time, she made demands of her own. Tentative. Gentle. But demands nonetheless.

When her tongue slid along his, an incoherent sound of approval emerged from his throat. Encouraged, Viola sucked his tongue deeper into her mouth, savoring his tangy taste.

From the first, the carnality of what they did staggered her, but this extended beyond that into a realm of experience that she'd never imagined. She curved into his body, as her frantic grasp on his shoulders eased into a caress.

Their lips launched a playful duel. Need sharpened into a powerful pulse between her legs. The ferocious potency of their actions made her quake and moan.

When he withdrew, they were both trembling. "We must stop," he said, and she thrilled to the desperation in his hoarse voice. "We must stop, or I won't be able to."

But his hand stroked up and down her back in a way that set her blood racing. When he spoke, he was so close that she felt his breath on her face.

"You make me hear music," she whispered.

Then she realized that she really could hear music. Supper must have ended. She'd lost all awareness of time.

"I didn't mean to go this far," he whispered. "But as soon as you stepped into my arms, I was lost."

"So was I." With an almighty effort, she dragged her hands down from where they tangled in the curls at his nape.

Viola still wore her long gloves. She knew it was wicked, but next time, she wanted to touch him without any gloves between them.

Would there be a next time?

"Damn it, I don't want to let you go."

"You must, or we'll cause a scandal." She heard a fatal lack of conviction in her voice.

"For pity's sake, Viola, help me to do the right thing here."

"Then you'll have to take your hands off me."

"I will." His hold settled on her hips. "I will…"

This time, the kiss flared into passion in an instant. Viola tumbled headlong into a sensual world that not long ago had been so foreign. Now it lured her like an open bottle of brandy lured a drunkard.

When Toby finally drew away, her head was swimming. He caught her face between his hands and peered down through the darkness.

"You'll come to the park tomorrow?" Ardor roughened his voice in the most ravishing way. "Early?"

"Yes." She paused. "But I can't kiss you."

The moon came out in time for her to catch the glint of his teeth as he smiled. "I'll do my best to get rid of your groom."

"You can't. If I break too many rules, Juliet will send me back to Wiltshire."

"Then I'll have to find some other way to get you alone."

She should protest. This attraction swept her out into dangerous waters indeed, and as Juliet pointed out, Viola had the most at stake in any flirtation.

But she'd never experienced anything to rival Toby's kisses. Having sampled paradise, she couldn't wait to do it all again. The secret rebel inside her had snatched control of the reins. Where this wild ride would lead, she had no idea. She prayed that it wasn't to ruin and disgrace.

It was too late to pull back. She had a fatalistic feeling that it had been too late to pull back from the second a stranger crashed down at her feet.

"Yes," she said on a long sigh. "Make it soon."

"I will." He kissed her again.

For a brief instant, she surrendered to the magic. But she'd come back to reality long enough to understand that it was risky to linger. So far, they'd been lucky to avoid discovery, but she couldn't rely on that luck continuing.

So this time, it was Viola who broke away. The effort that she needed to end the kiss was warning enough of how close she verged to throwing her cap over a windmill. "I have to go, Toby."

With a groan of frustration, he stepped back, too. She fought the urge to bridge the distance between them. Already, she was addicted to his touch. When he took her in his arms, she felt whole in a way that she never had before.

"Come out into the moonlight where I can see you. I fear you look like you've been kissing a fellow in the bushes."

"Funny, that," she said dryly, which elicited an answering grunt of amusement.

She extended her hand and he took it, as he backed out of the shrubbery toward the fountain. "I suppose you have a partner for this dance."

"Yes." She paused to identify the popular tune for a quadrille. "And for the one that finished before this one."

"I've kept you out here too long."

"Yes."

"I'm not going to apologize. I wish I could keep you out here until daybreak. I don't want you dancing with any of those undeserving sods. I want you dancing with me."

That sounded like jealousy. How very delicious.

"Oh, Toby..." She tilted forward, forgetting everything except how much she loved his kisses.

He straightened his shoulders and set his jaw. "Don't tempt me."

"You're having a terrible effect on my morals," she said in a low voice.

It sounded as if she was joking, but she wasn't. Not really. She'd never imagined that she was the type of girl to take silly risks with her person and her good name. But then, she'd never imagined that she'd fall headlong into a physical infatuation with a man either. It seemed that she didn't know herself as well as she'd always thought she did.

Toby smiled. "I hope so."

He released her hand and angled her face up to the moonlight. A vibrant silence descended, as he studied her the way her father pored over the text of *Macbeth*.

"Am I fit to be seen?" she asked in an unsteady voice.

"You're lovely." Even in the moonlight, she read tenderness in his expression. "You're always lovely."

The ridiculous truth was that when Viola was with him, she felt lovely. It was a gift that he alone gave her. "Thank you."

"And despite all those kisses, not a hair is out of place." He paused. "No, wait."

He adjusted the pretty gilt coronet that held her curls away from her face. Something about his effortless competence as he touched her made her feminine core contract with forbidden excitement. "That's better."

"Kiss me," she said in a low, yearning voice. "Just in case we never have this chance again."

What a demanding wench she'd become. If she adopted the habit of kissing Toby on a regular basis, she feared that she'd turn into a monster.

"I couldn't bear it if this is our only chance."

"I know. But..."

His hand was gentle as he caught her jaw and bent to take her lips. The kiss was gentle, too, although it sent now-familiar pleasure shuddering through Viola and made her reach blindly for his chest.

"Toby, I wish you didn't have to stop," she sighed, after he moved away with a reluctance that he didn't try to hide.

"So do I." He stroked her cheek, as he lowered his hand. "Let me make sure that we're safe."

# CHAPTER NINE

More than he'd ever wanted anything in his life, Toby wanted to linger in the shadows with Viola. Who had been as sweet as honey when she'd succumbed to his kisses. So sweet that the rake had skirted close to losing his head and forgetting where he was.

It was time that she returned to the ballroom. More than time. He didn't want her suffering any harm over their flirtation. He didn't want her suffering any harm at all. Especially at his hands.

He stepped onto the path. Blessedly empty. He ventured a few feet up to where the gravel curved away and found himself bumping into a lone female.

"Miss Dimchurch," he said without pleasure.

"Lord…Lord Renfrew," she said with a surprise that sounded genuine, although he'd witnessed enough of her tricks to have his doubts.

Thank goodness he'd gathered the shreds of his common sense and left Viola concealed in the bushes. He dreaded to think of the trouble that Marjorie would cause, if she knew that he'd been kissing another girl in the moonlight.

"What are you doing out here on your own?" They stood near a lantern, so he could see her much better than he'd been able to see Viola.

"I was..." Her voice trailed off, and he guessed that she must have been looking for him.

"Let me escort you back to the ballroom." He spoke at a normal volume, in contrast to the frantic, yearning murmurs that he'd shared with Viola. He hoped that Viola heard him and understood the danger she was in.

"Yes, thank you." Then Marjorie looked around, and he watched her expression change to a hardened determination that froze his gut to ice.

"Help! Lord Renfrew, what on earth are you doing?" Her shriek was high-pitched and designed to carry.

Toby jerked back in horror. "What the devil game is this?"

"No, please, don't do that!"

Feeling sick to his stomach, he saw her wrench at one filmy sleeve on her gown until it ripped. "Stop it, Marjorie," he hissed. "You'll bring the whole world down on us."

He retreated another step to stop himself grabbing the chit and giving her a good shake. But it was too late to save himself. He heard the crunch of numerous feet rushing across gravel.

Lord Edgecombe bustled around the bend in the path. "What's all this hullabaloo?"

Worse, his wife, the greatest scandalmonger in London, appeared at his side. As she took in Toby and Marjorie, the lamplight revealed her avid curiosity.

Celia Edgecombe stepped toward Marjorie and spoke in a sympathetic voice that didn't hide her interest. "What's the matter, dear?"

"Lord…Lord Renfrew tried to kiss me," Marjorie said in suitably failing tones.

"I most certainly did not," he snapped, drawing up to his full height and scowling at the growing crowd of observers.

"Fie, sir, you're ungallant," Marjorie said, as Lady Tierney came up to her side and placed a comforting arm around her. "How can you say that?"

"I say it because it's true." Although to his despair, as he looked around the faces surrounding him, he could see that nobody believed him.

"There, there, sweetheart," Lady Tierney clucked.

Marjorie began to snivel. Toby found the act deuced unconvincing, but he had the advantage of knowing it was a lie. A barrage of accusing glares focused on him. He could see that Marjorie's fantasies rang true to everyone else here. As Toby surveyed his audience, he felt trapped in an endless nightmare.

"Marjorie, you poor thing." It was one of Marjorie's minions. Letitia someone. "What a beast he is."

"Lord Renfrew asked me to meet him in the garden." The break in Marjorie's voice sounded infernally convincing, damn her. "He pressed his attentions upon me, yet now he calls me a liar?"

"The filthy cad," chirped another of the minions.

With every second, the crowd swelled. Toby heard shocked whispers, as those in the know passed on the scandalous news about Lord Renfrew taking liberties with Miss Dimchurch.

When he saw how skittish it made Viola, he'd cursed his bad reputation. Now he had more reason to rue his sins. His name for chasing the girls made people think it more than likely that he'd try to take advantage of Marjorie.

"Renfrew, what's all this?" Lord Tierney asked from the back of the crowd.

"Nothing. It's absolutely nothing," he grated out, as in despair, he recognized that he'd fallen right into Marjorie's clutches.

Be buggered if he meant to stay there.

The crowd parted, and he found himself staring at Marjorie's father, Sir Dexter Dimchurch. Someone must have fetched him from the ballroom. "What in Hades is happening here?"

"Your daughter is having a fit," Toby snapped.

"He tried to kiss me, Papa," Marjorie wailed, diving away from Lady Tierney to fling herself upon her father's bosom. "I tried to stop him, I really did."

Sir Dexter glared at Toby. "If you've despoiled my girl, you know what you need to do, young man."

The Dimchurch title was so new, it stank of the tanneries where Sir Dexter had made his fortune. If Marjorie snaffled the rich and noble Earl of Renfrew as a husband, it would be a major coup.

"She's lying." Toby said in a cold voice. "I didn't lay a finger on her."

"Then why is her dress torn?" Celia Edgecombe asked.

He gritted his teeth. "She tore it herself," he said, knowing how unlikely it sounded.

"I expect you to call on me tomorrow, Lord Renfrew," Dexter said, barely able to hide his glee.

"I've done nothing wrong."

"What a villain," Letitia said in carrying tones.

"You'll be cast out of society if you don't act the gentleman, Renfrew," Freddie Edgecombe said. "Come now, if you liked the chit well enough to sneak her away for a cuddle in the bushes, surely you like her well enough to marry her. It's the price of pursuing a lady of good character, lad."

But Marjorie wasn't a lady of good character. She was a deceitful weasel, and the thought of spending the rest of his life with her made Toby break out in a cold sweat.

"I didn't pursue her. I didn't touch her." He hardened his tone. "I will not be forced into wedding this woman under any circumstances."

"Papa, do you hear what he says?" Marjorie howled, and this time Toby really did believe that she was crying in earnest.

"Now, now, girl, don't take on so," her father said, patting her back, before addressing Toby on a completely different note. "You've impugned my daughter's honor, sir. If you don't intend to restore her good name, there's only one resort remaining to me. Name your seconds."

"Don't be absurd." Toby ground his teeth in irritation. "I have no intention of fighting a duel, just because your daughter is a scheming little witch."

Perhaps honesty wasn't the best policy in this case, because Sir Dexter straightened and stared Toby down over the sound of Marjorie's sniffles. "You will name your seconds, sir."

"This has gone far enough." At last, thank God, his cousin entered the fray. Leighton pushed his way through the people and stood beside Toby. "Miss Dimchurch, please gain some control over yourself. Sir Dexter, perhaps you and Toby and I can find a quiet room inside, where we can have a sensible conversation about this matter. A brouhaha does your daughter's reputation no good."

Sir Dexter refused to back down under Leighton's attempt to restore some calm to the situation. "This young man will marry my daughter, or he will face my bullet, my lord."

"My cousin doesn't deserve to be tried by the court of public opinion."

"He does if he's assaulted a virtuous lady at a society ball," someone said from the middle of the crowd. The observers remained very much on Marjorie's side.

But Toby refused to be bullied. He'd already spent too much time living under his father's thumb. Nobody was going to steal his freedom away again. He'd rather shoot himself than fall for Marjorie's nasty trick. "I haven't assaulted anyone, devil take you all."

Leighton shot him a meaningful glance. "That's not how it looks."

Bile soured Toby's mouth, as he realized that his cousin wasn't convinced of his innocence either. The ring of hostile glances made him realize that he was a stag surrounded by a pack of hounds.

Damn him, he should have done something about this blasted mare's nest well before this. He'd always treated Marjorie as a bit of a joke, however annoying she was. By heaven, he didn't feel like laughing now.

"Lord Renfrew didn't assault Miss Dimchurch," a cool, steady voice said from behind him. "She's lying, just as he says she is. For the last half hour, he's been with me. When his lordship encountered Miss Dimchurch, he'd just stepped out to check that we could slip back into the ballroom without attracting notice."

It was rescue, but a rescue that came at a price he couldn't countenance. Speechless with horror, Toby whirled around to see Viola standing on the path. In the lamplight, she looked pale and gallant and determined.

Marjorie raised her head from under the shelter of her father's arm. "What is she doing here?" The spite in her voice attracted a few questioning looks.

Viola ignored the girl. Keeping her attention on Toby, she stepped forward. "I was close enough to hear everything that happened. Lord Renfrew offered Miss Dimchurch no insult before she started shrieking her head off."

"Don't do this," he whispered, reaching for her, before he realized that touching her would only make things worse. "Please don't do this."

Shocked murmurs rose from the crowd. After this, the gossipmongers would have a field day. Toby could hear people repeating "Viola Frain" over and over as the identity of his defender became public knowledge.

"I have to." The gaze that Viola leveled on him was steady. "I won't let people call you a liar and a seducer and a coward, when I can save your reputation."

"But what about *your* reputation?"

She didn't answer. Instead, she squared her shoulders and addressed the crowd like a queen. Despite Toby wishing to blazes that she'd stayed hidden in the shrubbery, he couldn't help admiring her. She was so brave. He'd liked her from the first, but until now, he'd had no idea of her true quality.

Yet his actions brought this remarkable woman to destruction. His father had been right. Toby Sutton was a complete waste of time. Better that he'd never been born, rather than live to ruin Viola's life.

"Miss Dimchurch has only just come along the path. Lord Renfrew didn't have time to molest her, even if he had the inclination. His lordship was too honorable to mention my name in his defense, but I'm willing to swear on a Bible that he did no wrong to Marjorie Dimchurch."

"But what about the wrong he did to you?" Celia Edgecombe asked in an insinuating tone that made Toby want to wring her neck.

Toby stepped closer to Viola and seized her arm in a purposeful grip. There was no help for it. He knew what he had to do.

He struggled to plaster a smile on his face, hoping that the uncertain light would hide how sick he felt. "A newly engaged couple can be forgiven for seeking a little privacy."

When Viola jerked, he tightened his hold. "Toby, you can't—"

Toby spoke in a carrying, confident voice, before she could land them all in the soup. "I'm overjoyed to announce that Lady Viola has tonight agreed to make me the happiest of men."

Marjorie broke free of her father and surged forward. "No! It's not true. It can't be."

Sir Dexter grabbed her back with a roughness that made his daughter stagger. "Are you playing one of your stupid tricks, Marjorie?"

"That rat-faced little slut shan't have him!" Marjorie was past worrying about anything, except Viola usurping what she saw as her rightful place. "It's not fair."

"Shut your mouth, you useless hussy."

"I won't—"

The impact of Sir Dexter's hand connecting with his daughter's cheek echoed through the night and elicited a gasp of outrage from the crowd.

"Papa, you don't understand." Marjorie raised a shaking hand to her face. "I was—"

"I don't want to hear any more."

"But—"

Toby moved fast enough to catch the man's arm before it could descend once more. "If you hit your daughter again, sir, I *will* shoot you and laugh while I do it."

"You bastard!" Dexter glared up at Toby, who was at least six inches taller. "You dare to put your hands on me?"

"I dare." Struggling to control his temper, he turned to Marjorie. "Perhaps it might be better if you stayed with friends tonight, Miss Dimchurch."

The girl gaped at him, as if he emerged from a different world. "You've forgiven me?"

No, by heaven, he hadn't. But all those years suffering his father's brutality meant that he couldn't stand around to watch a lout abuse someone smaller and less powerful. Even if that someone was a designing shrew.

Kate pushed her way through the listeners and took Marjorie's arm. "Miss Dimchurch, you're welcome to come back with us."

"Thank...thank you." Marjorie sounded uncertain. "If you'll permit me, Papa?"

Looking defeated and bitter, Sir Dexter waved her away with a contemptuous gesture. "Get out of my sight."

Toby stepped back. Sir Dexter no longer looked likely to explode into violence, thank goodness. Which did nothing to change the frightful quandary that he and Viola were in.

Leighton addressed the audience with his best Earl of Shelburn arrogance. "I believe you've all had more than enough entertainment for the evening. As you now know, a private tryst between a newly betrothed couple has blown up into a public matter. I believe it's time Lady Shelburn and I took Miss Dimchurch home. Toby, perhaps you should escort Lady Viola back to the ballroom and consign her to her sisters' care. At least no real harm has been done."

Leighton sounded so certain, yet Toby knew that he was wrong. Great harm had been done, and he could blame most of it on his own carelessness. It wouldn't be too bad if he alone paid the price, but he was grimly aware that he dragged innocent people down into the pit with him. Even Marjorie, for all her treachery and her reckless gamble, was less at fault than he was. When all this blasted nonsense started, he should have made it clear to her that her quest to marry him had no chance of succeeding.

He ought to be bloody horsewhipped.

Toby sighed. Self-castigation could wait. Now it was a case of getting Viola out of the public gaze – she'd hate it, he knew – and doing his best to live down an almighty scandal.

He bowed to her with a genuine reverence that the night's chaos couldn't dilute. "May I accompany you inside, my lady?"

She let him lead her through the crowd. Only when they reached the terrace and had some privacy did she speak. "Toby—"

"Tomorrow," he said quietly. "We'll sort everything out tomorrow."

When he had to try and fix this unmitigated disaster. Heaven help him.

# CHAPTER TEN

*W*hen Smith announced that the Earl of Renfrew was calling at the Lorimer Square house, Viola stiffened up like a cat cornered by a growling dog. She was sitting with her sisters in the morning room, and they hadn't long finished breakfast. Not that she'd managed to eat much. Just as she hadn't managed to sleep much last night, after Juliet and Portia bundled her home like a dirty secret.

She rose to her feet and sent her sisters a helpless glance. "Should I see him in here?"

Smith stared into space. Viola had no doubt that all the servants knew about the previous night's events. Gossip spread even faster below stairs than it did in London's drawing rooms. "His lordship requests an interview with Lord Portdown, my lady."

A surge of panic made Viola stagger. She felt she was caught in a raging tide and it was too late to try and swim to safety. "Oh, no."

Juliet stood, ignoring Viola's jumpiness. "Is my father awake yet?"

"I believe he is, my lady. He's in his dressing room, practicing his lines for the reading at his club."

Next week, Lord Portdown gave a lecture about Shakespeare's sonnets. For the present, he abandoned the Greeks in favor of the Bard.

"I'll go and see him first," Viola said.

Their father, as far as she knew, remained unaware of the disaster that she'd brought down on the family. He'd been in bed last night when the three sisters arrived home in a subdued huddle. Nobody had had the heart to wake him with the news of Viola's fall from grace.

"No, I'll go," Juliet said. "The story will come better from me."

Viola knew that she was a coward to agree. After all, none of this was Juliet's fault. But she nodded just the same. "Thank you."

"Please show Lord Renfrew into the library, Smith, and let him know Papa will be with him in due course," Juliet said.

"Very good, my lady." The butler bowed and left.

Viola's shaking hands twined at her waist, as she struggled to control the queasiness churning in her stomach. "Papa will hit the roof."

"Not if I've got any say in it," Juliet said. "If he'd kept an eye on you, we wouldn't be facing this dilemma. I assume that his lordship will want to talk to you, once he's finished with Papa. Perhaps you should go upstairs and change into a nicer gown."

Because they all knew that Toby was here to propose, and Juliet wanted to place as much of a gloss on the occasion as the difficult circumstances allowed.

After Juliet left the room, Portia glanced across at Viola, who had slumped into a chair. "Are you all right, sis?"

Viola swallowed the bile that flooded her mouth. While Juliet might blame Papa for the scandal, the fault was hers. "You know, Juliet hasn't scolded me once for what happened."

In fact, neither of her sisters had mentioned anything beyond practicalities, since Toby had delivered Viola to their care in Lady Tierney's ballroom. It had proven a remarkably quiet ride home in the carriage, although Viola had felt the weight of her sisters' disapproval and disappointment all the way. Thank heaven they only had to travel as far as the other side of the square.

Once they arrived back at the house, Viola had trudged upstairs, feeling as if she'd committed murder. She supposed that she had, if she counted her reputation and her sisters' marital hopes as victims. As her maid undressed her, she'd remained silent. Then blessedly alone at last, she'd flung herself on her bed for a good cry, followed by a sleepless night where her frantic mind replayed every disastrous minute from the preceding hours.

What cut sharpest was the way humiliation had sullied the greatest joy that she'd ever known. Kissing Toby had been marvelous. What had come afterward hadn't been.

"When you came in from the garden last night, you looked like you were about to crack into a million pieces," Portia said.

"I felt like it."

"We'd just heard what was happening, and we were coming out to get you."

"I think the whole world will have heard by now," Viola said glumly.

"At least Renfrew has the sense to know that the sooner he acts, the sooner we can scotch the scandal."

"Yes." But at what cost?

She glanced down at her faded pink muslin gown. It was an old favorite, but unsuitable for receiving a suitor. She'd dug it out of the back of the wardrobe this morning, hoping it might provide some comfort.

Juliet was right. She needed to put on a more appropriate dress. "I'll go upstairs."

"No need to hurry. If I know Papa, he'll leave Renfrew to cool his heels, before he comes downstairs to read him the riot act. He's never very active first thing in the morning. Or at least not until he's had a couple of cups of strong coffee."

Portia smiled to ease the ominous atmosphere. It wasn't a very convincing effort, but Viola appreciated the attempt.

She let herself out into the hallway, but instead of going upstairs, she stiffened her backbone and marched toward the library's closed door. She felt like a guillotine awaited at the end of the corridor, instead of a handsome young man who intended to ask for her hand in marriage.

At the sound of the library door opening, Toby looked up from the cup of coffee that he was holding but not drinking. His stomach plunged to his boots, as he prepared to face the father of the girl he'd dishonored and to make atonement for what he'd done.

It wasn't Lord Portdown who came into the room. It was Viola.

"You..." He lurched to his feet so abruptly that lukewarm coffee sloshed into the saucer. "You shouldn't be here, Viola."

She hovered by the door and leveled a troubled gaze upon him. "Lately I seem to be making a habit of being in places where I shouldn't be."

He stepped forward, very careful to keep his movements slow and his voice quiet. It was the way that he'd approach a frightened horse. Viola looked ready to shatter at any unexpected action. He had a sudden memory of her impressive coolness when he'd first met her. His blasted ineptitude had destroyed that, plague take him.

"I'll come and see you, once I've spoken to your father." Toby had no doubts that Lord Portdown would accept his offer to marry Viola. Last night's fuss left none of them any choice.

He took in her paleness and the marks of sleeplessness. Since the fracas, he'd felt guilty. Now the proof of how his behavior had distressed this gallant, wonderful girl made his gut clench with self-hatred. How badly he'd wronged her.

He wished that he'd broken his damn fool neck when he fell out of that godforsaken tree. But he was bitterly aware that he couldn't turn back the clock.

Viola crossed her arms and took up a defensive pose. "You don't have to marry me."

"Yes, I do."

"It's not that bad." He hated the drowning despair that he read in her lightless gray eyes. "I can go back to Wiltshire for the rest of the season. I've always been happy in the country. I never expected to make a splash in society."

An unamused smile twisted his lips. "You've made more than a splash, I'm afraid."

One hand sliced the air. "If I leave London, people will forget the scandal. Eventually."

"In about twenty years, maybe." He paused, trying to stifle his hurt at the realization that she preferred a life of shamed isolation over marriage to him. Not that he could blame her. No woman of sense would want to take on such a rapscallion. And despite the evidence of her recent behavior, Viola remained a woman of sense. "Thirty, for sure."

She struggled to smile. "I can read a lot of books in thirty years."

While she was trying to be brave, he could see that it took an almighty effort. "So we've sorted you out."

His dry response made her eyes widen. "Exile doesn't seem like such a punishment."

"If you say so."

Her shoulders lowered, as she sucked in a huge breath. Relief, he supposed. It had to be relief. Why on earth would she want to marry him? "I knew you'd understand."

To his regret, he understood better than she thought. He had no right to feel pique at her lack of enthusiasm for taking him as a husband. A rascal like him was fine for a few kisses in the bushes, but she'd be insane to harness herself to such a loose cannon. "But people other than you are tied up in this infernal mess. What about Juliet? What about Portia?"

Her brief animation faded. "Nobody should blame them for what happened."

"Nobody should. But they will. Granville has a reputation as a high stickler. Will he want to wed a woman whose family is tarred by scandal?"

"Juliet's magnificent. He'd be lucky to have her as his duchess."

"Undoubtedly, but he might think twice about taking a disgraced debutante into his family when he weds her sister."

"I'll stay away from London." Viola backed off, until she bumped into the closed door. "Nobody in society ever needs to see me again."

Despite everything, vast tenderness flooded him. He kept his voice kind. "That's not good enough."

"It will have to be." Her lips flattened. "Juliet will forgive me. And so will Portia."

"They might. But what about me?"

She frowned in puzzlement. "What about you?"

"My reputation is hanging by a thread."

"But everyone knows Marjorie was lying. You didn't accost her in the Tierneys' garden."

"I didn't. Because I was too deuced busy, corrupting another lady's virtue. If you don't marry me, I'll be forever tarred as a man of no principles."

"The world already knows about your taste for lightskirts."

He hid a wince. "For lightskirts, yes. But I've never ruined a virgin from a good family."

"You didn't ruin me," she said sharply. "We shared a few kisses, but I'm as pure as the day I was born."

Not quite. He remembered how delightfully she'd followed him along sin's path. She wasn't half as innocent as she'd been when he whisked her away into that moonlit glade. Those few kisses had awakened Viola's powerful sensuality, until her innocent enthusiasm threatened to immolate him in frustrated desire.

"Gossip will say that you gave me more than a few kisses."

"I won't be in Town to hear it."

"I will be. Unless general disgust with my behavior drives me into exile, the way it drove Byron into exile last year. Juliet and Portia will still be in London. Your father will still be in London."

"Most of the time, Papa lives in a dream world."

"Perhaps. But do you really want to hide away for the rest of your days? Especially when you're living down a scandal that only arose because you've got more courage and character than is good for you."

He spoke gently, but he saw that every word landed like a blow. By now, she was ashen and tears glittered in her eyes. He felt like hell that he'd made her cry, although the heaviness around her eyes hinted that these weren't the first tears that she'd shed since their last calamitous encounter.

"But..." Her throat moved as she swallowed. When she forced the words out, her voice was clogged with emotion. "But if you have to marry anyway, what was the point of saving you from Marjorie?"

Toby didn't bother to hide a shudder. "I'd much rather marry you than Marjorie."

He'd hoped that might lighten Viola's tragic air, but she kept staring at him as if the world was coming to an end. He supposed that her world *was* coming to an end. "But you don't want to marry anyone. I refuse to trap you into a wedding that you'd never contemplate without coercion."

"You speak as if I'm guiltless, and you're entirely to blame. When I kissed you, I was well aware of the risks. In truth, out of the two of us, I bear most of the blame because I'm more worldly-wise."

"But I didn't have to agree to come outside with you. After agreeing, I didn't have to linger."

"Justice insists you're the innocent party. In every sense of the word."

"Justice is wrong. I wanted to kiss you. And because of that, we're in this dreadful bind."

The words that he spoke welled straight up from his unworthy heart. "If I'm going to marry anyone, I'm proud to marry the girl who stepped forward to defend me last night."

Viola made a sound halfway between a sob and a laugh. Closer to a sob, if he was honest. "I knew you were too honorable to say that you couldn't have been kissing Marjorie because you were kissing me instead."

Startled, he looked directly at her. Was it possible that she was yet again trying to protect him from the consequences of his actions? That put a completely different complexion on matters, if it was true.

Perhaps she wasn't as opposed to becoming his wife as he'd first thought. So far, all her demurrals focused on what their escapade had cost him, not her.

"Most people don't credit me with having any honor. That's why they were so quick to judge me at fault, when Marjorie played her nasty little trick."

Viola's jaw set with determination. "Then they don't know you at all."

Her certainty shocked Toby. "Taking you outside last night wasn't an honorable act."

"I went of my own free will." Her stubbornness was a great improvement on her desolation when she'd come in, thank God. "You keep talking about what happened, as if I had no agency in what we did. You weren't a wicked seducer. I was more than ready to kiss you. Then from an excess of chivalry, you were so desperate to save my good name, that you nearly fell into Marjorie's trap. I'd say that was honorable to the point of stupidity."

His short laugh held a grim note. "If you're determined to depict me as a hero, who am I to argue?"

"You're mocking me."

"No. On my soul, I'm not."

"You *are* a man of honor. I've never been so impressed in my life as I was when you stepped up to stop Sir Dexter from hitting Marjorie. Anyone an ounce less principled might decide she deserved what she got."

He shifted uncomfortably. "Nobody deserves to be hit."

"See?" She went back to blinking away tears. "You're a hero."

"It wasn't half so heroic as what you did when you came out of the bushes."

Her shoulders slumped. "We're still trapped, though, aren't we?"

Toby had a sudden poignant memory of how vivid she'd been in his arms last night. It bloody well broke his heart to see her so defeated.

He studied her. "After I've spoken to your father, will you accept my offer of marriage, Viola?"

She wrapped her arms around herself, looking too vulnerable for his liking. He fought the urge to embrace her. "You don't want to marry me," she said in a dull voice.

"I wouldn't entirely say that. I like you. A lot." He sighed with impatience when his confession made her jerk with surprise. "Why does that amaze you? I've been on your trail since we met."

Her lips turned down. "All of four days ago."

"Sometimes you know straightaway." He took a risk. "I had a feeling that you liked me, too."

"You know I like you. Why else do you think I kissed you?"

That sounded promising. Toby ventured a step closer. He really needed to touch her, or else he'd go mad. "If we're married, we can kiss twenty-four hours a day and nobody will say us nay."

Kiss, and other things. Perhaps the rewards for wedding Viola might outweigh the duress.

To his relief, that sparked a smile verging on natural. "We'd have to stop to sleep."

The promise of having her in his bed made him bite back a groan. Once she was his wife, sleep wouldn't be a priority.

Toby encircled her upper arm with one hand. She was as taut as a fishing line with a monster salmon on the end.

"Do you really hate the idea of marrying me?" He forbore pointing out that it was too late for either of them to choose another path, not if they wanted anything like a normal life.

"No." Large gray eyes met his. "But I can't bear to force you into something that you don't want."

Relief flooded him. Both at her answer, and what it revealed about her motivation. His guess hadn't been a million miles away from the truth. Her principal objection to their engagement was fear that he loathed the idea of wedding her.

His hands slid down her bent arm, until she straightened it and let his fingers tangle with hers. Despite their dire situation, touching her had the familiar effect of calming his troubled spirits. "I can imagine worse fates than a lifetime with you."

Her anxious gaze remained unwavering, which didn't stop her from allowing him to draw her into the center of the room.

That felt like a victory. He'd feared that if he said the wrong thing, she might take to her heels. Then she wouldn't stop until she was back at Afton Park, contemplating a nun-like future. If Viola Frain hid away from the world forever, the world would be the poorer for it, by Jove.

"You're just making the best of our terrible circumstances."

He smiled, surprised that his strongest impulse right now was to kiss her. Although why should he be surprised? He'd wanted to kiss her ever since he first laid eyes on her. "I can bear my martyrdom. I'll only remind you of my saintly goodness once an hour or so."

She gave a choked giggle. "Now you're just being charming."

"I can't help it. Haven't you heard? Toby Sutton is a devil with the ladies." He stepped closer. "Now, I really have to kiss you."

"But if Papa comes—"

The rest of what she meant to say disappeared under the touch of his lips. There was that immediate sweetness that he recalled from last night. A sweetness that promised an endless well of pleasure.

He kept the contact light. Right now, she needed comfort not passion. Although when her willowy form sagged against him in swift surrender, passion crept closer.

He sighed with satisfaction and slid his arms around her waist.

"By God, Juliet warned me. Get your hands off my daughter, sirrah!"

The angry voice seemed to come from another world. The real world that was full of thorns and explosions, unlike the heaven that Toby found in Viola's arms.

With a squeak of horror, Viola struggled free. "Papa!"

Lord Portdown stood in the doorway, his face like thunder. Then to Toby's astonishment, he burst into laughter. "If it's like that, you and I need to have a serious talk, Renfrew. Viola, go and find your sisters. This young man and I have things to settle."

Viola was blushing like a rose. "Yes, Papa," she said in a subdued voice and left Toby with the man he hoped would become his future father-in-law.

# CHAPTER ELEVEN

hrough all his profligate years in London, Toby had never had to account to an angry father for his many sins. In the main, because the women he chased were aware that any liaison with the Earl of Renfrew would be strictly temporary.

The moment he saw Viola, he'd recognized that he was swimming out into dangerous waters. Yet she'd been so damned irresistible, he couldn't stay away. Now they were both likely to drown.

Yet here he was, about to request Viola Frain's hand in marriage. While the scandal was regrettable and he hated that circumstances compelled Viola onto this path before she was ready, he wasn't nearly as angry about being cornered into a proposal as he'd expected to be.

By God, if Marjorie's nasty little stratagem had succeeded and he had to front up to the odious Sir Dexter, he'd be as sick as a parrot. A lifetime with Marjorie didn't bear thinking about. Whereas a lifetime with Viola was...almost appealing.

He understood that he'd need to give up his dissolute ways and act like a responsible man instead of a self-indulgent boy. He'd have to do his best to establish some domestic happiness. Which was a problem, when he had no more idea of what domestic happiness looked like than a newly whelped tiger cub did.

On the upside, his bride was a lovely girl who showed a promising talent for kissing. Better, he'd claim sole rights to take that lovely girl to bed.

Right now, the likelihood of his attentions to his wife producing offspring was too terrifying to contemplate. That prospect skulked in his mind like a monster brooding at the center of a labyrinth. But Viola was good and sensible, and he could already tell that she'd grown up in a more nurturing environment than he had. With luck, she'd do the childrearing and any brats would take after her instead of their ramshackle father.

So he faced Lord Portdown with a touch more optimism than he'd believed possible last night. An optimism that shriveled with the man's first words.

"Young man, you're not the suitor I'd have chosen for my daughter. Given what Juliet told me this morning, your recent behavior only confirms my opinion."

For a second there, Toby had wondered if this might be easy. He now had his answer. Lord Portdown regarded him the way the head gardener at Kew looked at a slug on the begonias.

"I don't deserve Lady Viola—"

"You've got that right," Lord Portdown snapped. Viola had taken his pretense of amiability away with her when she'd left. "How dare you lure an innocent girl into a tryst? Even worse, how dare you allow her to be discovered and shamed?"

"I'm at fault, my lord, and saying that I never meant scandal to tarnish your daughter's name is no excuse, although it's the truth." Toby squared his shoulders and met Portdown's eyes, gray like Viola's, but much, much colder. "I harbor the greatest respect for Lady Viola."

That declaration brought no visible softening to the other man's expression. "Fine way you have of showing it."

"If I could change what happened last night, my lord, I would." Which wasn't entirely true. He wouldn't miss out on kissing Viola for the world. Despite everything that had happened since. "But I can't. Now I hope that you'll give me the benefit of the doubt, and allow me to do what I can to restore your daughter's good name."

Not to mention his own, by God.

For a deuced awkward interval, Lord Portdown surveyed him with critical attention. Then with a faint growl, he retreated to the imposing chair behind the desk. "At least you've acted fast to resolve this matter. I hope you intend to ask for Viola's hand. I haven't been outside the house yet to hear the tattle, but according to Juliet, you and my daughter made fools of yourselves in front of half the ton."

"I would count myself the luckiest man in London if you give me your permission to propose to Lady Viola."

"All very pretty, I'm sure." Lord Portdown looked no more convinced. "But you're a rake, sir, and rakes make it their business to bamboozle honest folk with fine words."

"In this case, my words express my true feelings." Toby shifted from one foot to another. "My admiration for Lady Viola is sincere."

"What about her admiration for you? You're a handsome cove, and I've no doubt that you're quite the buck in the disreputable circles you move in. But Viola is a woman of character and intelligence. You'll need more than a comely face to keep her happy. If you imagine that you'll marry my girl and just go back to your bad old ways, I'm inclined to send you to the devil. Viola can take a tour of the Continent, until the worst of the fuss dies down. Juliet and Portia might face a bit of talk, but I won't let my daughter be wretched, just because a villain got his filthy paws on her."

Growing up, Toby had endured innumerable lectures from his father. This proved a painful reminder of those occasions. Except that he couldn't doubt that Lord Portdown spoke out of love for his daughter, whereas the late Lord Renfrew had felt nothing but contempt for his son. Not to mention that Toby was well aware that he deserved this dressing down more than he'd deserved his father's anger. At least on most occasions.

He gulped in a deep breath and spoke from the bottom of his reprehensible heart. "Lady Viola is the best girl in the world. I promise that I'll do my damnedest to make her happy."

Lord Portdown subjected him to another of those gimlet stares before he sighed. "See that you do. Sit down and give me an accounting of your circumstances. Scandal or no scandal, I won't let Viola marry a fortune hunter. And keep in mind that I'll look to confirm everything you say with a second party. You may have pulled the wool over my daughter's eyes with your Town bronze, but I'm nowhere near so ready to fall for a manly air and a ready smile."

Toby knew that he'd earned both the castigation and the suspicion. But he was a proud man, and it was difficult to accept the derision without protest. "All I can say, my lord, is that time will prove you've misjudged me."

Portdown responded with a skeptical snort and waved at the chair in front of the desk. "I hope to heaven you're right."

So did Toby. He gritted his teeth and lowered himself into the seat. He could already tell that the next half hour was going to be unpleasant.

In a tangle of nerves, Viola waited for Toby in the morning room. After her father's dismissal, she'd rushed upstairs to change into a gown fit to be seen outside the family before she hurried downstairs again.

Then she found herself waiting. And waiting.

"For heaven's sake, stop fidgeting, Viola," Portia said from where she sat near the unlit hearth. It was a sunny morning. The weather hadn't got today's news that Viola's world disintegrated into chaos.

"Papa seems to be talking to Lord Renfrew for a long time." She'd already paced the length of the room a hundred times. Now it was a hundred and one.

"A marriage requires a lot of arrangements," Juliet said with her usual calmness. She sat on the window seat, bent over her embroidery.

Viola wrung her hands and started another circuit of the room. "This isn't how I wanted my life to go."

Juliet's needle stilled, and she raised her head to direct a stern look at her youngest sister. "Then you shouldn't have sneaked out to kiss a notorious rake in the garden, when most of the ton were on hand to catch you in the act."

Viola paused, more puzzled than annoyed at the reprimand. "That's the closest to a scolding that you've given me since last night. I was sure that you'd tear strips off me, once you found out."

"It was too late for a scolding to do any good." Juliet sighed, as if she carried the weight of the world on her shoulders. For once, Viola couldn't disagree. "You knew you were taking a risk. Now you're paying the price."

"Lord Renfrew did his best to keep me out of trouble," Viola said.

"Yes, well, I'll admit from what I've heard, he tried to do the honorable thing, before you made your presence public." Juliet sounded as if she'd swallowed a lemon.

"Marjorie was—" Viola began.

"Telling a lot of lies. Yes, so I gather. She's at least partly to blame, poor little fool."

"Poor little fool?" Portia asked on a rising note. "She deliberately set out to trap Renfrew."

"But now everyone knows that she's a liar," Juliet said. "After this, what chance has she got to make a decent match? To establish a place in society? She took an awful risk, too, but nobody is stepping up to restore her to popularity."

"I couldn't let her horrible accusations go unchallenged." Viola came to rest in the middle of the room. How much longer would Toby be? He and Papa were taking a dickens of an age to make an agreement.

"Very principled. But the fact remains that if you'd stayed in the ballroom like you should have, there wouldn't be a problem."

"Juliet, we said we weren't going to nag and add to Viola's troubles," Portia said.

Juliet sighed, with impatience this time, and set aside her needlework. "I never nag." She caught the meaningful glance between Portia and Viola. "I call that rich, given—"

Juliet's protest faded to silence, when Smith appeared in the doorway. "Lord Renfrew requests a few moments alone with Lady Viola."

Viola's heart transformed into a boulder, a boulder that plummeted into her stomach. Not that Smith's announcement came as a surprise. She knew that Toby was about to propose. When she'd slipped in to see him earlier, he'd made her realize that she had to accept his offer. For everyone's sake.

On her way out, Portia paused at her side and gave her hand a brief squeeze. "Courage, sis. You look like you're about to collapse."

"I don't want to collapse," she whispered. "I want to disappear."

She waited for Juliet to say something snide about making her bed and having to lie in it. But to her surprise, her older sister stopped to give her a hug. Juliet in general wasn't a demonstrative woman, so the gesture was both unexpected and touching.

"You said you like him, and you're no fool," she said in encouragement. "You never know. This might all work out for the best."

Juliet was even less inclined to be optimistic than she was to make physical gestures of affection. This uncharacteristic behavior had the opposite effect to the one intended. It left Viola utterly terrified and convinced that she was about to make the worst mistake of her life.

Then her sisters were gone. Along with Smith. Toby stood before her, regarding her with such uncertainty that she feared she'd grown two heads.

"Are you all right?" he asked after the door closed, leaving them together.

"Yes," she said in a wavering voice.

"You don't look it. You look ready to cast up your accounts."

"I'm...I'm not going to be sick." Her voice came from far away, and the room turned misty in a most alarming fashion.

"Pleased to hear it." Toby strode forward to take her arm and help her down onto the window seat. "Damn your sisters."

Uncomprehending, Viola tried to focus on his face, but it was hazy, too. "My sisters?"

"Yes. Last time I saw you, you looked as if you'd come to terms with the dreadful prospect of marrying me. They've clearly alarmed you into catatonia."

"I don't—"

His hold on her arm tightened. "Breathe, Viola."

Her vision was narrowing. His hand closed around hers and through her panic, she recognized that he was here and he wasn't going to let her down.

"Breathe, sweetheart."

The endearment pierced her distraction as nothing else could. At last, she gulped in a mouthful of air. Straightaway, the room's details emerged from the fog. The room and Toby's concerned face. He sat beside her, staring at her as if he feared for her sanity.

"I'm...I'm sorry," she said unsteadily. "I'm acting like a goose."

"It's been a difficult time." He paused. "I fear it's going to get more difficult."

"Oh, dear." She studied him. "Was Papa beastly?"

He shook his head and brought her hand up for a kiss. No gloves today. "No more than I deserved."

"I can't bear it." The warmth of his lips went a long way toward restoring her grip on reality. "He bullied you into offering for me."

Toby smiled. That helped, too. She'd feared that he'd be furious at this abrupt change to his plans. But he seemed resigned to his fate.

Viola wasn't quite at that stage yet. She'd never thought much about marrying. She'd imagined that when she found a man she liked, it would happen. Everything would be gradual and orderly and respectable.

An inferno of kisses, a scandal, and a quick wedding to smother that scandal hadn't been on her horizon.

She supposed that Toby felt equally at a loss. Although he was kind enough to hide any resentment.

Now he spoke with a touch of urgency. "We don't have long to talk. I'm sure your papa fears that I'll take advantage of you if I'm unsupervised. Have you changed your mind about having me? I hope you haven't. I know our situation isn't ideal and you feel like you hardly know me, but I swear I'll do my best to be a good husband. I'll dedicate my life to caring for you. You said that you trust to my honor. Well, trust to my honor in this. I'll do everything in my power to be worthy of you, Viola."

Viola swallowed to ease a jammed throat. And swallowed again. The time had arrived. She had to make a decision. Although she was grimly aware that she'd relinquished any choice last night, when she emerged from the shrubbery.

"I haven't changed my mind," she said, grateful that her voice was steady. "I'll be your wife, Toby. "

Overwhelming emotion flooded his features. Relief, she supposed. As he'd told her, so much relied on a quick marriage. "Thank you."

"Kiss me." She studied him. "I'm not afraid when you kiss me."

"Viola…" He slid his arms around her waist and gathered her up, but the door slammed open to reveal Lord Portdown and the opportunity was lost.

# CHAPTER TWELVE

The ancient stone church at Afton was crowded for the wedding of Lord Portdown's youngest daughter, Viola, to Tobias Sutton, Earl of Renfrew. Despite an engagement that had only lasted five days, the village ladies had done the couple proud. Arrangements of spring flowers provided bright splashes of color against the worn gray stone, and the woodwork gleamed with polish.

Toby waited at the altar, wondering how in Hades he'd ended up here. A week ago, the thought of marriage hadn't entered his head. Yet here he was, about to claim a pure girl of impeccable bloodlines as his countess. The grim thought arose that for once in his life, his father would approve of his choice, even if he wouldn't approve of how Toby had arrived at this moment.

Since Viola had accepted him, grim thoughts had abounded. He knew that he wasn't worthy of her. He knew that he took on responsibilities that he wasn't convinced he could live up to. He knew that the world watched, expecting him to prove an abject failure as a husband.

"Cheer up, old son," Leighton said from beside him. "That Friday face is only going to make the talk worse. It's a wedding, not a funeral."

"I wish I'd had a chance to speak to Viola before the ceremony," he muttered.

The Frain family had decamped for Wiltshire the day he'd proposed. He'd been busy since, organizing a special license and making a quick visit to Brazey Castle to ensure that everything there was ready for the bride's arrival.

Last night, he'd ridden into Afton, hoping to assess how that bride felt about marrying him. But it was clear that there was a general conspiracy to keep them apart. He and Viola had sat together at dinner, but hadn't managed a second's privacy.

What he'd seen of his betrothed wasn't reassuring. She'd looked frightened and despondent. Had she lost weight in the few days since he'd last seen her? Surely not. But she'd been wan and quiet. She fretted about this rushed union, he could tell.

"You'll have plenty of time alone after you're wed," Leighton said.

Toby sighed. "That will be too late."

"You can't pull back now." His cousin regarded him in horror. "That would be beyond the pale."

"To blazes with you, I don't want to pull back," Toby snapped, drawing a disapproving glance from the vicar who stood a few feet away.

Leighton lowered his voice. "But you think that Viola might?"

"Why the deuce would such a grand girl want to marry a dog like me?"

"Because she wants her good name back?"

"It seems a hell of a price to pay for a couple of kisses in the moonlight."

Leighton sighed with long-suffering patience. "Toby, I know you're suffering an attack of the blue devils right now, but from what I've seen of Viola, she'll make the best of things."

"She'll have to make a silk purse out of a sow's ear if she marries me. My father said—"

"Your father was a close-minded, stiff-necked bastard, for all his academic reputation." Leighton spoke with some force. "There was always more good in you than bad, even if he refused to see it."

Toby gaped at his cousin. "You didn't like him?"

"I despised him. He was a prissy old bore, too convinced that his every word emerged as pure gold. And he treated you abominably. Now forget him and concentrate on making this gorgeous creature you're about to wed a happy woman. In the process, you may find some happiness yourself."

"Spoken like a contented husband," Toby said glumly.

"I can vouch for the bliss of taking a good woman to wife. I know you're expecting a disaster, but you and Viola have as good a chance as any other couple who come together as man and wife."

Except they didn't. They hardly knew each other, and they'd been forced to marry in circumstances that placed a pall over their future. Nonetheless, Toby appreciated that Leighton was doing his best to bolster his failing spirits. Although he couldn't help feeling that his cousin started from a false premise. Leighton believed that every marriage could offer the same fulfillment as his to Kate.

"I hope you're right," Toby said with no conviction at all.

"And stop tugging at your neckcloth. You don't want to step up beside Viola, looking like you slept in a hedgerow."

He didn't. However grubby the state of his soul, he always did his best to dress like a gentleman. "It's too damned tight."

The muttered curse brought another disapproving glance from the vicar.

"No, it's not. Leave it be."

He swallowed yet again. His throat was as parched as a desert. He wished to Jericho that he had a hip flask with him. But he owed Viola better than to speak his vows, stinking of liquor.

"She's late." His hand rose toward his neckcloth. With an effort, he lowered it, although his fingers curled and uncurled with the need to loosen that bloody noose around his neck.

"No, she's not." Leighton rolled his eyes. "By heaven, cuz, I hope this is the one and only time I have to stand up with you for a wedding. You're crankier than Richard when he's missed his afternoon nap."

Perhaps luckily for Leighton – and the vicar's nerves – Toby was saved from responding to that piece of effrontery. There was a rustle through the congregation, and the organ started to play the Largo from *Xerxes*.

A strangled cry jammed in his throat. This was wrong. He wasn't fit to be this glorious girl's husband. He'd bring her to ruin. All his father's predictions about what a useless lump he would become were about to come true.

"If you cast up your accounts, Viola will never forgive you," Leighton hissed from beside him. "It's too late to wriggle out of your obligations."

"I'm not about to be sick," he muttered back.

No, he was about to take to his heels. Better a scandal now than a lifetime of misery for Viola. In the long run, she'd thank him.

Panicked, he glanced back at the door. Three beautiful women lingered in the flower-adorned archway. Two eye-catching blondes, Juliet and Portia. And in the center in a simple, pale green gown, the loveliest of them all. The woman who was about to become his bride, for good or ill. The woman who looked pure and perfect, and far, far too good for a rogue like him.

Leighton was right. It was too late to escape. Not just because he'd made promises that he couldn't in honor break.

More than promises stopped him running away. Just the sight of Viola made him ache with longing. She might be too fine for him, but that didn't stop him hungering to possess every single inch of that graceful body. Even more, he wanted her to share her soul with him. When up to this stage, he'd had no truck with souls. Including his own.

In a few minutes, he and Viola would speak words that united them for all time. He'd take her into his care, and they'd create a future together.

While Juliet twitched the filmy veil covering Viola's pretty honey-colored hair and Portia passed her a bouquet of pink peonies, he made a private vow. He would dedicate the rest of his life to doing right by this magnificent woman.

When he watched Viola walk up the aisle, an unfamiliar sensation unfurled in his heart. He had a strange feeling that it might just be hope.

"She's a vision," Leighton murmured beside him. "You're a lucky man."

To his surprise, Toby replied without a hint of guilt. "I am indeed."

As they left the church under a shower of rice, Toby took Viola's arm with an air of proud possession. Behind them, the organ played triumphantly and bells pealed in jubilation.

Toby was laughing as he led her up to the carriage and helped her inside. She found her seat in the flower-bedecked vehicle, while he paused to accept the storm of congratulations. He leaped up beside her, a footman closed the door, and they were on their way to the house where she'd grown up.

"You're in a better mood than I thought you'd be," his new countess said with a hint of sourness unusual in a bride. But then, despite her pretty dress and the just-concluded ceremony, he supposed that she didn't feel much like a bride.

"And you're not." Toby cast her a searching glance. "What is it, Viola? Suffering a fit of the collywobbles?"

"Collywobbles doesn't do my feelings justice."

He smiled. "I'm sure. Have you spent the last five days torturing yourself about the wedding?"

She met his gaze. "Haven't you?"

He shrugged, although of course, he had. "What's the point of stewing?"

"But what are we to do? We made all sorts of promises in there that aren't true."

Hiding a wince, he took her hand. "I meant what I said. You're more than welcome to all my worldly goods, and I have every intention of cherishing and honoring you. I'll be faithful."

Very deliberately, he avoided mention of the other vow, the one about love. That took him into perilous territory that he wasn't ready to enter.

Troubled eyes continued to consider him. "I don't think I could bear it if you weren't. I certainly couldn't bear it if everyone knew you'd strayed. And they would know. They always know." Her heavy sigh depressed his spirits. "But you're not the faithful type. Or you never have been until now, according to the gossip."

Gossip be damned. He kept his voice cheerful. He didn't want to fuel his bride's crisis. "I've never been married before."

"Are you saying that you'll change?"

"I suspect I won't be able to avoid changing. Neither will you." He watched her go pale. "And now, plague take it, you're thinking about the wedding night."

Her eyelashes fluttered down, and she lowered her voice. "I've been worried about that since you proposed. I fear I'm going to be such a disappointment in that department. Actually, I fear I'm going to be a disappointment in every department, but particularly in that one."

He couldn't help laughing, a soft chuckle loaded with fond exasperation. "You silly widgeon, that's about the only thing I haven't worried about."

Her eyes widened as she glanced up. "Really?"

"Really." He lifted her hand to place a kiss on her knuckles, just near the place where a gold ring now gleamed. She'd worn gloves into the church but hadn't put them back on. "From the first, we couldn't keep away from each other. I saw you, and I wanted you."

"You did?"

"Yes. And I have an inkling that you might have felt the same, although you're so sweet and innocent, it took you a little longer to recognize the itch for what it was. You liked kissing me, didn't you?"

"You know I did." Faint color tinged her cheeks. "That's why we're in this mess."

Right now, Toby didn't want to view their union as a mess. "Then I'll wager the finest horse in my stables that you'll like the rest."

"Only a horse?" To his relief, she sounded more like the forthright woman that he knew her to be.

"I'm dashed fond of my horses." He kissed her hand again. "Let's do our best to rise above the circumstances of our betrothal. Everyone..." Perhaps not quite everyone. "...is predicting disaster. Wouldn't it be a daisy of an upset if we prove them wrong?"

After all, Leighton said that they had a chance of happiness, and Leighton was a clever man.

"Another vow?"

He nodded and tightened his grip on her hand. "Another vow."

"I'm still nervous."

"You've never done this before." His smile was tender. "You know what's going to happen?"

"I think so. Although when Juliet talked to me, she was at a disadvantage, not having any practical experience either."

Ah, so the fair Juliet and her duke hadn't anticipated their wedding vows? That was interesting, although not surprising. Plenty of couples did, but the oldest Frain sister was a pattern card of propriety. Toby should have known that she'd follow the rules.

"So she concentrated on the mechanics, not the pleasure?"

Leaving the church, Viola had been as white as a gardenia. Now she was blushing.

"I suppose so." When he shifted on the leather seat and bit back a groan, his bride shot him a puzzled glance. "What's wrong?"

Self-mockery edged his short laugh. "It's devilish arousing, talking about our wedding night. Perhaps we should change the subject."

"Oh." Her gaze dropped to his lap where he swelled against the biscuit pantaloons that he'd worn for his wedding. Juliet must have managed to convey at least one thing accurately.

"Oh, indeed."

"That's..."

"Yes." Toby released her hand and shifted as far away as he could. But the carriage wasn't big enough for him to avoid the sweet drift of her scent or the knowledge that all Viola's luscious warmth was now his to possess.

Not the most appropriate thought, five minutes before he presented her at their wedding breakfast. He ground his teeth and tried to concentrate on long division. It didn't help.

They'd been traveling up the long drive to the house. Now gravel crunched beneath the wheels, as they rolled into the turning circle at the foot of the magnificent double staircase.

The haze in front of Toby's eyes faded, and the turbulence in his blood subsided. He released a long hiss. "Let's sit here quietly for a little while, so we don't beat everyone to the party."

To his relief, Viola laughed. So far today, she'd been too nervous for humor. "I'll wager that you've never before suggested sitting quietly."

He laughed at himself. "You know, I doubt I have. You've wed a human hurricane." With all a hurricane's mindless destructive power, according to his father. With some effort, he banished the memory of his sire's hectoring voice.

"It's exciting," she muttered, as if admitting to a shameful secret. "*You're* exciting."

Startled, he looked at her. "You don't mind my reprobate ways?"

She shook her head. "When I'm with you, it always feels like an adventure."

"Well, damn me..."

Then she had to go ahead and spoil it all. "Goodness knows what our children will be like. The country won't know what hit it."

*Children.* That word extinguished his inappropriate arousal. And the infernal tragedy of it all was that there would be children, because he already knew that he wouldn't be able to keep his hands off his beautiful bride.

God help England. God help Viola.

Most of all, God help him. Because if ever a fellow promised to provide his offspring with an inadequate example, it was that out-and-out scoundrel Toby Sutton.

# CHAPTER THIRTEEN

S o she was married.

Viola leaned back against the red leather seats in the luxurious traveling coach that would carry her from Afton Park to her new home at Brazey Castle in Hampshire. Both the ceremony and the wedding breakfast were over. For the first time since she'd agreed to marry him, she and Toby were about to spend an extended interval alone with each other. At last, they needn't fear discovery or censure for being together.

Anticipation rippled up her spine, as she recalled Toby saying that now they could kiss all day and nobody could stop them. She'd spent the last five days in an agony of nerves, but the opportunity for more kisses had remained a bright spot amongst all that seething trepidation.

After they'd spoken their vows in the church, Toby had kissed her. It had been a mere brush of his lips, over in a second, but powerful enough to blast her with heat. And to remind her of what those lips could do when he had time and privacy to demonstrate his skills.

"What are you thinking about?" Toby sat beside her, holding her hand. He'd taken it when he helped her into the coach. As they bowled down the long lime tree-lined drive to the estate's gates, he hadn't relinquished the contact.

Silly to blush when they'd already enjoyed a passionate embrace and he'd do more than kiss her tonight. But blush she did. "Kisses."

His clasp on her hand firmed, as he responded with a grunt of wry amusement. "That's a relief. I feared that you might be contemplating throwing yourself out of the carriage."

She turned her head to stare at him. "I don't hate that I married you." She studied his face and took a risk in asking for honesty. "Do you hate that you married me?"

"I don't like that you were forced into it."

"But what do you feel for yourself?"

His lopsided smile set her susceptible heart somersaulting. "I feel like I've won a wonderful girl as a bride and that I'm a deuced fortunate sod."

She hoped to heaven he wasn't just being gallant. He sounded sincere. "Despite how we came together?"

He shrugged. "I suspect that before too long, I'd have offered for you anyway. I liked you from the first and sneaking you away for secret kisses was bound to lose its charm over time."

"We only did that once, and it turned into a disaster."

Toby sighed. "Perhaps if we stop thinking of our wedding as a disaster, it will be a step forward." His voice was low and earnest.

"Do you mean it?"

"About changing how we define our union?"

"No. The bit about offering for me."

"I want you, Viola. I wanted you when I was halfway up that elm tree and I saw you. Even a rake like me knows that I'd need to produce a wedding ring before I got you into bed."

She liked that he hadn't been toying with her in London. However daunting it might be to know that they'd share a bed tonight. "Wanting and liking form a good basis for a marriage."

They didn't add up to love, but for pity's sake, she'd only met him a week and a half ago. She'd be in alt if love came along, but it was too early to know if it would.

"I hope so." He raised her hand for a teasing kiss. "Not a disaster in any case."

"Definitely not," she said in a faint voice. "You're being very sporting about all this."

In the depths of her moping, she'd feared that Toby would hate her for trapping him into this marriage. But as she studied those remarkable features, she caught no shadow of resentment. A little uncertainty perhaps, but that was expected when they remained strangers in so many ways.

"Perhaps I should send Marjorie a thank you note."

Viola gave a horrified snort of amusement. "That might be going overboard."

Marjorie had spent two rather awkward days with the Shelburns, before leaving London to stay with a great aunt in Scotland. Elizabeth had written to Viola with the latest gossip, including the way society had closed ranks against the chit.

At least Marjorie hadn't gone back to her oaf of a father. Right now, given that Toby didn't seem too angry about the wedding, Viola found it in herself to pity the girl.

"When I saw you enter the church, I almost felt in charity with her. You made a beautiful bride, Viola. I should have told you before."

When she'd caught Toby's intent expression as she walked up the aisle, she'd felt beautiful. Her lifelong doubts about her looks, especially in comparison to Juliet and Portia, always faded under his open admiration. "We haven't had much chance for private conversation."

While they'd mostly stayed together at the wedding breakfast, people had surrounded them. Given that a scandal sparked the marriage, Viola had feared that her wedding day would be a shabby affair, tainted with shame and prurient curiosity. But everyone had seemed happy for her. In his speech, even Papa had unbent enough to welcome Toby into the family.

"No, and we started talking about bed sport, the moment I got you to myself after the ceremony."

She blushed again. "It's been on my mind."

"Mine, too."

A charged silence fell. Although Viola didn't feel nearly as awkward as she had when she'd set off from the church.

After spending an inordinately long time staring out the carriage window, she turned back to Toby. "How long does it take to get to Brazey Castle?"

"About six hours. We should be there in time for dinner."

"I'm looking forward to seeing my new home."

"Don't get your hopes up." She didn't understand the shadows dimming his eyes. For a while there, he'd looked reconciled to his fate. "It's a damned mausoleum."

"Oh," she said uncertainly, hearing his acid tone. "Don't you like it?"

"No. And I don't think you will either."

Goodness, what on earth was waiting at the end of this journey? "I rather liked the idea of living in a castle," she said in a reedy voice.

"If you want to go somewhere else after you've seen it, I'm more than willing. We could go to Paris or Vienna. Or Rome. Or the Highlands. With a bit more time, I'd have done a better job arranging a proper honeymoon."

"I've been eaten up with curiosity to see your – *our* – house. In Papa's library, I found a book of etchings that included a charming picture of Brazey."

"Artistic license," Toby said shortly. "We don't have to live there. We can live in London. Or I can buy an estate somewhere else, if you prefer."

Her puzzlement grew by the second. "But Brazey is the family seat."

"Yes."

She turned to stare out the window again. They were coming up to the first tollgate on the road east to Hampshire. It felt symbolic, as if this barrier marked the shift from Viola Frain of Afton Park to Viola, Countess of Renfrew, chatelaine of Brazey Castle. Whatever that meant. The house she'd seen in the picture had looked like a place that a man would be proud to call his own. But Toby's tone conveyed anything but pride. He sounded like he loathed his family home.

"I'm sorry." He kept hold of her hand, his thumb stroking her skin. "That added a plaguey dismal edge to our day."

She glanced at him. "Is it derelict?"

That made him laugh, if with more of that bleak note that chilled her. "Good God, no. You haven't married a poor man. I promise I'll put a decent roof over your head."

They fell quiet, as the coach stopped at the tollgate before it rolled onward. But to what?

Since agreeing to marry Toby, Viola had worried about so much. Now it seemed that she needed to worry about tonight's destination.

Their conversation had reassured her on many counts, not least that her new husband wasn't bitter about having to marry her. Viola straightened her backbone against the swaying movement. She told herself that if she must bear with mice and spiders and dust and a leaky roof tonight, she could cope. Reaching an understanding with Toby was more important than bricks and mortar.

She heard him sigh beside her. "Are you tired? If you are, you can rest your head on my shoulder and sleep for a while."

It was clear that he didn't want to talk about Brazey Castle anymore. Her lips turned down. "Actually I'm too keyed up to sleep, even though I've barely caught a wink these last few nights."

"I'll make it up to you, I promise."

She summoned her courage. He liked it when she was brave, she'd learned. "You could start making it up to me now."

Toby caught on quickly. The rather desolate expression in his eyes vanished in a flash, replaced by blatant masculine interest. "Oh?"

She licked dry lips, as she met his brilliant gaze. "You said that we could kiss all day if we married. It was one of the reasons I agreed to have you."

The satisfaction in his smile sent excitement zigzagging through her. "Then never let it be said that I'm not a man of my word."

# CHAPTER FOURTEEN

oby was much happier thinking about kissing his bride than he was talking about that damned funereal pile, Brazey Castle. He'd be overjoyed if the pestilential edifice sank into a bog.

Nonetheless he chided himself for failing to sound at least a little enthusiastic at the idea of introducing his new countess to the estate. When he provided an honest assessment of the place, Viola had looked so disappointed.

Something that he hoped wouldn't disappoint her were a few more lessons in kissing. Perhaps he might coax his wife to experiment beyond kisses. After all, they had hours before they reached Brazey. And for the first time, he had every right to explore the sexual awareness smoldering between them.

So he tugged down the blinds, turning the carriage interior to twilight. He removed the stylish hat that he'd bought for his wedding and placed it on the seat beside him. Leaning back, he stretched his long legs out into the well between the seats.

He smiled at her. "Come and sit on my lap, sweetheart. I think a cuddle is just the thing."

She paused to take off her bonnet and set it on the seat. She'd changed out of her pretty wedding dress into a light blue traveling ensemble that darkened the gray of her eyes to the color of the sea on a silvery day.

With a bit of wriggling and balancing against the vehicle walls, she settled her lovely soft rump on his lap. His dick responded with predictable alacrity, although he had no intention of taking his new wife in a moving carriage.

For Viola's first time, she deserved a bed – or at least a surface that didn't bump and rattle. So as Toby twined his arms around her, he told himself to settle down.

At first, she was tense, but when he did nothing beyond hold her, she gave a weary sigh. She sagged against him and snuggled her head into his chest.

He rested his chin on the pile of silky blonde hair and relished her yielding warmth. Gradually, the restless demons inside him calmed, the way that they always did in Viola's presence.

As he luxuriated in her nearness, peace descended on the carriage. The perfume of flowers filled his senses. And the now-familiar essence of Viola herself. He closed his eyes and absorbed the sweetness.

The creaking of the carriage and the pounding of the horses' hooves provided distant music, as his breathing eased to match hers. She fitted against him so perfectly. When they shared a bed, it would be magic.

The day's troubles receded. And the worries that had preyed on him during his short engagement. He'd feared that Viola would feel coerced and afraid and distressed. But it seemed that, like him, she was willing to give their relationship a chance to unfold.

If anyone had said to Toby before this that a woman of sense was a damned fine choice as a bride, he'd have scoffed. Until he met Viola, he'd valued women for their beauty and their willingness to forsake morality.

Not to mention that he could never have imagined a woman of sense evincing a scrap of interest in a fribble like him. If she did, she couldn't, by definition, be a woman of sense.

But Viola was without doubt a woman of sense. Hadn't she proven it with her measured reaction to a future with him? No tears. No hysterics. No storm of blame for a dilemma that was entirely his fault.

Even better, she liked him, and she was pretty. He got the best of both worlds.

Toby should drop to his knees and thank his Creator for the gift of such an exceptional wife. But right now, his bride occupied his lap and he had other, more profane matters on his mind.

"Don't go to sleep." The silence had developed a distinctly somnolent quality.

She nestled closer. "I could, you know." She sounded drowsy.

What a beast he was. He should let her sleep. She'd already told him that she'd been fretting into the midnight hours. He owed her fireworks tonight, to make up for all the trouble that he'd caused.

But before tonight, there was the present. When he had time and privacy to share a hint of the raptures awaiting.

He tightened his grip. "Wouldn't you rather kiss me?"

Toby felt her husky chuckle as much as he heard it. She tipped her face up. "Yes."

That was another of the many things he approved of in Viola. She wasn't coy. The eyes that she leveled on him glowed like moonlight. There was no mistaking her curiosity.

"That's the ticket."

"At the Tierney ball, everything went mad, but I've often thought about how wonderful it was before Marjorie arrived."

So had he. It was one of the few things about this whole situation that prompted faint optimism. Kissing Viola had been heaven. Everything that followed? Not so much.

Toby leaned closer, so close that her face blurred in his vision. "Shall we see if it's still wonderful?"

"Yes, please," she whispered, tilting forward with a gentle encouragement that he couldn't resist. He closed the minuscule gap between them and pressed his lips to hers.

There was the immediate enchantment that he remembered. That same indescribable feeling of rightness, as if he'd been born to kiss Viola Frain.

With a soft sigh of surrender, she raked her fingers through his hair to bring him closer. He needed no further invitation. His mouth opened over hers, and he slipped his tongue between her lips to taste the hot, honeyed interior.

With another of those damned arousing little moans, she drew his tongue deeper. The kiss flared into sizzling heat.

Toby angled Viola against his arm, giving him better access to her mouth. He devoured her with all the hunger that had tormented him since they'd first kissed. Only now did he admit quite how excruciating the delay had been. No woman had ever put him in such a fever.

At the Tierney ball, she'd been disarmingly shy and unsure. Now her clumsy eagerness lit an inferno in his blood. He sucked her lower lip into his mouth and gave it a quick nip. When she started, her hip bumped his straining erection. He groaned at the agonizing temptation and groaned again when she imitated what he'd done and nipped his lower lip. The spike of arousal threatened to blow off the top of his head.

For a long while, if not the full day that he'd promised, their mouths conducted a passionate duel. A duel that left them both victors. Through the thunder in his head, Toby noted her growing confidence. And her growing adventurousness. She soon caught on to the delight to be found if she imitated his actions. The encounter changed from him kissing her to a mutual feast that threatened to immolate him.

When his shaking hand landed on the swell of her breast, she gasped into his mouth. He curved his fingers around that luscious roundness, but it wasn't enough. He needed to see her before he went insane.

Only with the greatest reluctance, Toby raised his head. Viola offered him such a banquet, he barely knew where to start.

"Let me touch your breasts," he said roughly, his hand flexing on her bosom. Through several layers of material, he felt the impudent thrust of a beaded nipple.

Hazy eyes dwelled on him. Her face was flushed, and her lips were full and glistening after those fierce kisses. Unable to resist, he sought another taste and lost himself once more.

When he finally drew back, they both panted with excitement. He swallowed to ease the restriction in his throat. Viola's wholehearted surrender awakened every masculine impulse. How could it be otherwise? He had an abundance of red blood in his veins, after all. More than that, her innocent ardor touched his heart. She left herself so vulnerable. There was no calculation or attempt to shield herself. He swore that he'd do his best never to betray that trust.

As they stared at each other, she caught his hand and shaped it to her breast. "Please…" she whispered.

"You're too good for me," he said, meaning it beyond her current generosity.

With unsteady hands, he began to undo the line of buttons down the front of the close-fitting pelisse that did such a deuced good job of outlining Viola's graceful curves. Viola's breath caught, expanding her chest under his touch in a most pleasing fashion.

As he fumbled his way to the third button, she gave a choked giggle and lifted her hands to brush him aside. "Honestly, Toby, anyone would think you'd never got a girl out of her clothes before. And we both know that isn't the case. Let me."

With a sheepish smile, he allowed her to take over. "It must be different with a wife."

Toby had a suspicion that lots of things were different with a wife. If he wasn't so crazy with lust right now, that insight would terrify him.

"Clearly," she said with a hint of dryness, as she sat up and made short work of undoing her buttons. The pelisse fell open to her waist, revealing a matching blue gown beneath.

Toby growled in frustration. "Why do beautiful girls wear so many damned clothes? It's downright inhuman."

She gave a chuckle of such surpassing dirtiness that his cock twitched. "So that rakes need to do a bit of work before they get their reward."

The blue dress revealed the top of her breasts, but no obvious way to get past the fabric to the skin beneath. "Can I tear it?"

"You most certainly can't," she said on a shocked laugh. "It was a wedding gift from Juliet. Anyway, it's too pretty to destroy."

He gave another groan. So far this seduction of his bride was a turbulent mixture of pain and pleasure. "Devil take it, Viola. If you let me tear it, I'll buy you a whole new wardrobe. I'll take you to Paris and let you go berserk among the modistes. You can spend every penny I own. I won't utter a single word of complaint."

"What an impulsive creature you are." She sent him an amused glance. "I refuse to let you beggar yourself for the sake of a few seconds' delay."

"If you knew how I suffered…"

She looked unimpressed. "You'll survive."

He gave a sigh of theatrical despair. "I've wed a hardhearted wench, who will drive me to drink before she's done."

To his regret, she crawled off his lap and kneeled on the seat. "Not if I've got any say in it."

God help him, the schoolmistress tone sparked another zap of arousal. He was joking – mostly – about his torment. But the idea of his wife ordering him about in the bedroom in such an authoritative way threatened to melt his brain. "How does it help if you move further away?"

"I'll come back." She cast him an impatient look. "I promise."

"Viola, this is torture. You…"

All capacity for speech abandoned him, as he watched his wife balance against the swaying coach and pull off the pelisse. The dress beneath outlined every elegant curve. She turned on the seat, presenting him with a slender back and a row of hooks and eyes that looked to his desperate eyes like a maze.

He couldn't resist leaning forward and tasting the pale nape under the upswept mass of old-gold hair. As he tasted her skin, he dragged a deep breath into his lungs. Her alluring scent was strong there and left him feeling like he'd swallowed a whole bottle of brandy.

She leaned back. "Can you undo me?"

He caught her shoulders in shaking hands and spoke in a rasping voice. He hated to Jericho what he was about to say. "I can't undress you, plague take it, much as I'd love to. What the deuce will we do when we get to Brazey? I can't carry you into the house half-naked, however many wicked fantasies that fulfills."

"Oh, Toby…" She shivered, as if she, too, found the image he painted arousing.

He couldn't help kissing her nape again, pausing to nip her before letting his lips drift across to where her neck met her shoulder. His hands slid around to cup her breasts. Things had improved since she'd taken off the coat. The gown's filmy fabric allowed him to pluck at her nipples.

"Oh, Toby," she said again, in such a melting tone that he ground his teeth to keep hold of his control. "That's lovely. Don't stop."

With a huff of amusement, he continued to tease her breasts. "It's even nicer without a pestilential dress in the way."

His hand delved under the bodice to caress a pearled peak. He played with it, until Viola squirmed and her breath emerged in a husky sob. "That's sinful."

It was. He'd had sex in a carriage before, but there was something extraordinarily titillating about seducing his innocent wife while the vehicle bounced along the road and the countryside sped past outside. So titillating that he had to struggle against flinging her down on the narrow seat and having his way.

But Toby retained just enough self-control to hold back. Witnessing Viola's excitement was some consolation. He wanted her avid for the marital act by the time he came to her tonight. When he and his exquisite young bride would set fire to the sheets in the gloomy suite of rooms assigned to the earl.

"If you…" She began breathlessly, then stopped to whimper in delight as he scraped a nail over the pointed tip.

He pressed his face into her hair and smiled with satisfaction. By God, she was responsive. It augured well for conjugal relations. "Yes?"

"If you undo the first few hooks, we can pull down my bodice. When we get to Brazey, you can do me up and I'll wear my coat. Even if I'm a bit crumpled, nobody needs to know what we've been doing."

"I do so love a practical woman," he murmured into her silky hair. "Although shredding the rag seems more convenient."

"Not really. My maid would notice."

"She'll probably notice anyway. However hard I try to restore you to respectability, you're going to be rumpled."

She gave another of those salacious giggles. "The way you say 'rumpled' sounds so decadent."

Toby laughed, as he pulled back and began to undo the top hooks. His hands were no more adept than they'd been earlier. Touching her breast under her gown had undermined his failing control. "Rumpled and disheveled and untidy and ruffled." Deliberately, he lingered on the consonants and rolled his Rs, growling like a damned Frenchman.

She sighed. "Oh, yes."

He hauled Viola back onto his lap and took her lips in a voracious kiss. She met him as an equal and arched to crush her breasts into his chest.

His hands slid up and down her back before lowering to knead her lush rump. He pressed her into his groin and raised his hips to rub against her. This time, his groan was long and agonized. "By Jericho, Viola, I've never wanted a woman the way I want you. I'm beginning to question the wisdom of what we're doing."

"We could...consummate the marriage here," she said in a small voice.

Dear God, the temptation of her. How could he resist? But she was his wife. A hurried tumble in a carriage wasn't an adequate introduction to sexual congress for the new Countess of Renfrew.

"No, you're a virgin. You deserve time and attention. Not to mention stability."

Her laugh was strained. "It would be terrible if we fell off the seat in...in the middle of everything."

"It would." He was worried about hurting her, too. He'd never bedded a virgin before, but he gathered the first time could be painful. He wondered if Juliet had mentioned that. He didn't want to ask, in case Viola's earlier apprehension resurfaced. He liked it much better when she was all soft and willing, as she was right now. "But we can do a few other things."

He caught her mocking glance through the dimness. "We're already doing them."

"Some of them."

Her eyes rounded. "Do tell."

"Even better, I'll show you." A fiendish grin curled his lips. "But first..."

Her bodice sagged over her full bosom. As he brushed the material down to reveal a sheer white shift above a half corset, his mouth went as dry as the

Sahara. The sight of her breasts swelling against the transparent cambric was cursed stirring. Her skin was so creamy and smooth, and the nipples under their frail covering were the color of ripe raspberries. For a long moment, he enjoyed the delectable vision of his wife lying in his arms in complete abandon.

Suddenly impatient with barriers, Toby swept the shift out of the way. His chest contracted. By heaven, she was exquisite. His gaze drank in the burgeoning curves and their crowning peaks. "Viola, you're glorious."

She flushed hotter and raised her hands in instinctive modesty.

"No. Let me see you." Then he added, although he never pleaded with his lovers, "Please."

Indecision crinkled her forehead before, with a trust that squeezed his heart, she lowered her hands. "Very well," she responded in a raw voice that made his balls tighten.

"Thank you," he said fervently.

With reverence, he kissed the slope of one breast. He'd spent far too long during the last week and a half, wondering what Viola looked like naked. Now he had an inkling, and the glory rendered his most fevered dreams inadequate.

His lips trailed down to nuzzle at bare skin, until he drew one beaded point between his lips. He already knew that she tasted like heaven, but something about putting his mouth on her secret flesh added extra spice.

She moaned and combed her fingers through his hair. The slight tug added to the sorcery. He growled encouragement, before he shifted his attention to the other breast. While she'd been shy at first, he sensed no hesitation now.

The thought of secret flesh made Toby burn to discover the most private parts of her body. He shifted to relieve the weight of his arousal and positioned her until her legs splayed across the seat.

Suckling at her breast, he reached down to catch the hem of her dress and draw it up. She made a faint questioning sound against his lips. This time, when she pulled his hair, the action was insistent.

He lifted his head and drank in the sight of Viola in his arms. Lord above, if only he had the skill of Titian to capture this sensuous beauty and keep it forever. But he was no artist, so he had to etch every detail in his memory. When he was an old, old man, he'd feel young again, every time he summoned up this irresistible image.

She was rosy and heavy-eyed. "Toby, what are you doing?"

"I said there was more I could do. So I'm doing it." He glanced down to where her raised skirts revealed two slim legs in royal blue half boots and white stockings gartered at the knee with pretty sky-blue ribbons. Under the froth of petticoats, he caught a tantalizing glimpse of the lace edging on her drawers.

All these intimate hints were enchanting. No other man had touched Viola like this. By God, if he had any say in it, no other man ever would.

"My Lord above, though, you're wearing a lot of clothes."

"No more than is normal," she said faintly. "Is it really so troublesome?"

In truth, he didn't mind that all this lovely wrapping enclosed the splendors of his wife's body. It was like opening a wonderful present. And having to slow down reminded him that he'd promised to wait.

He'd see that they both had a *very* early night.

"Not for a man of my abilities," he said lightly, dropping a kiss on her bare breast.

"Oh?" Her gasp expressed endless feminine interest. "Juliet didn't tell me about any of this."

"There are some nice surprises in store. Now, part your legs for me."

Viola obeyed with a speed that met with his approval. She gasped again, when he found the slit in her drawers and at last placed his hand on her sex. Female musk tinged the air. Toby wasn't alone in finding this encounter deuced arousing.

She was sleek and ready for his caresses. It was time to give her a taste of what a man could do with a sweet, generous girl in his arms. With slow enjoyment, he stroked her cleft and lingered on the tiny pearl of flesh that would set her onto the road to heaven.

# CHAPTER FIFTEEN

*V*iola shuddered, helpless under the shocking caress. That storm of passionate kisses and Toby's attentions to her breasts made her shake with desire. A molten weight settled in the pit of her stomach, and an ache pulsed between her thighs.

Reaction jolted her, as he concentrated on one particularly sensitive place. Her heart, already racing, threatened to explode, and her vision went foggy as bolts of searing heat streaked through her. It had been disturbing enough when he'd suckled the peak of her breast. This ventured leagues beyond her experience.

When he'd kissed her in the Tierneys' garden, she felt like she toppled into an entirely new world. What he did now threatened to blast her into the sun.

"That's...that's sinful," she stammered, hating to sound so prim.

He responded with another of those alluring laughs that always sounded laden with affection. He kissed her briefly and despite her confusion, she couldn't help kissing him back. She began to think that even if she was declared dead, she'd kiss Toby back.

"We're married." He kept smiling, as he stroked the most private part of her. "Church and society give us full permission to take our pleasure."

"It feels sinful," she almost wailed, while magic rippled through her.

"All the better. There's nothing like a hint of the forbidden to add a piquant edge to seduction."

"This goes beyond piquant," she protested, although the conviction faded from her voice. Now that she'd accepted the idea of his hand between her legs, she started to enjoy the extraordinary sensations.

When Toby met Viola's gaze, his expression was serious. "Trust me."

How many women had he spoken those words to? The sad fact was that when he looked at her that way, Viola couldn't deny him. She suspected that must be true about the other women, too.

To her wicked regret, he started to pull his hand away. "Viola?"

"Don't stop," she choked out and caught his wrist in an unsteady grip. With every touch, something momentous edged closer. If he left her poised on the brink of this unfathomable chasm, she couldn't bear it.

"Ah, sweetheart," he said in a long exhalation of satisfaction.

She was sure that he'd called those other girls fond names, too. Despite that, the endearment made her silly heart caper around like a newborn lamb in spring sunshine.

While his lips covered hers, she felt a pleasurable stretching at the junction of her thighs.

She jerked back. "Are you—"

"Yes," he groaned.

He'd pushed his finger inside her. How bizarre. Yet wonderful, too.

His finger slid in and out, setting up a powerful rhythm that set her blood thundering. She gasped, and gasped again when the pressure deepened. He must be using two fingers.

Breathing in erratic gusts, he shifted her against his shoulder. That freed one hand to cup her breast and toy with her pointed nipple. Sensation assailed her from every direction.

That indescribable feeling spiraled tighter and tighter, until she feared that she wouldn't survive the tension. He withdrew his fingers from inside her and returned to that special place, rubbing it hard. In an incandescent instant, the world shattered into bliss. With a titanic shudder, she tumbled across some invisible barrier into blinding light and blazing heat.

"Toby!" Viola clung to his neck, as the world around her dissolved into flame.

For a long time, she remained suspended between the stars. When she floated back to the reality of the luxurious traveling carriage rushing through the spring countryside, Toby held her safe in his arms.

"How do you feel?" he asked.

"Marvelous." With trembling hands, she tugged her sagging bodice over her overflowing breasts. Surprising how much effort that took. "All my bones have turned to honey."

"I'm glad."

She frowned. He sounded strained, instead of like his insouciant self. "Are you all right?"

His features were drawn, and visible lines ran between his nose and mouth. His smile was a ghost of his usual effort. "I think you should move away and close your eyes."

"Why?"

A twist of his lips. "Because I need to find some relief."

Her curious gaze dropped to where his male parts pressed against the front of his breeches. "It's painful?"

"Yes," he forced out. "And it's worse when you look at me."

"Can I help?"

His laugh was strangled. "No, I can take care of myself. But I don't want to frighten you, after such a capital beginning."

"It was capital, wasn't it? But I hate to think of you suffering."

"I'll live." Another grim huff of amusement. "Although right now, it doesn't feel that way."

When Viola shifted off his lap, audible relief edged his sigh. "I said I don't mind if we...do it here."

"Your first time deserves patience and care. At this minute, I'm incapable of either. I hadn't realized quite how I'd feel when I watched you climax. I should have. Your kisses stop me in my tracks, after all."

She liked to hear that. She also liked having a word for that blazing rush of sensation. Climax was a perfect term for the spectacular ending to his breathtaking caresses. "Can I watch?"

He looked startled. "You'll be repulsed."

She shook her head. "So far, everything we've done has been unfamiliar and a little bizarre, but I haven't been repulsed. Not once."

He closed his eyes, as he placed his hand over the bulge in his breeches. A long exhalation escaped him.

"I'm curious." She went on, her wondering stare settling on his concealing hand. "I've seen statues and etchings in books, but I imagine a real...male member doesn't look like marble."

"It damn well feels like marble," he grated out.

"Will you show me?"

His sigh sounded like another groan. "If you insist."

He ripped at the buttons fastening his tan breeches. She caught a brief glimpse of proud flesh before Toby curled a shaking hand around himself.

Viola licked dry lips and shifted on the seat. There was something exciting about watching him touch himself. He tipped his head back to rest it on the wall of the carriage, and he began to move his hand up and down. The rhythm he adopted was an inevitable reminder of his fingers inside her.

He breathed in hoarse grunts that matched the timing of his hand. She now recognized the strong animal scent tinging the air as male arousal.

Before she thought to stop herself, she reached out. "May I touch you?

His hand stilled, and his whole body went rigid, not just the part he rubbed. "You're not scared?"

"I'm nervous," she admitted. "But this is so interesting. And…stirring. You have no idea what it's like to be a respectable young lady. Nobody tells us anything about the important things in life. When Juliet said humans mate the way animals do, I didn't believe her at first. I hate living in ignorance. Not only that, it's dangerous. Think of the trouble a girl could get into, just because she doesn't know enough to protect herself."

Toby gulped visibly. "I'm too distracted to discuss deficiencies in female education."

"But it's an issue. Even for me, and I've had the run of Papa's library since I could read."

"Loads of warnings for the unwary in Shakespeare," he said in a constricted voice.

"Yes, but I'm only starting to understand them."

"Can we talk about this later?"

She gestured to where he held himself. "Is that nice?"

"Yes," he muttered. "But it's a poor substitute for being inside a woman one...desires."

"Thank you for answering me properly. There's nobody else I can talk to about this."

Her hand opened and closed, as if she already shaped it around his hardness. The sight of him stroking his member revived her earlier tumultuous feelings. The secret hollows of her body went soft and liquid, as though she dissolved into warm syrup.

"You're welcome." He sounded gruff, as if he was angry.

Despite Juliet's best efforts, so much of what happened today seemed outlandish. But as Viola had told him, her principal reaction was rapt curiosity. "Would you like me to touch you now?"

"Beyond anything." His green eyes were almost black, and a muscle jerked in his lean cheek. He seemed on the edge of disintegration. "Although I can't promise I won't spill the second you do."

Viola wasn't quite sure what he meant when he talked about spilling, despite something in the way he said it making her shiver with anticipation. But by heaven, she'd like to find out.

She reached out, as he slowly lifted his hand. At last, she saw his impressive masculinity.

"My goodness," she gasped. "It's huge."

His distended breeches had given her an idea of his dimensions. But nothing prepared her for the sight of the powerful veined column rising to a flushed, rounded head. His organ emerged from the opening in his clothing with a primitive power that made the hollows of her body pulse with excitement.

His laugh sounded like it hurt. "Please don't faint."

"Don't be silly, Toby." She smiled. "I'm too interested to faint. What should I do?"

"Curl your hand around me."

"The way you did?"

"Yes."

"I won't hurt you?"

"It only hurts to want you so much."

She liked that answer, too. Viola slid along the seat of the rocking carriage. She extended her hand the last few inches and formed a fist around him. On a long, reverberant groan, he tilted his hips toward her.

Taking time to accustom herself to what she did, she bit her lip. He felt so vibrantly alive. Hot and hard. Silky skin over pure steel.

A drop of moisture glistened near the slit at the top of his organ. Heavy sacs descended below. The pictures she'd seen in books didn't do justice to this vital potency. Not to mention that the statues' parts hadn't been swollen and upright like Toby's.

His Adam's apple bobbed as he swallowed, and his hand clenched against the seat. "Move...your hand," he forced out.

At first, she was tentative, holding him in a loose clasp. As she lowered her hand, a nest of dark brown hair tickled her fingers.

"Tighter," Toby growled.

Firming her grip, she moved with more confidence. His shuddering exhalation indicated approval.

Soon she found a rhythm that pleased her and seemed to suit him. Just as she started to grow accustomed to the action, he grabbed her wrist and pulled her hand off him. "I can't..."

With greedy fascination, she watched him sit up and fumble in his pocket for a handkerchief. On a long, guttural growl, he lost himself in the square of white linen.

So much of what he'd said before now made sense.

A bristling silence descended, as he scrunched the stained handkerchief and shoved it back into his pocket with a touch of furtiveness, as if he was ashamed of losing control. Viola didn't feel like that at all. Seeing him succumb to his desire had been a moving experience. As she studied his now flaccid member, a vast tenderness rose inside her.

After he tidied himself up and fastened his breeches, he closed his eyes and tipped his head back. His rough breathing gradually quietened.

"Did I do it right?" she ventured to ask.

Toby lifted heavy eyelids and cast her an incredulous glance. When he spoke, he sounded like the man she knew, not the shaking, desperate stranger from a few minutes ago. "You were brilliant. I can't wait for tonight."

When he'd find that fierce release inside her body. After what had just happened between them, she could hardly bear the delay. "It's been such a—"

"Surprise?"

"That, certainly." The inescapable physical intimacy exceeded her most extravagant imaginings. "But revelation is a better description."

"A good revelation?"

"You've introduced me to a whole new realm. One I had no idea existed. Juliet made everything sound so...prosaic."

"Sort of in and out, and now we're man and wife in fact instead of just in name?"

"That's it exactly."

"We've only just started." His smile conveyed the tenderness that always left her longing. "I like that you're so bold. I always feared that I'd wed a milk-and-water miss who shrank from gross physicality."

Viola snorted. "You don't need to worry about that. This is the most interesting afternoon I've ever spent."

He pulled a gold watch from his pocket. "We're due at the inn to change horses. Would you like to stop for some refreshment?"

"Yes, please." Then with daring, "Although I'd like you to kiss me first."

"Demanding wench," he said, although he didn't sound as if he minded. "Come here."

She shifted closer and put her arms around him. He smelled earthy and delicious in a way that was new. She drew in a lungful of the evocative essence. "Then perhaps you need to do up my dress."

"Thank heavens I didn't rip it to shreds." He paused. "I'll take you to Paris anyway."

"I'd like that. I've never been out of England." A slow gloating smile curved her lips. "I'd especially like that, if going to Paris means we're stuck in a carriage for miles on end."

# CHAPTER SIXTEEN

It was evening before the traveling coach turned through the elaborate wrought iron gates and onto the winding drive that led to Brazey Castle.

Toby's arm curved around Viola, holding her close. She'd curled up on the seat beside him and fallen asleep after they left the Running Dog, where they'd stopped for a light meal and to change horses. Her sweetness and warmth were almost enough to combat the wave of bleakness overwhelming him at the prospect of several nights in his childhood home.

Why the devil had he decided to spend his honeymoon in this hellhole? In truth, hell itself would be a better choice. But everything had been such a rush after that horrid scene at the Tierneys', and something in him had decided to take his medicine first.

Viola would have to see Brazey at some stage. Better they got the worst over early.

Now he wondered what on earth he'd been thinking. But it was too late to go anywhere else, at least tonight.

"What is it?" Viola asked sleepily, stirring against him.

He dropped a kiss on her honey-colored hair. "We're nearly there."

To his regret, she sat up. He'd loved having her snuggled up against him.

"You've turned as stiff as a board. That's what woke me."

Viola meant no double entendre. He *was* as stiff as a board. The mere act of arriving at the estate turned him into a block of ice. "I'm sorry."

To his relief, she didn't pursue the subject. Instead, she raised her hands to her hair. "How do I look?"

He smiled. Or at least he attempted to. "Lovely."

That provoked a roll of her eyes. "Thank you. But am I fit to meet the staff?"

When they'd stopped at the inn, she'd looked rather disheveled, but the private parlor's mirror had helped to restore her appearance. Since then, sleeping on his chest had rumpled her again. Toby liked her rumpled, but even a rascal like him understood that a good first impression was vital. So he tucked up a few loose tendrils of hair and helped her to straighten her clothes. "Shall I put on your bonnet?"

"Yes, please."

After placing the chip straw hat on her head, he tied the wide royal blue ribbon into a bow with a flourish. Some nurturing impulse enjoyed performing such small tasks for his wife.

Leaning in, he gave her a quick kiss. "For courage."

That considering glance focused on him yet again. "Do I need courage?"

He wondered what she saw. His lurking fear that everything would go wrong the instant they set foot in the pestilential family seat? Everything always did. Why should his marriage, which so far showed signs of avoiding complete disaster, prove any different?

"One always needs courage," he said lightly. Or he tried for lightly. The doubt in his bride's expression hinted that he missed the mark.

Yet again, he blessed her tact as she turned to look out the window. Since leaving the Running Dog, they'd kept the blinds up. "I can't see the castle."

"You will around the next bend. My grandfather hired Capability Brown to design the grounds last century. He liked to play peekaboo games with the landscape."

Toby winced to see Viola's eagerness, as she leaned forward to catch her first glimpse of the house. The carriage followed a wide curve around the end of the lake, and the vista opened up to reveal Brazey Castle. The gothic monstrosity straggled along a high ridge and dominated an idyllic prospect of lawns and artistically sited copses.

The idyllic impression was deceptive, he was sickly aware. There had been no happiness in this location for at least the last fifty years. He couldn't imagine there had been much happiness before that. The very stones of Brazey Castle seeped misery.

"It's most impressive."

Her enthusiasm made him cringe. "The oldest part of the building dates back to the fourteenth century, but you'll be pleased to find that inside, it's more up-to-date than it looks."

Not much. His father had been above thinking about mundane issues like creature comforts.

"It's fit for King Arthur." Viola regarded him with a teasing smile. "Does that make me Guinevere?"

"If you are, I'm not letting that scoundrel Lancelot onto the property." He tried – he really did

– to sound as if he wasn't ready to order the driver to turn around and take them away. To anywhere.

London. Edinburgh. Timbuctoo.

Her laugh sounded dutiful rather than heartfelt. She curled her fingers around his, as if she sensed his turmoil. She probably did. She was smart and perceptive, and he had a suspicion that she understood him better right now than he wished she did.

Pride insisted that he didn't need her sympathy. But he couldn't quite bring himself to pull free. At Brazey, he was always cold. Viola's touch took the edge off the chill.

The carriage rattled up the hill to the walls surrounding the house. They rumbled across the drawbridge spanning a dry moat and rolled under the portcullis into the walled courtyard.

"Everyone has come out to greet us," Viola said in a failing voice. "Did you arrange this?"

Toby glanced out to see the staff lining the tall stone staircase leading up to the massive front doors. His heart sank anew. It had already dipped below sea level at the sight of his home.

He shook his head. "No. But it's over forty years since the castle had a new mistress. I'm guessing Robson, the butler, decided some ceremony was required."

"How kind of him."

"Yes," Toby said, with a flatness that he couldn't conceal.

He waited for Viola to question his lack of animation, but her grip on his hand firmed, before she released him to pull on her gloves. "Everyone has gone to such trouble. I hope I make a good showing."

"You always make a good showing."

A cynical smile twisted her lips. "I didn't at the Tierney ball."

"That was my baleful influence."

While he sounded like he was joking, he wasn't. Because as the coach came to a stop in front of his home, he couldn't help fearing that his wife's life was about to worsen because of their association.

The sad fact of the matter was that some stupid part of him would give anything for the chance to be a genuine hero to Viola.

Her usually ebullient husband's reaction to their arrival left Viola baffled. Most men would be cock-a-hoop to bring a new bride to such an awe-inspiring abode. Yet Toby acted like he was going to a hanging – a hanging where he played the starring role.

Even his reluctance to get out of the carriage was telling. A footman had opened the door, yet Toby remained sunk in gloom in the corner.

Heavens above, was she about to move into a ruin? Surely not. From this angle, the castle was a monumental structure, and Toby had already assured her that the roof didn't leak.

Her instincts told her that her husband's funk stemmed from more than mere architecture. She recalled the few times that he'd mentioned his father. The frozen expression on his face reminded her of his reactions then.

The day of one's wedding was a daunting moment to discover that one had been mistaken from the first. She'd imagined that she'd married a certain sort of man. Now she uncovered complications that she hadn't counted on.

"Toby?" she prompted when he didn't move.

His jaw hardened, and his mouth thinned. For pity's sake, he looked ready to fight an invincible enemy, rather than set foot in his family home. "I'm sorry, Viola. I was woolgathering."

If he was, the wool was threaded with broken glass. Viola had difficulty relating this stern stranger to the man who had given her such pleasure only a couple of hours ago.

A sour lump of disquiet settled in her stomach, as Toby climbed out of the carriage and turned to extend his hand. There was a mystery here, and something told her that unless she got to the bottom of it, stormy weather lay ahead.

Now wasn't the time for questions. Those would have to wait until she and Toby had some privacy. So she plastered a smile on her face, accepted Toby's assistance onto the cobbles, and allowed him to escort her toward a sweeping staircase that looked about a thousand years old.

An aged man with gray hair and stooped shoulders came down to meet them. "My lady, my lord, welcome to Brazey Castle. I hope your journey was pleasant."

Viola cast Toby a glance, hoping to catch a glimpse of the charming scoundrel who had scandalized London. She knew where she stood with that man. But he still looked like he attended his best friend's funeral.

"Thank you, Robson," Toby said. "I appreciate that you assembled the staff."

The man bowed. "We're all overjoyed to welcome her ladyship to her new home, sir."

Viola took in the double row of servants, extending all the way up to lofty wooden doors that could have graced Camelot. She swallowed to moisten a dry mouth. She wasn't sure she was up to handling her husband. She certainly wasn't equipped to assume her place as mistress of Brazey.

At a distance, the idea of living in a castle had seemed like a romantic fantasy. This evening, standing amid acres of medieval courtyard under what felt like hundreds of curious eyes, she couldn't help but wonder what she'd taken on.

*Chin up, Viola.*

She braced her shoulders. Best to start as she meant to carry on, so she smiled at the butler. "Thank you, Robson. How kind of you to ask everyone out to meet me."

Was that a slight relaxation of the butler's formal manner? He bowed again. "Not at all, my lady. We're honored to serve the new Countess of Renfrew. Allow me to introduce the staff. And may I wish you and his lordship congratulations and many happy years together?"

"Thank you." Pretending that she was Juliet, she allowed Toby to escort her up the stairs, with frequent pauses to speak to each servant. This was the sort of situation that her formidable sister took in her stride, after all. Viola had a sinking feeling that she might have to spend the rest of her life pretending to be Juliet.

None of the names stuck in her mind, but she hoped in time, she'd find her way. None of the names, except Robson and his wife, the housekeeper, who was the only person to do more than bow or curtsy and murmur good wishes.

"We're so happy to have a mistress for the house again, my lady. The castle needs a family in residence to make it a real home."

"I'll do my best," Viola said, as the idea of creating that family added yet another level of apprehension to what proved a nerve-racking experience.

"I'm sure you'll help Lady Renfrew to find her feet, Robbie," Toby said beside her, sounding human for the first time since they'd left the carriage. The nickname provided the only hint that these people who served him were more than strangers.

"I'd consider it a privilege and a pleasure, my lord. And may I, too, wish you every happiness with your new bride?"

"Thank you." Viola would feel better if he'd responded as if that idea was more than a distant possibility.

She and her husband passed under a pointed stone arch and into a great hall lit by tall stained-glass windows catching the last of the daylight. Perhaps it was the sunset, but Viola couldn't contain a gasp of dismay at the gloom. Despite huge fires burning in two massive fireplaces at either end of the cavernous room.

"It's—" she began.

"Dark and dreadful and dreary. I did warn you." Toby spoke in an undertone, before he turned to Mrs. Robson, who had followed them inside. "Please show her ladyship to her apartments. Robbie. We'll have dinner in the dining room in an hour." He turned to Viola, who found his sudden lordliness almost as intimidating as this echoing chamber. "Or would you prefer a tray in your room?"

Eat alone? Heaven forbid. The ghosts might get her. A place like this was bound to be haunted, if only with the unhappiness that she saw in her husband's eyes. Afton Park had always been a contented home. Even so soon after setting foot inside, she could tell that Brazey Castle wasn't.

"No, I'd like to have dinner with you."

"Very well." Toby looked marginally jollier about that, before spoiling it by releasing her arm. She struggled not to reach after him. His touch provided the only genuine warmth in this sprawling building.

He turned back to Mrs. Robson. "There's another carriage on the way with my man and Lady Renfrew's maid, as well as most of the luggage. I'll have a brandy in the library now before I go up to my apartments. We'll both need hot water."

"Very good, my lord," Mrs. Robson said. "My lady, if you'll come this way?"

Viola would much rather cling to Toby, but she raised her chin and told herself that a short separation wasn't going to kill her. She wished she was sure about that. "Thank you, Mrs. Robson."

The woman led her up a huge oak staircase, stained black to add to the general murk, and down an endless corridor to a suite of rooms, decorated in the style of half a century ago.

"I expect you'll want to do out the apartment, my lady." Mrs. Robson crossed to straighten an invisible crease on the faded blue and cream chintz bedspread.

"The rooms are lovely." At least they were light and airy, and the furniture was elegant. Everything downstairs looked like it was built for a siege.

"These rooms haven't been occupied since his lordship's mother passed away twenty-five years ago. God rest her sweet soul."

Her husband had never mentioned his mother. A shock to recognize that he, too, had grown up without maternal influence. "You were here then, Mrs. Robson?"

The woman smiled. She seemed friendly, and it was clear that she was fond of Toby. That alone made Viola like her. "Dear me, yes, madam. I'd been housekeeper ten years. I came as maid to her ladyship, when she left Capstone Abbey to marry the late earl back in 1775. I married Mr. Robson two years after that."

That implied that Toby's parents had been married a long time before he was born – and he was an only child. Or the only surviving one. Viola suspected a sad story there, too.

Perhaps she could ask her husband to show her around the house tomorrow. Something told her that all this family history had a significant bearing on her future contentment. "So you've been here most of your life?"

"Indeed. Although with no members of the family in residence, it's been very dull since the late earl passed away. The staff are so pleased that his lordship has married, and to such a pretty young lady. And that he's brought you here to Brazey. The house is crying out for a woman's touch."

Viola couldn't but agree. "I'll do my best."

"You're just what the castle needs, madam. And just what his lordship needs, too."

Right now, Viola was too busy feeling inadequate to believe that. She wondered if the staff knew about the scandal precipitating her marriage. Surely they must. Toby would have traveled with some of his London servants, when he came down to prepare the house for her arrival. A coachman and valet at the very least. They wouldn't be slow to share the gossip.

Mrs. Robson had been here throughout Toby's childhood. Viola suspected that the woman could advise her on how to proceed with the stranger that her husband had become at Brazey. But this was no time to find out, and Toby's pride would smart, if he knew Viola had quizzed the staff behind his back. So she merely smiled and thanked the housekeeper for her kindness.

"Would you please send a footman to show me to the dining room before dinner?"

"Very good, my lady." The housekeeper curtsied and left. Her departure was followed by the appearance of Jenny, Viola's maid, along with the rest of the luggage and the promised hot water.

Viola had no chance to dwell on the strangeness of her arrival, before she was getting ready for her first meal in her new and rather oppressive home.

# CHAPTER SEVENTEEN

*I*n the end, it wasn't a footman who arrived to escort Viola to dinner, but the earl himself.

She was sitting at her dressing table in her bedroom as Jenny placed the last pearl pin in her hair, when there was a knock at the door to the far side of the room. Viola had assumed that led to a dressing room or a sitting room. The countess's apartments were huge. She hadn't yet explored them.

When she called out permission to enter, Toby came into the bedroom. He looked distinguished in a beautifully cut black coat and buff trousers.

"That will be all. Thank you, Jenny," she said to the maid, who curtsied and left them alone.

Toby walked up behind her, and their gazes meshed in the mirror on the old-fashioned white and gilt dressing table. He continued to look troubled, she noticed, and older than the man she'd known in London.

"Smile at me," she said in a small voice.

"I'm sorry." He sighed. "It's not much of a way to start our life together, is it?"

He set one hand on her shoulder, bared under the scooped bodice of her green satin dress. It was one of her favorites. She'd put it on to lift her spirits. So far, it wasn't working.

"You're as nervous as a cat on a stove," she said, hoping to provoke a smile.

None appeared. Although as always, his touch made her heart swell against her ribs. "We can go somewhere else tomorrow. It's a bit much expecting you to cope with the horrors of Brazey Castle on the same day that you had to face a wedding with me."

"I enjoyed being a bride," she said, surprised that she meant it.

"You'll enjoy it more if we set up house somewhere cheerier. Let's go up to London. We can decide where we want to head from there."

That prompted a heartfelt groan. "I've had quite enough of traveling. Despite your best efforts to divert me along the way."

A lifetime with this man stretched ahead. Something inside her insisted that solving his issues with his inheritance was the only way forward. Viola could only do that here at Brazey.

A sardonic smile twisted his lips. "I live to serve."

"And the staff are so happy that you're here." Toby might be as prickly as a hedgehog with this return to Brazey, but Viola saw nothing but devotion and a hope to be of use in the servants.

His mouth twisted. "They'll get over it."

She placed a hand over where his rested on her shoulder. "Now that we're here, I'd like to stay. At least long enough to see the castle."

As she'd told Toby, curiosity was her prevailing fault. She needed to fathom why a man who was all laughter and devilry in London turned into this grim-faced stranger in the country. Her acquaintance with Toby started off with *As You Like It* and ended up as *Hamlet*.

He sighed. "It's deuced dismal."

Right now, Viola suspected that word described her future, too.

"It doesn't have to stay dismal. We could redecorate." Despite everything, she couldn't help laughing at his confused reaction. "Hadn't you thought of that?"

He shrugged and to her regret, moved away to prowl restlessly around the room. Amongst the delicate chinoiserie, he formed an intrusive masculine presence. At the sudden memory of what they'd done to each other in the coach, excitement heated her blood. She was rather looking forward to further masculine intrusions.

"I've been too busy avoiding the place to think about curtains and cushions." He paused. "Anyway, it's always been like this."

"Since the Dark Ages, I'd say." She twisted around on the stool to watch him pace. There was more than a hint of the caged tiger about his movements. If he had a tail, it would be lashing. "Although if you like it this way, I won't interfere."

The look he sent her was mocking. "You know damn well I don't like it."

The question was why that was the case, but while she'd gathered a few clues, they didn't add up to an adequate explanation. She shrugged with an appearance of nonchalance that didn't reflect the uneasiness weighing down her heart. "Then we'll change it."

Toby surveyed the pretty room with an attention that included a large measure of surprise. "These chambers could definitely do with updating."

"Actually, they're the nicest rooms I've seen so far."

"I hadn't set foot here for years, until I came in this week to make sure there are no mice."

Viola put on a horrified voice. "Mrs. Robson wouldn't permit a mouse on the premises."

"No, by George, she wouldn't." His features relaxed a fraction. "She and Robson were very kind to me when I was a boy. But she never put up with any nonsense."

Viola observed him, aghast. Something told her that the butler and his wife had provided the only kindness he'd known in this house.

Toby had already admitted to a difficult relationship with his father. His mother had died when he was little more than a baby.

Was it possible that the coldness at the heart of Brazey Castle stemmed from a complete absence of love?

Her voice softened. "We can leave this room as it is, if it brings back memories of your mother."

When he faced her, his eyes were sad. Once, she'd never have imagined they could look like that. "I used to sneak in here when I was a child to try and pick up some impression of her. But my father caught me one day and had the doors locked."

Oh, dear. The thought of that lonely little boy was too poignant for words. Yet he'd hate that she pitied him. He'd hate it to his marrow.

Telling herself that she wouldn't under any circumstances cry, she turned back to the mirror and fiddled with a curl that didn't need adjusting. She refused to spend her wedding night sniveling like a nitwit.

"What are your apartments like?" She hoped that he didn't notice the husky edge to her question.

"Hell's antechamber," he said shortly, venturing back to stand behind her. "This evening, I'll come to you here, if you don't mind."

Viola promised herself that tonight she'd do her best to give him at least one bright memory of his home to place against what sounded like a lifetime of unhappiness. Which was all very well for her to say. Despite those ecstatic moments in the carriage, she remained a rank amateur. Whereas Toby was used to experienced lovers who knew how to satisfy a man.

Dear Lord, didn't she already have enough to worry about? She'd do her best. If she made a shambles of her wedding night, she just had to hope that she got better with practice.

She wanted Toby. He wanted her. That was a good start.

Unless his edginess had extinguished his desire.

Viola made herself smile, although she wanted to wrap her arms around him and tell him that he was no longer that neglected waif. "If that means I'm not spending my wedding night in hell's antechamber, I won't mind at all."

At last, a grunt of amusement escaped, however grim. "I'm sorry, sweetheart. I should have taken you to Paris."

The "sweetheart" eased some of Viola's tension and self-doubt, and her voice emerged more naturally. "Paris can wait. I'm not sure your cook can. Shall we go down to dinner?"

"Not just yet. There are two things I need to do first."

She watched him in the mirror. "Oh?"

"Actually, three." He slid his hand into his coat and pulled out a long, blue velvet box. "I haven't given you your wedding present."

She didn't move to take the box. "I didn't get you anything."

"You're gift enough, Viola." He sounded like he meant it. Perhaps he did still want her.

"I might say the same to you."

"You might," he said doubtfully. Before she could argue, he opened the box to reveal what looked like a thousand diamonds.

"Goodness gracious, Toby."

"Let me fasten them on you. I know it's just the two of us for dinner, but if you wear this, it would please me." He set the box on the dressing table and scooped up the rope of glittering stones in one long-fingered hand. "A little sparkle won't go astray."

Viola couldn't but agree. "I'd like that."

His fingers brushed her sensitive nape, a reminder of the thrill when he kissed her there. He removed the gold locket that she wore and placed it on the dressing table. He draped the looping diamond necklace around her neck. A few seconds to fasten it before he stepped back, his expression openly admiring.

"Just as I pictured. You make a magnificent countess, Lady Renfrew."

"They're lovely," she said breathlessly. She'd never owned anything as extravagant in her life. "Thank you."

He dropped a kiss on top of her mass of curls. "My pleasure." He delved into his pocket again and brought out a small square box covered in scuffed leather. "And there's this. I should have given you your engagement ring before the wedding, but we couldn't find a minute alone. We've done everything else topsy-turvy. Giving you the betrothal ring after the ceremony fits the pattern."

"I didn't think about an engagement ring." She stood to face him. "You're much more organised than I am."

He opened the box and palmed the contents before she had a chance to see. "Hold out your hand."

When she obeyed, he took her hand. The contact felt significant in a way that she couldn't quite define.

"This is the Renfrew ring. It's been in the family for over two hundred years." The eyes that focused on her face were grave, when once she'd thought Toby Sutton incapable of seriousness. "You don't have to wear it. If you don't like it, I'll buy something more up-to-date. But it's tradition for this ring to mark the marriage of the current earl to his countess."

"All of a sudden, I'm feeling very feudal," she said in a hushed voice.

This time, to her relief, he gave her a proper smile. "Glad to hear it."

He slid a heavy gold ring onto her finger, just above the wedding band that she wasn't yet accustomed to wearing. As he released her, she spread her fingers to display the ring.

It was a large ruby set in heavy chased gold, ancient and beautiful and subtly foreign.

"Toby, it's superb." It was. But it seemed too old and valuable and...significant for Lord Frain's youngest daughter to own. "I'm not sure I do it justice."

He caught her hand and brought it to his lips. "You most certainly do."

She shivered with response. "It even fits."

The Renfrew ring seemed to mark the changes in her life unlike anything else, including her wedding. Taking possession of this ring announced her transformation from often-disregarded youngest daughter to chatelaine of Brazey Castle.

"So you like it?"

"It's gorgeous. Thank you."

"It came into the family, when one of my forefathers wed a Spanish lady who served Catherine of Aragon." He kept hold of her hand. "Now to the third thing."

Viola cast him a teasing glance. "Not more jewelry? I'm already feeling overwhelmed."

"Not more jewelry. I'd like to kiss you."

Her foolish heart melted. Silly to blush with pleasure, but she did. She stepped closer and twined her arms around his neck. "You don't need to ask permission for that."

"I've never been married before." The strain had ebbed from his expression, she was glad to see. He linked his hands around her waist. "I haven't yet worked out how to go on with a wife."

"Kisses are a good start."

He brushed his lips across hers. Coming to Brazey had awoken all Viola's insecurities. She needed more than a brief contact. With an incoherent protest, she caught his head to bring him back for a more thorough exploration.

She'd learned enough about kissing to coax him to cooperate. She nipped his lower lip and flickered her tongue against the seam in a request for more. With a low growl, he took charge of the kiss. For a long while, hot, velvety darkness enveloped her.

By the time he raised his head and stared down at her with heavy eyes, she felt giddy.

"Shall we cancel dinner?" he murmured.

For a reckless instant, Viola considered saying yes. But she wanted to turn Mrs. Robson into an ally, and telling the housekeeper that she'd wasted her efforts tonight didn't seem the best way of achieving that. So laying her hand on Toby's cheek, she smiled. "We have all night ahead."

He smiled back. She was glad that he looked more relaxed. It seemed that kissing was a good strategy. She needed to remember that. "Sustenance might be a smart idea?"

"Yes." The cheek under her palm was smooth. He must have shaved before he came to her. Such personal knowledge of him felt like a delicious secret.

"I could live on your kisses alone."

Her heart performed another of those unsettling flips. "Toby, that's so romantic." Then she burst out laughing. "No need to look so disgusted."

He kissed her again, and this time she didn't extend the embrace. When he took her hand, it was enough to note that the frozen expression was gone. She'd made a start in her quest to restore some happiness to his forbidding childhood home.

# CHAPTER EIGHTEEN

"Shall I leave you to your port?" Viola set down her spoon and fork. Mrs. Gibney, the cook, had supplied an excellent treacle tart with custard to finish their meal.

As Toby viewed his pretty wife, he couldn't help thinking that diamonds became her. They reflected the sparkle in her bright gray eyes. The first hint of a sparkle in this house during all his years of living here.

To his surprise, their first dinner at Brazey Castle had been enjoyable. Not because of the food, although that had been top class. Since he'd inherited, he'd made sure that the kitchens produced palatable meals, unlike the tasteless stodge that his father had preferred.

No, the meal had been a pleasure, because Viola didn't seem to find the dark paneling and the severe portraits oppressive and she'd been her usual entertaining self. A couple of times, he'd found himself laughing, which was a new experience in this sepulchral chamber.

Toby caught the eye of a full-length portrait of the previous earl. He directed a silent "fuck you" to his father's unfriendly ghost. "I might ask for the liquor tray to be set up in your rooms."

"Oh." Her lashes fluttered down, and color brightened her cheeks. She knew that he'd just admitted how impatient he was to have her. Although for pity's sake, that shouldn't surprise her.

He captured the hand that she rested on the white damask tablecloth. "Are you afraid?"

"A little. Although what we did in the carriage helped."

That was what he'd hoped. "I'm glad."

Toby squeezed her hand, feeling the Renfrew ring press against his palm. He wouldn't have said that he possessed an ounce of family pride, but something in his soul exulted to see the heirloom on Viola's pale slender finger. He felt like he claimed her forever.

For a long interval, Viola studied him. Toby wished that he could hide how Brazey affected him, but it was impossible. He detested every single stone in the place. Only reluctant duty to his noble name stopped him from leveling the whole edifice to the ground.

He released her and rose to his feet. "Shall we go?"

He'd borne his father's critical, painted stare for as long as he could. Anyway, he had a beautiful and ardent young bride to bed. Right now, he had somewhere better to be.

"Yes." She stood and stepped away from the table. They'd eaten at one end of the endless stretch of polished mahogany.

"Why are you smiling?" she asked.

"I'm thinking what an excellent countess you make."

It was true. She was young and inexperienced, but she was also smart and brave. She'd grace her new role to perfection.

"I hope so."

He came around and took her arm. "You're perfect in my arms anyway."

She slanted a questioning glance at him. "I'm a little worried about the competition."

He frowned. "I promise that I'll never betray you."

"I believe you." Her lips formed an unhappy line. "But you've done this so often, and I've never done it once. I fear that I mightn't measure up."

He swept her into his arms and kissed her with an unabashed carnality that left them both trembling.

Misty gray eyes blinked up at him. "That was…"

"A foretaste of what is to come." He gave her another quick kiss. He couldn't get enough of those soft, sweet lips. "You could never disappoint me. You're like a flame in my arms, and I long to burn with you."

She looked dazed. "Toby…"

"Trust me."

"I do," she said. "I have. I will."

"In the carriage."

"And in the church, and when I agreed to marry you, and when I went into the Tierneys' garden with you."

"I let you down then."

She shook her head with a conviction that went some way toward easing his lingering guilt. "No, you didn't."

"Well, I won't let you down tonight." Or he'd do his utmost to ensure that he didn't.

He avoided the portrait's sanctimonious glower. His father had loved to lecture Toby about his failings. But his father was dead and gone, and Viola was staring at him as if he'd hung the stars in the sky.

Who would he rather believe?

"Take me upstairs, Toby. I want to become your wife in truth."

Wearing a red silk dressing gown embroidered with gold Chinese dragons, Toby knocked on the door separating the earl's apartments from the countess's. Hearing a murmur to enter, he stepped through into Viola's rooms.

Massed candles lit the space to gold. The heavy brocade curtains with their designs of peacocks and pagodas were drawn, creating a cavelike atmosphere that, unique in his experience of Brazey, approached cozy.

Viola sat in the fourposter bed, looking very slender and small against the pile of pillows and the tall, carved headboard.

Toby paused to drink in the beguiling picture. Her flimsy rose-pink silk nightgown did little to hide the lush breasts that had so enthralled him in the carriage. Her gilt hair cascaded around her white shoulders, catching the candlelight. He was surprised at its abundance, now that it was released from confinement. His hands curled at his sides, as if he already buried his fingers in the silky opulence.

"Please say something," she said in a reedy voice.

Heaven help him, he was gaping at her like a rustic visiting London for the first time. She must be scared to death.

Toby made himself smile. "Your beauty stops me in my tracks."

The tension in her delicate features relaxed, and she gave him a shy smile. "How lovely."

"No, you're lovely." He crossed to a chest against the wall where, in accordance with his instructions, several decanters and plates of delicacies were set out. After pouring two glasses of brandy, he carried them over to the bed. As he sat on the edge of the mattress, he extended one in her direction. "Shall we make a toast to our future?"

"I've never had brandy before." As she took the heavy crystal glass, the sheet dropped below her waist, offering a breathtaking glimpse of a lithe female body draped in pink silk.

"A night of firsts," he said, then cursed himself. Right now, she almost looked at ease. He didn't want to say anything likely to spoil that.

"Yes." She raised the glass. "Here's to new beginnings leading to happy outcomes."

Happy outcomes? By heaven, he was on board with that idea.

That didn't sound like she suffered a nerve storm. His smile became easier. While it was sure to prove too optimistic in the long term, he wasn't going to argue with her statement. "I'll drink to that."

He touched his glass to hers and took a sip. The spirit soothed his taut throat. Right now, he'd lay good money that he was jumpier than his bride.

He watched Viola try the brandy. She smiled. "That's rather nice."

"It is." Toby set his half-full glass on the bedside table and waited for his wife to put hers down beside it.

Catching the back of her head, he tilted her up for a kiss. He tasted the tang of spirits on her lips and beneath that, the evocative flavor of Viola herself.

Familiar now, but as alluring as ever. He took his time, using his tongue. At her swift and fervent response, excitement hardened his body.

Tonight at last, he didn't need to draw back from the ultimate prize. Tonight, this exquisite creature would become his.

He could hardly wait.

Still kissing her, he flung back the bedcovers and sank down onto the mattress next to her, turning her to maintain the heated contact of their mouths. His hand stroked one lush breast, until her nipple contracted into a beaded point. With a soft sound of surrender, she tunneled her fingers through his hair.

He sat, drawing her up with him and broke free of those intoxicating kisses. "Let me take off that fiendishly becoming nightgown."

"Yes, please." She raised her arms with a willingness that made his heart pound faster, when already it threatened to explode. Fire rushed through his veins instead of blood, he wanted her so much.

His hands trembled as he hauled the delicate silk garment over her head, ruffling that shining mane of hair to tangled magnificence. He let the pretty garment drift to the floor.

"Viola, you're splendid," he forced out, as for the first time, his gaze feasted on his wife's nakedness.

By all that was holy, she was a goddess. Her perfection beggared the fevered fantasies that had kept him awake and on edge during this last week.

Toby kneeled at her side and for a charged interval, the world stopped turning. What a lucky bugger he was. He couldn't think of a single thing that he'd done to deserve such a luscious bride.

His greedy gaze traced the sinuous feminine curves arrayed against the white sheets. Full breasts with pert pink crests. A narrow waist. Rounded hips. Long, shapely legs.

Taking his time, his eyes forged a path up past her breasts to her slender throat. Then higher, to dwell on red, kiss-swollen lips, before he met her shining gray gaze.

He watched her swallow, sign that she was more unsure than she admitted to. As if to prove that guess, she slid one hand across to cover the feathery light brown curls beneath the pale plain of her stomach. What an enchanting mixture of boldness and innocence she was.

"You've seen most of me before," she said unsteadily. "I shouldn't feel so shy."

"It's different when you're not wearing anything."

"It is," she agreed with emphasis. Hesitantly, she lifted her hand away from the junction of her thighs. Not that she'd managed to hide much.

"Shall I take off my dressing gown?"

"It only seems fair," Viola said faintly.

"Very well." Thank the Lord that he only had to loosen the belt. He wasn't sure that he was up to dealing with complicated fastenings.

Although he was up for plenty of other things, as his bride was about to discover.

Under that inquisitive regard, he fumbled with the simple knot. For the love of God, he was a man of the world. Yet he'd never felt at such a loss with a woman.

But then, no woman had ever mattered the way that Viola did.

He'd spoken a greater truth than he knew when he said that everything was different with a wife. What they did tonight launched their lives together.

It placed enormous pressure on him to get everything right.

Sighing with humorous impatience, she rose on her knees to face him. The movement set her breasts bobbing in a way that evaporated all the moisture from his mouth. Hell, he wanted her past all endurance.

"Here, let me. I can see your valet dresses you every day."

That made him smile, even as she released the belt with a couple of deft tugs. "You know what London's rakes are like. Useless for anything except seduction."

Which would surprise Holt, his valet, who always complained that Toby's self-sufficient ways left him with far too little to do.

She caught the lapels and pushed the robe away from his body. "Tonight, seduction is all I require."

He laughed and seized her for a devouring kiss.

After some enthusiastic participation, she drew back. "Stop distracting me. I want to look at you."

"I'm nowhere near as pretty as you are."

"So you say." She placed both palms flat on his bare chest. "Lie down so I can see everything."

This time, his strangled laugh held a note of protest. "Please don't take too long. I'm in a fever to have you."

"I'm happy to hear it," she said, although he could tell that she wasn't really listening. Instead, the intense attention that she focused on his naked body made him groan and close his eyes.

"Hurry," he grated out.

"But you're so interesting."

He'd discovered that "interesting" was his bride's favorite word. "I'll be more interesting if I catch on fire. That is until there's nothing left of me."

"You exaggerate."

He did. But not by much. "You'll be sorry when all you've got to play with is a pile of ashes."

"I'll take the risk." She paused. "You're quite hairy."

She kept catching him out and making him laugh. How could he revel in this encounter so much, when his balls were turning blue? "Not overly so, I believe."

"The statues didn't have any hair." She paused again. "Although our farm labourers have hair on their chests, so I should have expected it."

"Most remiss to imagine I'd be any different," he said in a failing voice.

Every time that he thought he'd hit the limits of his arousal, she did or said something to rack up his hunger. Maintaining a coherent conversation fast became an impossibility. Every drop of blood in his body rushed to his erect cock.

From the first, he'd found Viola entrancing. Lying bare as Adam in front of her while she talked about him in almost scientific terms was so bloody arousing, it amounted to torture.

"May I touch you?" she asked.

He should say no. He was too close to forgetting the care he owed her and jumping on her like a barbarian. "Yes."

"Excellent."

He braced for the brush of her hands, wondering where she'd choose to start. It turned out that she wanted to explore his chest.

Through a smoky blur of desire, Toby watched her lay her palms below his collarbones and conduct a slow exploration across his pectorals. When she rubbed his nipples, he bit back a curse.

"My goodness, you're so hard," she murmured.

She had no idea. A wordless growl emerged from his throat.

Viola raked her fingers through the curls forming a light cover over his chest and arrowing down toward his aching cock. "But your hair is soft."

She lowered her head and kissed a line down the center of his chest to his belly. His racing heart smashed to a clanging stop.

When her hair slithered over her shoulders and tickled his dick, fireworks exploded behind his eyes. He ground his teeth, battling the urge to drag her a few inches further, until that hot mouth closed over his prick.

Viola was bold and imaginative. Toby was sure that if he played his cards right, she might consent to that particular intimacy. But not tonight. The risk of frightening her was too great.

Even as passion stirred and yowled, he thrust his hand into her lavish hair and pulled gently. He couldn't bear much more, not without spilling. Damn it, this time when he gave up his seed, he wanted to be inside his wife.

"Viola sweetheart, you can do whatever you like next time, but right now, I can't wait. I want you too much."

She went still, although he felt her lips move on the burning skin of his belly. The kiss flooded him with molten heat, and he set his jaw so hard that it threatened to crack.

"Please," he said in a voice that he didn't recognize as his own. Another tug on her hair.

This time, she raised her face. In her piquant features, he caught desire and defenselessness, and something that looked like wonder. "Yes."

The short word was enough. Toby hauled her up for a ravenous kiss before he rolled her beneath him and settled between her thighs.

# CHAPTER NINETEEN

*V*iola slid her arms around Toby's long, glorious body and closed her eyes as she sank into the passionate kiss. He was as warm as a furnace, and she was painfully conscious of his member pressing into her thighs.

In between kisses, he shifted to the side to stroke her mound. His hands delved between her legs to explore her cleft. A liquid surge of response greeted him. Despite what they'd done in the carriage, the reaction remained unfamiliar. She gasped into his mouth, as he pushed one finger inside her, then two. After a short while, she felt something larger and harder.

He shifted until he was directly above her. "Bend your knees," he grated out, rising on his elbows to stare into her face.

Viola caught his shoulders and curled her fingertips into the sinew as she obeyed. His shoulders blocked the candlelight, so all she saw was the febrile glitter of his eyes. While she couldn't make out his expression, she heard his tension and she felt it in his body.

The tendons under her hands tensed, as he pushed forward with an inexorable power that terrified as much as it excited her. Only now that she lay beneath him did she realize quite how big he was in comparison to her frail female body.

Viola bit her lip, as pressure built between her legs. This wasn't like accepting his finger. He felt impossibly large and dominating, and she feared that he might rip her asunder.

"I'm not sure you'll fit," she rasped out.

She heard fond laughter, even through his strain. "Viola, you're adorable."

What a strange time to realize that she wished he *did* adore her. She wished with an agonizing longing that would alarm her, if she had an ounce of attention to spare.

Toby caught her hips and lifted her. She whimpered as her body stretched to accommodate the new angle.

"Are you all right?" His voice was a husky rumble. He trembled under her hands, and she realized that he battled to hold back until she became accustomed to their joining.

"I think so." The feeling was odd. Not altogether comfortable, but endurable.

"Try and relax."

Her snort was dismissive. "I'm not feeling relaxed."

"Let me see if I can help." His hand toyed with that sensitive place.

Intensifying the caresses, he kissed her again. It took her longer than usual to get into the spirit of things. But as always, in the end, she melted into the kiss and almost forgot the awkward intrusion between her legs.

She released her frantic grip on his shoulders and wrapped her arms around him. When he raised his head, she inhaled air sharp with their mingled scents.

Toby moved forward in one smooth glide. She whimpered as something tore inside her. When he settled deep, the brief sting faded.

"Oh, Toby," she sighed, as her body adapted to his size.

He watched her through the gloom. "Did I hurt you?"

"A little. Hardly worth a mention." As the shock receded, she became aware of how close they were. "I see now what the vicar meant when he said 'one flesh.'"

Toby kissed her again and shaped a hand around her breast. She murmured encouragement, as he rolled her nipple between thumb and forefinger. The yearning point hardened and zapped heat to where their bodies united. As her hips rocked in instinctive pleasure, he went deeper. When she'd thought that he was already as far inside her as he could get.

This time, the sensation approached pleasure rather than discomfort. She gasped with surprise against his seeking lips and flicked her tongue into the hot cavern of his mouth. When he sucked on her tongue, she experienced another of those evocative tugs on her womb.

This verged closer to those extraordinary responses that he'd aroused in the carriage. She stroked the long, powerful line of his back. Tracing his spine and gliding down to clutch the firm globes of his buttocks.

He broke the kiss and raised his head. "Ready for more?"

The memory of pain had ebbed. Instead, Toby's body filled her, leaving no room for fear. She gave him a quick kiss. "Yes, please." She frowned. "What is it?"

"I like it when you show me you want me." He wriggled, and awareness sizzled through her. She'd moved so far past nervousness that she was hungry to discover what lay ahead. Married life proved more interesting by the minute.

He kissed her twice more. Astounding the power of these quick kisses. Every time their lips met, she adjusted to his possession in a most enjoyable way.

When her hands flexed on his buttocks, he moved. Another twinge of desire. "I do want you. I think I did from the first, but I was too innocent to realize what it all meant. I certainly couldn't think about anything but you. When I did, I imagined your kisses and your hands on me. It was most improper."

"Not improper." Viola caught a flash of white teeth, before he kissed her again. "Perfect."

He released her breast and rose on both elbows. She sank into the mattress beneath him. Every time he moved, sparks showered through her veins like shooting stars.

"Am I hurting you?"

"No, I like it."

"Good." His muscles firmed under her palms, as he slowly pulled free. Her moan resonated with unabashed pleasure. The sensation of him sliding inside her with such controlled languor was extraordinary. More extraordinary when he thrust forward with another impressive demonstration of control. This time, her body's resistance was thrilling instead of painful. It felt like he possessed every inch of her.

"Toby, that's wonderful," she murmured, bowing up to take more.

"Hold on to me." His voice was rough as gravel.

He began to shift in and out, burying himself to the hilt with every plunge. Viola had discovered a profound pleasure in accepting his body, but as he continued, she discovered an echo of that unprecedented response that he'd summoned from her in the carriage.

Soon it was more than an echo. Hunger and pleasure coiled inside her. She felt like an eagle circling higher and higher on a thermal, until all of creation spread out beneath her. Through her rising crisis, she realized that his control had started to fray. His movements became choppy, and he gasped for air.

Her breath caught in her throat then exploded free, as she tipped over into the soaring heights of rapture. She cried out at the glittering wonder of it all.

In helpless ecstasy, her body spasmed around Toby's. Her hands clenched in his buttocks, as she sought some solid anchor in a world that reeled in a wild, pagan dance.

Through thundering pleasure, Viola felt him jerk. Liquid heat flooded her. His groan was a raw, primal, unforgettable sound in her ears. He moved again, before slumping over her with an exhausted sigh.

He was heavy, but she didn't mind. She lashed her arms around him and closed her eyes, as quaking joy gradually retreated, followed by a transcendent peace that she'd never known before.

The lunatic race of her heart steadied, as she drifted back to earth from that spectacular flight to the edges of the universe. Toby's face was buried in the hair that clung to the side of her neck. As his breathing slowed, she stroked his back.

Like clouds across a sunny summer sky, idle thoughts wafted in and out of her mind. When she finally caught hold of one, it was an acknowledgment that she was happy. Despite all the chaos and confusion and heartache that led up to her marriage, she and her new husband shared more than duty.

He stirred at last, and she was surprised that she regretted the separation of their bodies. When he'd first pushed inside her, he felt alien and overpowering. No longer.

At Viola's faint complaint, Toby rose on one elbow to survey her. "How are you feeling?"

When she touched his cheek, his whiskers prickled under her palm. "Like a queen."

A smile creased his face. "You're a miracle in my arms."

Her fingers flexed in a caress. "I pleased you?"

"Beyond my wildest dreams." His voice lowered to a velvety rumble. "Never doubt it."

That was a huge relief. "I'm glad."

Such an inadequate response to the night's awe-inspiring events. But how could mere words encompass that sublime experience?

She wasn't sure who moved first, but they were kissing. His kisses always captivated her, but after what they'd just done, the meeting of their lips held a special significance. He took her in his arms and rolled over, until she sprawled across him. Her muscles felt like they'd turned to silk. She wondered if she'd ever stand up again.

When she started to lift away, he caught her head between his hands. She felt him inspect her through the dimness, as if he sought the answer to some eternal question. "Well, wife, have we made a fine start?"

Draped over him like this, his chest hair tickled her breasts. She smiled without trying to hide her joy in what they'd done. Although in this shadowy corner, there was no guarantee that he'd see her expression.

"A very fine start, my husband." It was the first time that she'd called him that. Viola now felt like a wife, instead of the shy girl who only that morning had stammered her vows at Afton Park.

Toby kissed her again. This time with more tenderness than passion.

It was strange that gentleness brought tears to her eyes in a way nothing else had on this eventful night. She'd felt desire and satisfaction, but the poignant longing that dug its claws into her as she kissed him now was new. And dangerous, she feared.

No word had been spoken of love. Not in London. Not since they'd been wed. But Viola had a grim presentiment that when Toby laid his hands on her willing body, he laid claim to her susceptible heart as well.

# CHAPTER TWENTY

*T*oby had started his wedded life in a most satisfactory manner, with a night of bliss unlike any he'd ever known. During those resplendent hours, he and his new bride had established a new understanding. He even nurtured a shred of hope that he hadn't dragged Viola headlong into a calamitous union.

But because this was that hellhole, Brazey Castle, everything went to blazes the next day at breakfast.

He and his wife were enjoying a repast in a morning room just as unappealing as the dining room. Yesterday's spring sunshine was no longer in evidence. The day was as gray as the pall that always descended on Toby's spirits when he set foot in his childhood home. Fires roared in the castle's hearths, although no fire on earth could take the edge off Brazey's air.

It was late, near eleven. London hours instead of country ones. Toby had started the day at dawn, making love to his beautiful bride, who showed a gratifying aptitude for the erotic arts.

But however much he might like it, he couldn't spend the rest of his life in bed with Viola. At some stage, the earl had to set foot outside the countess's apartments.

Which was when the trouble started.

"Where would you like to go?" he asked Viola, as he polished off the last morsels of a massive breakfast. Passion gave a man a healthy appetite, by George.

Viola had been more circumspect, choosing coddled eggs and a crusty roll, instead of his hearty selection of eggs and bacon and sausages and mushrooms. Now she set down her coffee cup and leveled a searching gaze on him. That particular expression had disconcerted him from the first, as if she saw past his surface polish to the inadequate human lurking beneath.

Except even a man as plagued by self-doubt as Toby recognized how eager she'd been for him last night. Perhaps she wasn't as displeased with her husband as she should be.

Or perhaps she made the best of a bad bargain. By God, he couldn't bear it if Viola thought he was a bad bargain.

"Toby? I said why do we have to go anywhere at all?"

He'd missed her reply to his question. In general, he avoided introspection, but something about Brazey always awoke his demons. And every one of them spoke in his father's frigid, clipped baritone. "I offered to take you to Paris, you'll recall."

Fondness seemed to tinge her smile. His heart flipped, and heat rushed through his veins. By Jupiter, she was pretty this morning, in her daffodil yellow gown and with her hair piled up in loose curls. She was the first spot of brightness that he could ever remember seeing in this doleful pile. He began to wonder if he could forget everything else and just carry her upstairs to that big bed in her apartments, where he'd visited heaven in her arms.

"I do recall, but we only arrived yesterday. The staff have worked so hard to prepare the house. It would be churlish to take off after only one day, don't you think?"

He bit back a response – admittedly churlish – that he paid his servants good wages to put up with his whims. As he glanced around the room, he noticed vases of flowers. He vaguely remembered flowers in the countess's apartments last night, too. He'd been too eaten up with desire for his wife to pay much attention. Flowers were a rare addition to the castle's dreary décor.

He also recalled, much as he wished he didn't, the household's warm welcome yesterday.

"They're used to me coming and going." Mainly going.

"But now you're married, and we're planning to establish our family here."

He already recognized that he was going to lose this particular debate, damn it. The contentment that he'd crammed into his soul last night as a bastion against future unhappiness drained away. "Brazey has never been a family home."

Viola's look was sharp. "That doesn't mean we can't make it one."

Toby sighed. "You're butting your head against a brick wall, sweetheart. Unhappiness was built into this place with the foundations."

He'd said too much, although only a fool would miss his dislike for Brazey, and Viola was the smartest person he knew.

"I refuse to bring my children up in an unhappy home."

"Then we need to buy another estate," he said shortly.

Her delicate jaw firmed in determination. "No, we need to fix this one."

She'd discover the futility of that statement, but it would take time. Toby supposed that he could remain here long enough to prove her optimism was in vain.

Then he'd take her to Paris.

He also had to admit that dragging his new bride on another long carriage trip would be inconsiderate. In the last few days, she'd traveled from London to Afton Park, then from Afton Park to Hampshire. He refused to be an inconsiderate husband.

This time, his sigh expressed audible surrender. He took a sip of his coffee before he replied. "I suppose we can spend most of our time in your apartments." *In your bed.* "I don't mind those rooms at all."

Her lips curved upward. "What a nice idea."

That brightened him up. "You agree?"

She greeted that with a derisive huff. "No, of course I don't."

No, of course she didn't. Feeling as though he was losing control of his life, Toby regarded his wife with weary affection. "We're newlyweds. We're allowed to be ravenous for each other. In fact, it's encouraged."

She laid her hand on top of his, where it rested on the table. Despite disliking the discussion's outcome, he couldn't ignore the immediate warmth that flooded him. He'd held her arm when he brought her downstairs, but he hadn't touched her since. And touching her rapidly became the most reliable method for preserving his sanity.

It was this bloody cursed house. The sooner they got away the better, before Brazey could poison the promising beginning that he and Viola had made to their life together.

But looking at his wife's expression – he'd long ago recognized that for all her self-effacing ways, she was stubborn – he resigned himself to a short stay in his ancestral home.

"I am ravenous for you, Toby," she said, which cheered him up a little. "But if we're to create a life together, we need to think about more than the lovely things we do in bed."

*Lovely things?* Even better. If he could coax her into his arms often enough, he might survive the next few days.

He laid his damask napkin on the polished mahogany. "You're going to ask me to show you the castle, aren't you?"

"I am." Viola bestowed another smile on him. She knew that she'd won. This particular argument, anyway. "Can you bear it?"

She sounded like she was joking, but he suspected that she guessed the huge concession that he made in agreeing to stay. "Anything for you, my dear."

"The perfect answer," she said lightly. But her hand squeezed his, as if she tried to infuse him with some of her confidence.

As Toby conducted Viola through what felt like an endless series of rooms, each more depressing than the last, she started to wonder if Toby's barely hidden aversion for this house was justified. This morning, after a night of such splendor that it beggared description, her aim of conquering Brazey's oppressive ghosts had seemed achievable.

She'd even imagined that she might be able to restore some pride in his family and estate to Toby.

Now, she wasn't so sure.

Some deep-seated instinct convinced her that if she couldn't heal his wounded soul, she and Toby had no chance of genuine happiness. And she was desperate for a contented life with him. She'd liked him from the first, and she liked him all the more, now that she'd caught a glimpse of the troubled spirit beneath his London polish.

Last night had been a revelation. His sweetness and his passion and his patience with her meant that she'd tumbled from attraction to adoration between one sigh of pleasure and the next. He was a man worth loving. He was a man worth saving.

As the interminable tour proceeded, she started to realize that saving wasn't too strong a term for the task ahead.

"There's only the long gallery to go," he said, his voice toneless. He'd withdrawn a little more from her with every room that they'd entered, starting with the library where he'd been as jumpy as a rabbit in a gun shop.

The gallery? Another bunch of forbidding portraits, she thought, muffling a groan. She'd developed a hearty dislike for Toby's father, who seemed to glare at her from every second wall.

Viola struggled to maintain her buoyant tone. "We may as well finish the tour."

"Then I'll take you to the stables. You'll like those."

"I'm sure I will."

He'd told her that he was fond of his horses. At least the stables might contain some life. Which wasn't fair to the staff, she knew, who had all greeted her as if she brought fresh hope. Having now seen most of her new home, she sympathized, however unequal she felt to the role.

They turned from yet another dark corridor into a long room. Tall windows faced out over the grounds. A line of paintings filled the opposite wall.

Toby started to tell her about these frozen-faced Suttons, starting with a bearded gentleman in an Elizabethan ruff. Like Toby's father, most of his ancestors were pale blonds with pinched features and cold eyes.

"I'm sorry if I'm boring you," he said, about half a dozen portraits into his lecture.

"You're not." Viola hadn't, in fact, been listening. "You don't look like anyone here."

"I take after my mother. She was an Anstey, the late Lord Shelburn's daughter. That's how Leighton and I are cousins."

Viola should have already worked that out. Although to be fair, she'd had plenty of other, more urgent matters on her mind since she'd agreed to marry into the Sutton family. "I'm rather glad. Your forebears are a formidable bunch."

Without visible pleasure, Toby regarded a painting of a unsmiling gentleman in a powdered wig. Smiles were absent from all the portraits.

In all this cold, unwelcoming house, the picture gallery turned out to be the coldest room of all. Viola had hoped that her tour would help her to understand Toby's background. What she discovered sent a river of ice down her spine.

What had it been like to grow up in these daunting halls? Under these critical gazes? With every minute, Toby's's disquiet became more comprehensible.

"They were bred to hold Brazey Castle for the kingdom. They did that right up to the Civil War, when the earl at the time lost his head for fighting for Charles I."

"But that was almost two hundred years ago. Life in England has been more peaceful since."

His smile was unamused. "I don't think my father got that message."

As they moved on, Viola stopped in front of yet another depiction of Toby's father. "He must have liked sitting for his portrait."

This one was larger than the painting in the dining room and featured the late earl standing with one hand on a globe and holding an open book in the other hand. The traditional attributes of the scholar.

"He did. He was a vain man, both of his looks and his intellectual accomplishments. He was proud that he'd bred true to the Sutton line."

By now, Viola was familiar with the austere family features and bloodless coloring. She didn't remark on the obvious correlation that Toby didn't look like a Sutton. Staring into that supercilious face, she was sure that Toby's father had made his disappointment apparent.

"He's handsome, I suppose," she said in an unenthusiastic voice.

"He certainly believed so." Toby surveyed the painting with an unreadable expression. "I thought you'd like the library."

This time, she didn't hide her shudder. "It gave me the creeps."

"Really?" Toby sent her a startled look. "I loathe it, but then that's where my father meted out my punishments."

Something in his voice told her that had been a frequent occurrence. Poor Toby. Growing up in this luxurious but joyless house, all alone with a man she already knew had been a self-righteous bully.

"It felt overpowering. I couldn't imagine anyone taking a book down from those shelves, just for the sheer pleasure of reading."

A snort of ironic amusement greeted that. "Good God, no. Books were far too serious for entertainment. I was never allowed in there, unless it was to pay for my latest trespass. Most of the books are locked up behind glass anyway. There's some priceless manuscripts in the collection. The last thing that dear Papa wanted was my grubby paws on his treasures."

As they'd wandered the dim corridors of Brazey Castle, Viola's mind had been working. Now she turned to Toby, ready to launch her plan to make a home out of this unpromising pile. "What college did he attend?"

"He was at King's at Cambridge. He got a first."

"Good for him," Viola said flatly. "Let's clear out the library and donate the books to his old college. If the collection is as exceptional as you say, they'll be glad for the gift. We can start again and buy books we like."

"The Herbert Sutton Memorial Gift?" Toby looked thoughtful. "The pater would have liked that. He never thought I was a fit custodian for his library, and he'd love the idea of scholars consulting his books into perpetuity."

A smile of wicked satisfaction curved Viola's lips. "I don't think we should call it the Herbert Sutton Collection. I think we should call it the Tobias Sutton Collection. After all, you're the one making the donation."

"Papa would turn over in his grave."

"Good."

Guiding her around the house, Toby had been subdued, becoming more so with every room they entered. Now delight sparked in his eyes, and he looked like the man who had taken her flying to paradise last night. "What a...fiendishly appropriate suggestion. I left King's with a very undistinguished degree. I rather like the idea of my name gracing the annals of learning."

"So do I."

"I'll get my secretary on the case straightaway." He caught her hand and hauled her close for a passionate kiss.

By the time she struggled free, Viola was laughing. She was flustered and pleased and distracted. Toby's kisses always turned her a bit silly. "What was that for?"

His arms encircled her waist. "Isn't a man allowed to kiss his brilliant wife?"

"He is. But what if the servants see us?"

"Haven't you noticed? The staff are being tactful and leaving us alone."

Actually, now she thought back, during the whole long morning, she hadn't seen a single maid or footman. "How very nice of them."

"And now..." Toby checked the long room with its polished wooden floors. "...I've finally found something in this house that meets with my approval."

Puzzled, Viola looked around, too. All she saw was acres of dingy paintings and the iron-gray sky outside. It had just started to rain. She was very glad that she'd persuaded her husband against traveling today. It would be miserable on the road.

While she'd never say that she'd enjoyed her morning – she'd been torn between outrage and a sorrow for Toby so sharp that she wanted to cry – she wasn't at all sorry that she'd insisted on seeing the house. While he'd been reticent about a childhood that must have been lonely and violent, she'd read more into what he didn't say than what he did. She now knew her husband so much better than she had – and what she'd learned threatened to break her heart. And made her more determined to bring changes to his life and home.

"I hope you're going to say you approve of your charming new wife," she said lightly.

Toby gave her a wicked smile. All of a sudden, he looked like the out-and-out scoundrel that she'd first fallen in love with. While the man she'd discovered since was a thousand times more fascinating, she found the libertine breathtakingly exciting.

"That goes without saying."

"Nonetheless, you could say it."

His kiss was brief but thorough, and put her off balance again. "I'm enchanted by the lovely girl who was generous enough to accept such a rapscallion as a husband. I particularly like her devious mind."

"Goodness me, have you ever praised a girl's mind before?" Viola said faintly.

"And her bosom is a work of art, too."

She kept laughing, as he drew her across to one of the wide window seats. "That sounds more like you."

"It's time to renew my acquaintance with what I discovered last night."

"And this morning." He'd woken her at sunrise for another fiery ride to the stars. There had been no discomfort at all, just oceans of pleasure that sweetened her blood to syrup.

"And this morning." He perched on the tapestry upholstery and stared up at her with the devil in his bright green eyes. "But now I realize that I'm unworthy of the fraternity of rakes."

"Oh?" Familiar liquid heat stirred in the pit of her stomach. If he was talking about more bed sport, she was eager to cooperate. She hoped to heaven that it wasn't a mile back to her apartments. She'd lost track of where they were in the house.

"To think that I've been in this gallery a thousand times, and I never before noticed how convenient these seats are."

She didn't need to ask what they were convenient for. Toby was as keen to have her as she was to be had. Even so, shock jolted her.

"Someone might see us from outside." The window overlooked a formal parterre with a fountain.

Toby's grunt was disdainful. "Nobody will be out in the gardens in this weather."

"What if a servant comes in?"

"I told you, the servants are allowing us privacy, God bless them."

He firmed his grip on her hand and drew her closer. Her heart raced with a mixture of excitement and trepidation. Despite that incandescent encounter in the carriage after their wedding, she hadn't contemplated congress outside a bed. "There isn't room to lie down."

"We don't need to lie down."

As always, her curiosity stirred. Lord above, Toby introduced her to such intriguing new experiences. "We don't?"

His expression intensified. If his eyes got any hotter, her clothes would catch alight. As her desire turned restless, she shifted from one slippered foot to the other.

"Take off your drawers, Viola." The teasing note frayed, and she realized that he was already hard for her. How very…gratifying.

She leaned in and kissed him, and this time, she tasted desperation on his lips. His interest had risen with astonishing swiftness.

Basking in Toby's avid gaze, she stepped back and hauled her skirts up.

"You have lovely legs. No wonder your father gave you the breeches parts in his productions."

"Thank you," she said. "Just my drawers?"

"For the moment."

She untied the strings at her waist and let the sheer cambric garment slip to her ankles. As she stepped out of her drawers, her skirts drifted down again.

When she dared to glance at Toby, she saw that he'd opened his breeches and now stroked the impressive column of flesh that had given her such pleasure. Her breath caught, as she took in his size and power. She rubbed her thighs together to ease a surge of desire.

"It feels wicked to do this in daylight," she stammered, venturing closer.

"All the better to see you with, my dear," he said with a theatrical villainy that made her giggle.

"You're looking rather wolfish." Viola's hands closed at her sides, as she fought the urge to touch him. In the carriage, she'd loved taking hold of all that virility.

A flash of something that she didn't understand lit his eyes, as his hand continued its lazy movement up and down his member. "I certainly look forward to eating you."

He must be talking about giving her more of those sizzling kisses. How wonderful.

Toby released his rod to spread his hands against the seat. "Come here and sit on my lap."

Anticipation turned her knees to water, as she closed the small distance between them. "Like I did yesterday on the way here?"

He caught her hips. "No, straddle me."

Astonishment held her still. "You want…"

"I do."

"Is that possible?"

"Very much so." A crease marked his cheek as he smiled. "Not something Juliet mentioned?"

"She only talked about beds." And not much about that.

"Beds have their uses." Toby's smile broadened in a way that would alarm her, if she wasn't in such a lather to feel him inside her. "Not to mention chairs and walls and sofas and floors. And right now, window seats."

"Heaven help me," she squeaked, her secret places clenching with carnal longing. Gingerly she slid over his lap, too aware of how close she came to his breeding organs.

"Put your knees on the seat and hold onto my shoulders." His voice was rough with strain.

She'd promised to obey him, hadn't she? Shaking hands curled over those brawny shoulders. She folded her legs to rest her knees on either side of his hips. He retreated until his back bumped into the mullioned glass behind him. The extra space aided her precarious balance.

Her grip tightened, as he shoved aside the mass of skirts and petticoats separating her naked nether regions from his. His hand explored her cleft, making her tremble and gasp. When he discovered she was already wet, he sighed with brazen satisfaction.

"Rise up on your knees and take me, sweetheart."

This was where she thought he was going, odd as the whole situation struck her. But everything that he'd asked of her so far had resulted in rapture. Perhaps this would, too.

Viola moved up and positioned herself above his member. He rewarded her with a long hiss of approval, as she sank over him with an ease that surprised her. After all, this was only her third experience of physical intimacy.

This variation wasn't just possible. It promised to set her on fire.

She met Toby's dazed eyes and managed a smile, as her body eased to fit around him. At this angle, he filled her in the most enthralling fashion. Even better, the gray light pouring through the windows revealed every shade of his reaction. He looked fierce and serious and purposeful in a way that thrilled her to the bone.

She leaned in for a quick kiss and circled her hips to take him deeper.

# CHAPTER TWENTY-ONE

*D*ear God, she was going to kill him with pleasure. Toby's fingers dug into her hips, as he closed his eyes and rested his head back on the mullioned window behind him. He succumbed to dark heat and radiant warmth, and a connection that surpassed all his wide experience. Until he'd bedded his wife.

Viola was so hot and snug around him. He bumped up in a silent request for her to move. She took the hint, performing that spectacular twist once more, before rising in a leisurely glide that threatened to shatter him.

He gritted his teeth and told himself that he'd hold back until she found her peak. Despite his balls feeling ready to explode.

With a low moan that echoed in his bones, she sank. Toby's eyes cracked open to catch her wonder, as she discovered the potential of this position. Her face was brilliant with excitement.

He released one hip and buried his fingers in that luxuriant mass of hair. "Come here," he growled, dragging her forward into a succulent kiss.

She rose to take him again. Every undulation sent an earthquake roaring through him. When she accepted his full length, the connection became transcendent.

He lowered his hand from her head to her breast, squeezing it through the pretty yellow muslin. She muttered encouragement against his lips and tightened around him. Volcanic sensation pummeled him.

She tore her lips free of his and, panting, began to move faster and faster. He gripped her hips and helped her to establish a rhythm. At first, she'd been cautious, but lost in this turbulent storm of arousal, she was at the mercy of ascending pleasure.

One last time, she lowered and shuddered over him in an eruption of female pleasure that splintered his control. With a groan, he released his desire. Even while he pumped into her, she slumped onto his chest in boneless satisfaction.

"That was just wonderful, Toby." His shirt front muffled her voice.

"It was," he murmured in return, lashing his arms around her as her spasms eased.

Since they'd met, she'd offered him an irresistible peace. But he rapidly discovered that no peace compared to holding his wife close after they'd found ecstasy together.

After a long, silent communion, he shifted. Despite Viola's drowsy protest, he moved to break their connection.

Once he'd fastened his trousers, he raised his feet to the seat. He bent his knees and arranged a somnolent Viola with her back against his heaving chest. One hand slid beneath her bodice to caress her breast, as a lazy tide of pleasure coursed through him. Tilting his head against the folded shutter behind him, he felt that, in spite of the cold, rainy day, he basked in sunlight.

Viola lifted her head to skim a quick kiss across his jaw. A gesture of affection rather than passion, but one that filled him with warmth. Before his rushed wedding, he'd focused on carnal matters. Odd to realize that the idea of his wife caring about him proved as powerful as the prospect of more bed sport.

With a smoothness that created its own caress, his hand left her breast. He caught her face and held her steady for a longer kiss that was a wordless expression of his regard.

By the time he raised his head, they were both breathless. She gave him a dazed smile, before resting her head on his chest. The action conveyed a trust that nobody had ever shown him. How odd that in all the world, only the clever, fascinating creature that he'd wed considered him a man of substance.

He hoped to blazes he never disappointed her.

His hold firmed, and he closed his eyes to enjoy the rarest of emotions in his wayward life, perfect contentment.

After a dreamy interval, Viola stirred and shifted to meet his eyes. "You know, if we weeded out the gloomiest portraits, this could be a beautiful room. The views over the grounds are lovely, but all those disapproving scowls make one reluctant to linger."

"You've been thinking about redecorating? After what just happened?" he asked in theatrical horror. "I must be losing my touch."

She released a dismissive huff. "Not at all. I loved what we did."

Mollified, he glanced around the gallery. This morning, it was only a large room, instead of a torture chamber. "My father used to drag me in here every week to tell me about my revered forefathers and to lecture me on how I didn't measure up."

"How old were you?"

He shrugged. "It started when I was five or six, I suppose. He made me stand still, when all I wanted to do was run up and down. The room seemed made for children's games."

That was another of Viola's gifts to him. He avoided discussing his miserable childhood, because every memory stung. But as he described those soul-crushing sessions in his late father's company, the queasy churning in his gut for once was absent.

"I agree." With a thoughtful air, Viola surveyed the gallery. "After hearing that, I'm even more determined to send some of these pictures to the attics. Starting with that vainglorious monstrosity of your father. I don't see why he should claim a dozen spots on the walls of this house. He's not the Duke of Wellington, when all's said and done. One painting is enough, and we'll put it in a dark corner."

Toby gave a short laugh. "More spinning in his grave."

Or burning in hell, if there was any justice.

"If he expected people to cherish his memory, he should have been kinder during his life."

Toby considered what she'd said. "He wasn't a man who valued the gentler virtues."

He braced for more questions. He'd revealed more today than he had before, but he wasn't sure that he was ready to spill every ugly, humiliating truth of growing up an unloved son in this grim house.

"Where's your mother? Shouldn't she be next to your father? The other couples are displayed together."

"The pater didn't want her beside him. He always spoke of my mother with utter contempt."

The same contempt that he'd directed at his unsatisfactory son.

Viola frowned. "Why?"

Toby shrugged again. "She was much younger than him and displayed too much Anstey frivolousness. Even worse in my father's eyes, she took forever to produce a child that lived past its first year. They'd been married fifteen years before I was born. Then instead of a real Sutton with a studious disposition and a suitably dour outlook on life, I turned out to be a frivolous Anstey."

Sorrow and pity darkened Viola's eyes to the color of the ocean on a cloudy day. "How very sad."

"That I'm more like Leighton's side of the family?"

"For your sake, yes, that is sad. You would have had an easier time, if you'd been the mealymouthed little prig that your father wanted." Before he could object to her pity, she went on. "But I was thinking of your mother. I imagine that she was gay and spirited before she fell into your father's clutches."

"According to the servants, she was just as you describe her. I don't remember. I was just two when she died, after yet another failed confinement. My father got her pregnant every year. I think her body just wore out."

"I suspect her heart was broken, too, if she lost all those babies. I can hardly bear to think about it."

"It's a tragic story, isn't it? And my father blamed her. He wouldn't have shown any consideration for her suffering. He didn't trust emotions. In his view, the world would be a better place, if automatons populated it."

"So she bore all that grief without one kind word from her husband. What a horrid fate for a pretty girl who must have been the toast of London during her season."

"Her doctor said that she was too fragile to carry another child to term after having me. But dear Papa..." He didn't bother to soften the bitter edge to his voice. "...had got his heir. Now he wanted his spare."

"What a pig."

Viola's vehement response surprised him. "He was a selfish, self-satisfied devil."

"Who spread misery to everything he touched. I'm so glad that you managed to stay true to yourself and grow up to be the marvelous man you are."

"Marvelous?" he echoed in bewilderment.

He'd never had a conversation like this in his life. Nobody had called him marvelous before. Well, not unless he was lying between their legs. He was used to women praising his sensual skills, less accustomed to compliments otherwise.

"Yes, marvelous."

He frowned, still feeling like he was an intruder in a world that made no sense. "Viola, don't tell me you're crying."

She pushed away and sat upright on the window seat. The light through the tall windows was stark on her distress, and Toby cursed himself for upsetting her.

"It's all just so awful. And so avoidable. With a little care, your mother might have lived to love you as you deserve. If your father had accepted you on your own terms, you might have developed a real relationship." Her words emerged in furious fits and starts, and emotion thickened her voice. She dashed her hands across her eyes, but that didn't dam the tears pouring down her cheeks. "He's the one who missed out."

Trying to work out whether his lovely and notably clever wife suffered a brainstorm, Toby drew his handkerchief from his pocket and passed it across.

"Thank you," she muttered, clutching it in a shaking hand and swiping at her overflowing eyes without noticeable effect. "You'll hate that I'm creating such a scene. Men hate howling women. Papa has no patience with what he calls female megrims, and with three daughters, he's had to put up with plenty."

Toby shifted to sit beside her and put his arm around her. With a gratifying lack of hesitation, she nestled into his side.

"You've had a difficult few days. Hell, you've had a difficult time since you met me." He strove to inject a lighter note into the conversation by adopting a pompous tone. "I can see that after sampling my incomparable lovemaking, you're overwrought. Most women lucky enough to enjoy my attentions are overcome. I bear it all with good-natured stoicism. It's the price of perfection."

His absurdity roused a watery giggle. "You're a fool."

"Your fool." He kissed the top of her head and brought her closer.

"I'm even-tempered most of the time. I promise not to spend our entire honeymoon sniveling over you."

He stroked her back and for once, when he touched a woman, he meant comfort not seduction. "I don't mind."

"You're too gallant." She started to sound more like herself.

"Not me. Not gallant at all. And I truly don't mind."

To his surprise, he wasn't just saying that. When his mistresses burst into tears, he'd been all too aware that they wanted something. Like jewelry. Or a new carriage.

But Viola cried for his sake. A different situation altogether. Not only different, unique. He couldn't recall anyone shedding a tear on his behalf. Yet after learning about his unhappy youth, his wife wept like a fountain.

So far, marriage presented a series of firsts. The first time somebody wept for him. The first time he shared his bleak history with a confidante he trusted. The first time he experienced genuine emotion with a lover.

Viola changed him. Already. Soon he'd have difficulty recognizing the man that he'd once been. Toby had an inkling that wasn't altogether a bad thing. After all, the man that he'd been was an aimless roué.

He'd be happy to sit here with his wife for the rest of the day, but too soon, she raised her head and released a soggy laugh. She wasn't crying anymore, thank heaven, but she was still in a bit of a state. "Let me put my drawers back on, then you can show me your mother's portrait."

She didn't wait for agreement, but stood and crossed to pick up the drift of white cambric. As she raised her skirts and tied the garment at her waist, he watched with stirring interest.

After that almighty climax, he should be satisfied for a while. But Viola had a special magic. The more he had of her, the more he wanted. That was a new experience, too. He always enjoyed the thrill of the chase, but his appetite never lasted, once he caught his quarry.

"Or we could stay here and extend your education," he said with manufactured idleness, as heat eddied in his blood.

Her lush mouth – by God, he could devote an eon to kissing her and count the hours well spent – twitched in an intriguing way, as if she liked the idea of dalliance. "First show me your mother."

First? That sounded deuced promising.

He rose and crossed to draw her into a luscious kiss that he hoped conveyed the extent of his appreciation. "If I'd known how devilish delightful marriage would be, I'd have compromised you the minute we met."

She giggled. "We broke the rules from the first, didn't we?"

"You were so clever to get us off the hook that day."

"We ended up on the hook anyway."

He couldn't interpret her tone. "Do you mind?"

She shook her head. "So far, I'm enjoying life as a wife."

"I'm glad." Which was an inadequate description for the wave of relief that swept through him. The strength of his reaction made his knees wobble. "Especially as this is all my fault."

"But Marjorie—"

"I shouldn't have assumed that she'd just go away. I should have found a way to tell her that I wasn't interested, and I was never going to be interested."

Viola didn't look convinced. "She needed to believe you."

"Nonetheless, I ought to have made some effort to control the situation. Embroiling you in scandal was the act of a villain."

Her gaze somber, she stood in his loose embrace and studied his face. "You know, if you keep showing me all these wonders, I might forgive you. At least a little bit."

"I'll show you." Self-mockery turned down his lips. "I fear that I'll show you so hard and so often, you'll get sick of the sight of me. Unless you haven't worked it out already, I'm mad for you."

Her smile was brilliant, and his heart leaped into his throat as he waited for some reciprocal declaration. Perhaps something stronger than "mad."

She shifted out of his hold. "Show me your mother."

Telling himself that he had no right to be disappointed, he took Viola's hand. That felt so natural, yet so significant. Much more significant than a mere connection of palms and fingers. They walked to the end of the gallery and stopped before a picture of a slender woman in the heavy embroidered silks and wide skirts fashionable last century.

"You weren't exaggerating when you said your father put her as far away as possible," Viola said.

"If he wasn't so puffed up with Sutton pride, I suspect he'd have stashed the painting in the attics or destroyed it altogether. But family tradition puts every earl and countess in the gallery, so he couldn't quite bring himself to exile her into the cold."

"She was beautiful."

"I've always thought so," he said softly.

"And she does look like you." Viola took her time to assess the painting. "It's a great work. The artist has captured something of her soul, I think. Burning it would be a crime."

Toby stared at the picture and tried to judge it as a piece of art and not the only likeness he owned of his dead mother. But it was impossible. "It's a Gainsborough. One of his best, I've been told."

"She looks lovely, but—"

"Wistful, too. Gossip was that she fancied a young captain, but a second son wasn't an eligible parti for Lord Shelburn's daughter."

"So instead they gave her to a dried-up old man and a life of misery."

He shrugged. "It's the way of our world. You know that."

"That doesn't make it right."

"No."

She sent him a quick smile. "At least I wed a vigorous young husband. I'm luckier than your mother."

He hoped to hell that she felt like that in a year. Or ten. Or fifty. He met the painted green eyes in the portrait. He saw those same eyes every time that he stood in front of his mirror to shave. "As a small child, I used to wait here for hours, begging her to talk to me. But she never did. One day my father caught me and whipped me for being feeble."

Toby kept his attention on his mother, in an attempt to avoid his wife's damned compassion. Compassion and curiosity.

Viola was curious about everything. A definite advantage when she joined him in bed. Less so, when she devoted that scalpel-sharp intelligence to his past sorrows. Then he felt like she peeled away the outer layer of his skin. Slowly.

He loathed people feeling sorry for him. He'd inherited the Sutton pride, if nothing else.

Why in Hades couldn't he keep Viola out? Good God, he almost begged her to pity him.

Her grip on his hand tightened. Despite everything, his rebellious heart softened at the gesture of affection.

"You know, I'm beginning to think that keeping even one portrait of your swine of a father might be too much," she said.

Toby turned to her in confusion. "You sound angry."

She looked it, too. "I don't like domestic tyrants, and he treated you appallingly."

Despite his discomfort with having old humiliations exposed, the unhappy child lurking in his heart settled. "You're breaking with tradition if you take down all his portraits."

He was half-joking, but Viola shot him a searing look. "Tradition hasn't done the occupants of this house one ounce of good."

Viola glanced back at the striking image of his mother and went on before Toby could object. Not that he felt the slightest desire to argue. "Your father must have bullied his wife as relentlessly as he bullied you. He made you unhappy, when you have such an immense capacity for joy. Not to mention, he's given you a lifelong hatred for your home."

It dawned on him that Viola was on his side. He couldn't think of anyone else who had so unequivocally leaped to his defense. She didn't see him as a total failure, the way his father had.

"Give her time, she'll find out in the end," said the jeering voice in his head that always spoke with his father's withering disdain.

But for once, he didn't accept that scathing verdict on his character and abilities. Because of Viola. Viola wanted to pack away every image of his odious papa. Viola wanted to remove the old man's doleful influence from the house.

Viola, who wanted him and who had called him both marvelous and magnificent.

By Jove, Toby would take her voice in his head over the pater's any time.

"It's a damned unwelcoming pile," he said.

"It doesn't have to be."

Toby surveyed his surroundings with a cynical smile. "I doubt a few cushions will transform it into a bower of bliss."

Viola's determination strengthened. "It's worth a try."

He laughed, admiring her optimism, however futile it might be. He drew her close for a kiss. When he raised his head, he looked around once more.

Amazement flooded him, as he linked his hands around Viola's lissom waist. "You know, tumbling you on the window seat has taken the chill off this room."

It was true. Perhaps cushions wouldn't make the grade as exorcists, but the magic of his body moving in Viola's did.

At last, she smiled. Although with a touch of her earlier fierceness. "This morning you said that you like the countess's apartments. Perhaps if you debauch me in every room of this house, you won't loathe the castle half as much."

A delighted smile turned up his lips. Not because he believed that she could banish the ghosts from Brazey, but because she suggested lots and lots of sex. "You've seen how many rooms there are. Are you up to the task?"

With a blush and a saucy smile that he found dashed arousing, she glanced down at his breeches. "Are you?"

The impudent question roused a splutter of choked laughter. "My Lady Renfrew, I am outraged."

Her glance was unimpressed. "No, you're not."

No, he wasn't. He was too busy blessing the day that an unreliable elm tree had dumped him at this bewitching girl's feet. "It might take us a while."

She shrugged. "We've got the rest of our lives." She sent him a thoughtful look. "I know where I'd like to start."

His cock twitched with interest. "Oh?"

She caught his hand and stepped back. The spark in her eyes made his heart crash against his ribs. "Yes, in that mausoleum of a library."

Another slam of heart to ribs. "Now?"

Her smile widened. "No time like the present."

Toby hauled Viola closer for another kiss, before he took the lead. Laughing, they ran through the long gallery and down the imposing staircase.

# CHAPTER TWENTY-TWO

It took them three days to make it into the dining room, as they pursued their quest to banish the ghosts from Brazey Castle. That had been number two on Viola's list after the prison of a library. But the string of dark, overly luxurious rooms in the master's apartments had distracted them. According to Toby, those chambers retained a particularly strong emanation of his vile father and needed extra attention.

She didn't mind. By now, she was so bedazzled under the onslaught of passion, she didn't care where her husband seduced her. Just as long as he kissed her and placed his strong, elegant hands on her and joined his big powerful body with hers.

Odd to think that less than a week ago, the marital act had been a frightening mystery. Now Viola was addicted to Toby's touch. And his spicy scent. And the rumble of his voice. And the rich sound of his laughter, which always defied their dreary surroundings.

So when the servants had cleared away the last of another shamefully late breakfast and left Toby and Viola alone with a fresh pot of coffee, she knew what the glint in her husband's eyes meant.

With a purposeful air, he set his cup back in its saucer. "Well, wife, what have you got planned for today?"

She met Sarah Sutton's bright painted glance and permitted herself a secret smile. Toby's mother's portrait had held pride of place in the dining room since the day that she'd first seen it. Viola had arranged for it to replace the picture of the late earl, which gave her indigestion.

"Perhaps we should call on the neighbors. We haven't done anything to establish ourselves in local society."

He made a discontented sound. "Local society be buggered. I'm only interested in my wife's company."

That was extremely nice to hear, but she couldn't resist playing with him a little longer. "We could take a walk. It's nice outside, and you haven't shown me all the grounds yet."

So far, they'd been too busy inside, although she and Toby had strolled in the parterre and he'd given her a tour of the stables. That had been a surprise. The heavy atmosphere that infested the house was absent. All was modern efficiency and contented horses and bustling grooms. Toby hadn't exaggerated when he'd told her that there, if anywhere, was where his heart lay at Brazey Castle.

"Bugger the grounds, too."

"We could go through some of the ledgers. I'm fiendish quick with figures." She fought to control a smile. "At Afton Park, Papa left all the accounting to me."

"Good for Papa."

How she loved to tease Toby. Especially when he knew that she was teasing him. The light in his eyes brightened, and something inside her loosened in anticipation. She'd wager half her generous pin money that the ledgers would remain unopened.

"Actually, I mean that about the ledgers."

He flung his napkin onto the table and stood. "You're welcome to them."

"I hope to be useful." She wasn't teasing now. "I don't want to be the sort of wife who is no help to her husband."

"Pleased to hear it." The devilish grin that curled his mouth intensified the wanton heat swirling inside her. "Stand up."

Viola had never liked taking orders, which had made for some strained encounters with Juliet over the years. But she placed her napkin on the table and rose to her feet with an alacrity that made Toby's smile widen.

He shifted the coffee pot to clear a space on the tabletop. "Come here."

That heavy, melting feeling inside Viola intensified. She shifted from one foot to the other in an excited shuffle, before she forced her rubbery legs to move. Toby stepped back and signaled for her to lean against the edge of the table.

He planned something special. She could already tell. That deliberately straight mouth told her that he was about to invite her into unknown realms. Realms he was sure that she'd like. Over the last few days, she'd become familiar with that particular expression.

Her breath emerged in choppy gasps, and her heart raced. She thought that she knew what he wanted to do. He'd already seduced her on all kinds of furniture. He'd revealed new possibilities for window seats and chairs and sofas, and on one memorable occasion the imposing desk in the library. Although the beds in the earl's and countess's suites had received plenty of attention, too.

They were yet to make use of a table. Today must be the day.

He leaned in, and kissed her with a passion that his outwardly calm demeanor belied. As always, she surrendered with helpless enthusiasm. His mouth tasted of coffee and him. Delicious.

When he pressed closer, the backs of her thighs met the hard edge of the table. The ruthless grip on her hips thrilled her. She loved his male strength. It spoke to a profound femininity in her soul.

"You should lock the door," she murmured against his lips.

"No servant is going to interrupt us." She felt him smile. "They're still being discreet."

Now she thought about it, it was odd that nobody had ever walked in on them. Even when they used public rooms for private acts.

She pulled a few inches away and caught his face in one hand. When she brushed her thumb across his lips, he sucked it into his mouth. The wet heat and pressure sent a bolt of painful arousal slamming through her.

"I've been too obsessed with what you do to me to pay attention to much else," she admitted.

When he bit down, the hint of pain sharpened her desire. She gasped and clutched at his shoulder, as she withdrew her thumb. Her tingling palm flattened on the polished wood table.

Toby nuzzled her neck. She was especially sensitive there. Heat zapped her, and her stomach constricted in wicked expectation. The scrape of his teeth made her shake and curl her fingers deeper into his shoulder.

He lifted her and set her bottom on the table with a bump. He released her hips to drag the filmy bodice of her pink muslin gown down, revealing breasts mounded over the top of her half corset.

A gloating smile illuminated his features. "Did I tell you I love your bosom?"

A snort of dismissive laughter. "Once or twice." *Every day.*

She adored her husband's unabashed admiration for her body. It meant that she started to appreciate it, too. Something that provided such breathtaking pleasure deserved more respect than she'd heretofore given it.

He cupped her breasts and squeezed. "Then let me tell you again."

As sultry heat settled between Viola's legs, she sighed. He pushed her shift aside to uncover her nipples and bent to take one pointed peak into his mouth. Another jolt of response. She curved forward to comb her hand through the silky abundance of his hair.

When he eased her backward onto the table, need gushed through her like a spring tide. Blindly, she fumbled for the front of his breeches. Through his clothing, she felt the insistent weight of his member. With a low murmur of approval, she shaped her palm to fit him.

He groaned and lifted his head from her breast. His eyes glittered with excitement. "Not yet."

"I want you." Her voice vibrated with need. Another thing that she'd discovered since her wedding was that Toby loved to hear how much she desired him.

"And I want you like the very devil. But first, there's something I'd like to do."

Oh? That sounded interesting.

"Lie back."

"You want to see me?" The first time that he'd viewed the secret hollows of her body, she'd just about died of embarrassment. The way he relished every single inch of her soon made her luxuriate in having his eyes on her cleft.

"Yes," he said on a long hiss that made the hairs rise on her skin.

Without protest, she spread her legs and stretched out over the table. "I feel rather like a pagan sacrifice," she said without resentment, as her gaze fixed on the green and white plasterwork on the ceiling.

"I certainly intend to make you burn."

"You always make me burn."

He set his hand on her knees and pushed up her skirts and petticoats. A charged silence descended.

"Viola, you're a wish come true."

A smug smile lengthened her lips. "My drawers never stay on for very long, so I thought I'd save you the trouble."

He dropped a kiss on her bare thigh. "I approve."

"I thought you might," she said in a scratchy voice. He'd just started to touch her, yet she felt ready to go up in smoke.

"I wish I'd known at breakfast."

"I knew." Her smile broadening, she pulled her skirts higher. "It was rather...titillating."

"I'm sure." He placed a row of kisses across her bare stomach, igniting a line of small fires.

Viola closed her eyes to savor the sensation. Darkness honed her other senses in a most diverting fashion.

She waited for Toby to come down over her and push inside. But his hands ran along her thighs, before she felt hot, moist breath on her sex.

Startled, she opened her eyes and instinctively tried to bring her legs together. But she encountered an obstacle.

"Toby?" she stammered, as she rose on her elbows to find him kneeling on the floor between her legs.

She'd seen desire in his face often enough over these last days to recognize its presence now. "You'll like this."

She didn't have to ask what "this" was, because at the end of the sentence, he leaned forward and with a voluptuous gusto that she couldn't mistake, he licked her cleft.

The sensation was odd. And shocking. Her hands formed fists, as she fought the urge to push him away. "That's...depraved."

Viola already knew that wouldn't persuade him to stop. He watched her face now instead of her sex. Given what he'd just done, that didn't diminish her jumpiness.

"Indeed."

"Why would you want to do...that?"

"Because it will give me pleasure." Before she could respond, he went on with more emphasis. "Because it will give *you* pleasure."

When she covered her sex with one hand, she blushed to discover how wet she was. Thanks to his mouth, but also thanks to her own building arousal.

He groaned again and briefly closed his eyes. "That's not helping."

"I don't understand...this," she said shakily.

The thought of him kissing her sex should repulse her. Part of her was repulsed. But something about the naked craving that she read in his features thrilled her, too.

"I know you don't."

She'd started to feel like she caught onto the pleasures that a man and a woman could find together. But it seemed that there was more. More than her imagination could encompass.

Her fingers curled over her mound, feeling the tickle of damp pubic hair. Forbidden curiosity made her shiver. She loved it when Toby touched her private places. Was it possible that she'd like it if she touched them, too?

The notion was so sinful, she snatched her hand away.

He smiled as if he read her thoughts. Heaven help her, he probably did. "It's nice to touch yourself, isn't it?"

"I'm sure I'm not supposed to," she said in a thready voice.

"You never pleasured yourself?"

"No," she said, appalled. Even more appalled, because the sybarite that she'd become over these last few days found the idea intriguing.

"It's not that outrageous. Most people do. I certainly did before we were married. First, it was because I wanted you and I was sure I'd never have you. After our engagement, I touched myself to find relief from how much I looked forward to our wedding night."

Papa? Juliet? Portia? Elizabeth Tierney? The Duke of Granville? Surely not. "I don't believe most people do."

"It's natural."

"For licentious young men, perhaps," she retorted with a hint of acerbity.

Spread out before him like a banquet for his delectation, she felt at a distinct disadvantage. Oh, and goodness, hadn't he said that he wanted to eat her? Their puzzling discussion in the long gallery now made sense.

She sat up and tugged her skirts down to cover her knees. "For pity's sake, don't look so downcast."

A grunt of self-derisive laughter. "But I am downcast."

"Because I won't excite myself while you're watching? Or because I won't let you put your mouth on me?"

"Both." He sighed. "You've been such an angel in my arms, not to mention so intrepid, that I hoped to introduce you to a new variation."

She shot him a chagrined look. "Now you make me feel like I've let you down."

"You could never let me down." He caught her chin and gave her a quick kiss that helped to soothe her ruffled feelings. "When I was alone in bed every night after we met—"

She frowned. "Alone?"

"Yes, alone." The question surprised him, she saw. "Apart from the ghost of the glorious Lady Viola Frain, who wouldn't leave me in peace."

"I thought a rake like you never slept without a lover."

"Actually, I rarely slept with a lover. We did what we wanted then parted ways. Even on the rare occasion when I set up a mistress, I'd visit her house before I came home or went to a gambling den or my club. I wasn't ready for domesticity."

She considered what he said, as warmth flooded her foolish heart. "So I'm the first woman you've actually lived with?"

"Yes. Very agreeable it's been, too."

That went a long way toward mollifying her. "I assumed that you continued your escapades until the day we stood up in church together."

He shrugged as if he wasn't turning her ideas about him on their head. For about the hundredth time since they'd wed, blast him. "I couldn't have the woman I wanted. I wasn't going to waste my time with women I didn't want."

She bit her lip and told herself that it would be absurd to cry. "Toby, that's the nicest thing you've ever said to me."

"Silly widgeon." He frowned. "I told you that you knocked me for six at first sight."

"You did." But she hadn't believed him. Not really. Now, she did.

He went on. "I used to toss and turn all night, thinking of what it would be like to kiss you and touch you and lie with you. I used to imagine how you looked without clothes. I used to think of my hands on your body and my mouth on your quim. I fantasized about how you'd taste and sound when I kissed you into ecstasy."

"Toby…" How could she remain immune? What he wanted seemed unnatural. Heavens above, it seemed more unnatural that he wanted to watch her touch herself.

She thought that she'd moved beyond self-consciousness. It turned out that she'd had no idea.

*So get some idea, Viola.*

The stern little voice reminded her that everything she and Toby had done so far had been wonderful. And she'd been new to it all. Juliet had done her best to prepare her, but her efforts had been lacking. Given her sister's inexperience, how could that be otherwise? Perhaps what Toby asked now was just another lesson in her sensual education.

"You're thinking about giving me my way, aren't you?" He sounded happier.

She laughed, despite her cheeks flushing hotter. "Yes, plague take you, I am. Although after this, I'll blush to look anyone but you in the eye. In fact, I doubt that I'll be able to look you in the eye either."

"You won't regret it."

"You're such a rogue, Toby. You whisper in my ear, and I'm so weak that I just go along."

"You can't resist me, I know."

She sighed, although she knew that he was joking. "No, I can't."

"Lie down, Viola. Let me ravish you. You know you want to find out what it's like."

She did. Despite being unable to imagine either of them enjoying such a bizarre experience.

Half-reluctant, she settled back on the table and with trembling hands pulled up her skirts. "Do your worst," she said faintly, closing her eyes, as if she might lessen her embarrassment by refusing to watch what he did.

She waited for some mocking response, but his tone was grave as he answered. Grave and fervent. "Thank you."

She mightn't understand, but she couldn't mistake how much he wanted to do this outlandish thing. Her hands closed into fists at her sides, as she waited for the intimate kiss. But he started by running his hands along her stockinged calves to linger at the sensitive place behind her knees. His caresses turned her muscles to jelly and pleasure streaked through her. She loved his hands on her body.

He ventured higher, past blue satin garters to her thighs. "Relax, Viola," he murmured, moving his hands up and down her legs.

Her response was a scornful exhalation. "Easy for you to say."

"I'm not doing anything I haven't done before."

When he bent his head, she felt the warm brush of his hair on her thighs. Every muscle tautened in expectation of his mouth on her quim.

It was a word that she'd only learned since her wedding. One of many new things that she'd learned over the last few days.

Toby nibbled a path along her legs, each nip setting off a small explosion of sensation. She exhaled on a long breath and her body relaxed. He was right, curse him. She couldn't resist him.

A low hum in his throat signaled approval. His hands hooked around her knees and when he pushed her legs further apart, she didn't object.

For a long while, he nuzzled and stroked her legs. Her hands uncurled until they lay flat on the tabletop. Viola floated in such a sea of bliss, she hardly noticed when he drew her forward. She slid as smoothly across the polished mahogany as a hand over silk. Her hips rested on the edge, and her legs dangled toward the floor.

The delicate nipping kisses continued, verging higher and higher. Occasionally over the past nights, he'd slowed the pace of seduction, until each second spun out into eternity. It made her feel cherished, as though he revered every part of her. This was like that, so not too unfamiliar at all.

When his mouth reached the inevitable end, her shyness had receded to a point where scruples felt distant and unimportant. His tongue traced her cleft before concentrating on that mysterious place that set her quaking.

She didn't fight the pleasure sweeping through her. When he caught her hips and lifted her to deepen his exploration, she moaned. His hands kneaded the soft cheeks of her buttocks in time with the brazen dance of his tongue.

Soon the waves of pleasure became more urgent. Her blood ignited to fire, and her heart galloped with rising excitement. The hot suction of his mouth on her sex sparked the journey to ecstasy.

All her doubts about what Toby did fled, leaving only burgeoning desire behind.

For the first time since he'd started, she bucked upward. With another low growl of approval, he pressed the tip of his tongue inside her. A rush of heat greeted his incursion. This time, her shiver had nothing to do with revulsion and everything to do with incandescent sensation.

"Toby, that's lovely." She tangled her fingers in his hair. His head bobbed in her grip as he tormented her.

She opened her eyes, expecting to see a fiery heaven instead of the ceiling. Then with dizzying speed, Toby dragged her toward him and set her legs over his shoulders. She tilted her head to see his face buried in her sex. By now, the sight was thrilling instead of alarming.

The tempest seized her, and she cried out as she soared into a blazing tornado of ultimate pleasure. She lost all grip on the everyday world.

After an eternity of rapture, her legs slipped from his shoulders to splay as loose as wet string on either side of him. Through her sated haze, she felt him stand. His long, hard member slid into her. She was so aroused, he moved with an ease that thrilled her anew. She clenched helplessly about him, still caught in the throes of that almighty climax he'd given her with his mouth.

Toby was right about this, too, blast him. Once she'd come to terms with the idea, she'd thoroughly enjoyed what he'd just done. The way that he lingered over her now told her that he'd enjoyed it, too.

Blindly, she grabbed his forearms, as he thrust, going full length with every penetration. As the first peak ebbed, she rose toward another. She feared that she couldn't survive more, even as her body dissolved into ecstasy.

Toby kept up those hard, deliberate thrusts. Again, she shattered into starlight, just as he groaned and filled her with his seed.

She melted into him, caught in the wild rush. Shaking, he dragged her up for a clumsy devouring kiss. Still joined to her, he collapsed into a dining chair that creaked under their weight.

Viola curled her arms and legs around him, as her climax became sweet aftermath. Toby groaned again and buried his head in her shoulder. For a long time, they rested in gasping recovery.

Viola closed her eyes and savored her husband's embrace. She loved everything that he'd done to her since they'd married. But what they'd shared today was exceptional. He'd changed her forever.

Toby raised his head and kissed her again. "Good?"

"Marvelous," she murmured. "But you knew it would be."

She waited for some exultant response, but instead he turned his head from side to side and smiled as he surveyed the room. "The ghosts have gone."

As Viola looked around her, she could only agree.

# CHAPTER TWENTY-THREE

he next four months sped by in a haze of voluptuous pleasure and growing closeness with the man Viola had married. Every day brought a new discovery, a new delight, a new surprise. She'd never been so happy. If every day also deepened her love for the compelling man who shared her life, that secret sorrow only made her blessings shine brighter.

Toby showed no signs of wishing to leave Brazey Castle. The plan to visit Paris had shifted to something they might do next spring.

It had taken Viola and her husband weeks to make love in every room in the castle, with the exception of the servants' quarters. They'd even made a few memorable visits to the kitchens and storerooms downstairs in the middle of the night, to avoid scandalizing the staff. And on one unforgettable afternoon, Toby had taken her up against the wall in the wine cellars.

When they'd launched their project, both of them had treated the idea as a bit of a joke. An excuse for her husband to debauch her when and where he wished – and she had no complaints about that. But the strange fact was that combating sad old history with passionate joy had done much to dispell the castle's oppressive atmosphere.

That, and spending a fortune on new furnishings. Toby had been dubious about the power of a few cushions to lighten the gloom. But he'd since admitted that a brighter, more modern décor leavened the brooding magnificence to something bearable for the mere humans who lived here. These days, Viola could step into the cavernous great hall without a chill inching down her backbone.

It had taken a little while, but Toby had lost that cold, bleak air that had haunted him when he'd first brought her to Brazey. These days, he looked more like the man she'd encountered amidst the chaos of broken branches and torn leaves.

Like that man, but not entirely. Because she'd soon discovered that while the lighthearted rascal was part of his personality, it wasn't the whole story. He was a man who laughed, but he was also capable of perception, generosity, and kindness. Toby Sutton possessed a bone-deep sweetness that he might try to hide, but which found expression in his every action.

And he was brave. Heartbreakingly so. Although he'd cringe if he knew how she saw through his devil-may-care grin to the wounds inflicted so long ago.

Her husband didn't say much about his unhappy childhood, but she'd picked up plenty of hints about the way that his father's contempt and cruelty had shaped him. She'd learned enough to understand his dislike of the house and the entrenched self-distrust, unexpected in such a dynamic, attractive man.

When they'd first wed, she'd feared that Toby resented making a lifelong commitment to a woman for whom he felt a mere passing attraction. Now she knew that he'd wanted her from the first, with a desire that continued to stun her. His doubts about their marriage stemmed from his fears that he might let her down.

Viola hoped that the late Earl of Renfrew fried in hell for his arrogance and callousness. If she could, she'd stoke the fires. She couldn't remember actively hating anyone before, but it hadn't taken her long to develop a virulent loathing for Toby's insensitive, vainglorious lout of a father.

As rapturous day followed rapturous day, she noticed that Toby became easier in her company and easier in his role as the earl. The staff seemed happier, too. Some of that was thanks to the ongoing presence of the lord and lady. Viola had soon recognized that the earl's long absence from Brazey was a burden to the people who lived and worked on the estate. But much of this lessening tension related to a contentment that seeped down from the earl and countess to the humblest scullery maid.

Over these last weeks, Viola had started to nurture a fragile optimism. That Toby might come to terms with his past. That Brazey might become a happy home. That her marriage had a chance of turning into the productive, supportive union of equals that she'd always believed was the best kind of match.

Lying satisfied in Toby's arms in the depths of the night, she permitted herself to hope that perhaps one day he might care for her as she cared for him.

They'd made a fine start. He liked her and enjoyed her company. If he found her annoying or boring, he wouldn't seek her out as often as he did.

He didn't only seek her out because he had an itch to scratch – although he did that often, too. Even four months after their first explosive joinings, she merely needed to glance at him sideways for him to rush her away for a tumble. His desire seemed to strengthen every day. It was as if feeding his appetite only increased it.

But beyond conjugal delight, he enjoyed talking to her and making plans and enquiring after her thoughts. She knew that he respected her intelligence. He appreciated that despite her quietness, she was a woman of decided opinions.

He'd changed her, too. As the overlooked third Frain daughter, she'd been too self-effacing when she arrived at Brazey. Now she carried out her duties as Countess of Renfrew with an aplomb that astonished her.

Toby's belief in her abilities lent her the poise to excel in her new role. Not only that, but four months of passionate marriage had convinced her that she was more than a bookish little mouse. She was a fulfilled and sensual woman, capable of seizing her future and holding the attention of a husband.

One of her greatest joys was how she and Toby worked together to transform Brazey and the estate into what they wanted. She'd never thought that she'd come to a point where she'd view the forbidding edifice as an opportunity rather than a disaster. But now she did.

The chance to turn the house into a family home, while paying due respect to its history, had brought her closer to Toby. Something that she'd feared – because gossip made such a meal of it – was that she and Toby were too different to establish a genuine partnership. But so far, the ton's predictions of catastrophe for the scandalous Renfrew marriage hadn't come to fruition.

Almost from the first, she'd loved Toby. How could she not? He was charming and handsome, and he needed her, even if he mightn't realize it.

Viola liked to be needed, she found. She also liked the idea that her steadiness lent direction to her glittering husband's wayward existence. Direction and purpose. To her surprise, this rambling, unloved, gloomy house supplied them with both.

Today, as summer moved into mellow autumn, she and Toby were busy restocking the library. It had been void of books, since Toby had donated his father's collections to a very grateful King's College. According to the Dean's latest letter, the Toby Sutton gift was already inspiring research.

*Take that, my dear father-in-law.*

Viola had arranged for her books to be sent over from Afton Park, and she and Toby had a standing order at Hatchard's in Piccadilly to deliver the latest novels. She'd been appalled to realize that the late earl's collection hadn't included a single novel. Or any book by a female author, for that matter.

As far as she was concerned, spotty students were welcome to the tomes that had once lined the shelves and glowered down at a boy more interested in football and horses than the funeral customs of long-dead Etruscans.

Now she directed a considering stare at the first volume of *Pride and Prejudice*, a favorite that she must have read about five times since it came out four years ago. "You'd like this one, I think."

Toby stood at the desk, unpacking a crate of new poetry. He glanced across to where she kneeled on the floor, surrounded by tottering piles of books. "Is it a kissing book?"

She laughed and put the leather-bound book aside, as she rooted around in the box for the other two volumes. "It's a romance. But it's funny."

These last months, she'd broadened his taste in literature, although so far, she hadn't managed to convert him to the wonders of a good gothic tale from the Minerva Press.

"I like funny."

He did. She'd already read him *Tom Jones* and *Don Quixote*. She'd indulged in some dreadful overacting to bring out the humor. Her father would be disgusted. Who knew doing all that Shakespeare would prove handy when it came to entertaining a spouse?

"I especially like funny when you're reading to me naked," Toby said in a thoughtful tone.

"I didn't get much reading done that night." Last week, after an energetic encounter in the earl's bed, she'd cracked open a volume of Sheridan's plays.

"After all, you were—"

"Naked. Yes, I know. Next time, I'll put on my dressing gown."

"Not on my account." He waggled his eyebrows in imitation of a leering villain. "I like you naked."

He liked that even more than a funny story, she'd learned. She shifted away from the box and stretched her legs out, leaning back on her arms as she studied him. "Toby, you can't possibly want to do that again."

His sigh didn't hide the interest in his eyes. Nor did his teasing. "You know I do. I always want to do that."

"But we went back to bed after breakfast." When he'd taken his time kissing her between the legs and launching her on another flight to heaven. Her reluctance to participate in that intimacy was a thing of the past. She'd discovered that she could use her mouth on his sexual organs, too. Before their first week together was over, all her shyness about erotic practices had dissolved.

"I was tired."

She greeted that with a contemptuous grunt. "No, you weren't."

After tasting her, he'd used her body with an unfettered enthusiasm that had thrilled her to the bone.

"Well, *you* were tired."

"I haven't had much sleep lately."

Yesterday afternoon for the first time since their wedding, she'd retired for an afternoon nap, and she'd slept instead of using that as an excuse to seduce her husband. She'd woken to discover Toby curled up at her side, watching her with an expression that had made her heart ache with longing.

She'd recognized desire, but she'd also noted a glow that looked like affection. Once she shifted to kiss him, desire had taken over. But for a charged moment, she'd wondered if perhaps Toby wasn't as far from loving her as she believed.

He put on a tone of mock complaint. "That's because you're always inciting me to do my marital duty. You'll have to ask Mrs. Gibney for more roast beef. I need to keep my strength up."

A wry smile turned down her lips. "Request noted." She held out her hand. "Help me up."

He crossed to pull her to her feet with his usual vigor. Viola gasped for air, swayed, and disappeared down a long dark tunnel.

When she returned to awareness, she lay on the carpet, with her head resting on Toby's lap.

He stared into her face, as if she was likely to vanish in a puff of smoke without warning. "My God, darling, are you all right?"

"What happened?" she asked woozily. The ceiling above her heaved in the most nauseating manner, and she had trouble focusing on Toby's features.

"You went out like a candle." He stroked her forehead with a gentleness that went a long way toward easing her swimming head and rebellious stomach. "I pulled you up, and you just folded at the knees and went down. Thank goodness I caught you before you hit the floor."

She frowned, struggling to understand what had happened. The fog in her brain wasn't cooperating. "I swooned?"

"You did. And nearly gave me a heart attack in the process."

"But I never swoon."

"Perhaps you're the one who needs roast beef." He was trying to make her smile, but the fear in his voice made the joke fall flat.

"Was I out for very long?"

"Long enough to make me panic."

"Toby…"

His lips compressed. "Probably only a minute or so. Going on a century."

Viola started to feel a little more like herself. She struggled to sit up, but his hands captured her shoulders. "Lie quietly for another second before I carry you upstairs. I'll get Dr. Purcell out to have a look at you."

Her vision had cleared to a point where she could read his reaction. Toby looked drawn and frantic. "I'm sure I'm all right."

"I'm not."

This time, she managed to escape his hold and sit up to look at him. "It's quite natural, I believe."

"For a perfectly healthy woman to faint? I don't think so."

Toby was too upset to pick up the hint. She snatched a nervous breath and placed a hand on her heaving stomach. This wasn't how she'd planned to do this, but circumstances had overtaken her.

She drew another breath. "Perhaps it's a good idea to ask Dr. Purcell to call."

Toby hadn't latched onto the truth yet. His face contorted, and he grabbed her hand. "Viola, what's wrong? Tell me. Is it my damned hunger for you? You're new to this. I should have kept my blasted hands off you. I'll never forgive myself if I've done you any harm."

She rolled her eyes. Over the past months, she'd developed a healthy respect for her husband's intelligence. Despite his frequent claims to being as stupid as a rock – his father's influence, she knew – he had a quick brain and a surprising amount of intuition. But it was apparent that seeing her collapse at his feet had turned his mind to soup.

"You haven't done me any harm, my dear clodpoll. I'm going to have a baby."

# CHAPTER TWENTY-FOUR

When Viola opened her eyes, the countess's chamber was shadowy, not just because the curtains were closed, but because twilight had drawn in. She rolled over in the large bed and found without surprise that Mrs. Robson was sitting in a chair beside her. She knew that it wouldn't be Toby.

After she'd fainted, he hadn't left her side, until Dr. Purcell arrived to examine her and confirm that she was carrying a child. If all went to plan, she'd have the baby in March.

Once the doctor had gone, Toby joined her for a light luncheon. In the library, she'd imagined that they'd end up in each other's arms before too long, but he'd started to treat her as if she'd disintegrate at the slightest touch. She'd been too downhearted to protest about him keeping his distance.

Because although her husband had said all the right things, expressing his great pleasure in her news, she knew him well enough by now to see that he put a brave face on a situation he couldn't change. He also didn't want to hurt her feelings, bless his kind heart and his thick skull.

But it was too late to deceive her about his reaction. She'd seen his face when she told him about the child. While he'd done his best to cover his immediate response to her announcement, she hadn't missed the horror that flared in his eyes. Unlike her, her husband didn't view the next generation's arrival as good news. As long as she lived, she'd never forget the way her heart had shriveled at that instant.

"Mrs. Robson, how nice of you to watch over me," she said in a husky voice, as she pushed herself up against the pillows.

Mrs. Robson put aside the mending that occupied her hands and smiled at Viola with the unconditional approval that had been lacking in Toby. "It's nice to sit down for a while, my lady. And his lordship didn't want you left on your own."

Not so much that he'd kept her company himself, Viola thought with a hint of sourness. "I must have slept for hours."

"The doctor said to let you rest." Mrs. Robson rose and poured her a glass of water. "Are you feeling up to some tea and a morsel to eat, madam? Mrs Gibney has baked some gingernuts. My old mam always swore there was nothing like ginger for settling a queasy stomach."

Viola accepted the glass and took a sip to ease her parched throat. "Yes, please."

She'd felt too disheartened to do justice to the cold collation that she and Toby had sat down to after Dr. Purcell left. Now she was hungry and back to herself enough to feel annoyed as well as troubled.

Mrs. Robson rang the bell. She must have arranged for the tray to be ready, because it arrived within minutes.

"Are you feeling better, my lady?" she asked, as she laid the tray on Viola's lap.

"Much better, thank you." After fainting, she'd felt horribly shaky. She'd never fainted before. She hoped never to faint again.

"I'm so glad."

Viola eyed the housekeeper, who returned to her chair. "I suppose you know what's going on," she said, once a cup of tea and a handful of delicious ginger biscuits had restored her spirits.

"I understand that we're expecting a happy event, madam."

*Not as far as the earl was concerned.*

"It's impossible to keep secrets from the servants," Viola said with a smile, choosing another gingernut and nibbling on it. Mrs. Robson was right. The ginger helped.

"It's wonderful news. You and his lordship have done so much to turn Brazey into a real home. A baby will be the icing on the cake. The house has been dark and dreary and empty for too long. Even when his late lordship was alive, there wasn't much light at Brazey, if you'll pardon my saying so."

Ah, it seemed that Mrs. Robson was at last ready to share confidences. Viola supposed that she shouldn't encourage the woman, but on the other hand, right now, she needed every weapon she could lay her hands on. She had a war to fight with her husband. A war that she wasn't at all sure she was capable of winning.

"My children will grow up with more freedom than his lordship enjoyed as a boy."

As Viola finished off the biscuit, Mrs. Robson stared into her lap with a pensive expression. She guessed that the housekeeper battled with her loyalty to the old earl, although it was clear that she hadn't liked him much. Nobody seemed to have liked him much.

"I hope that's true, my lady." She fixed her gaze on Viola. "In my opinion, the late earl was unduly harsh with the current master. Downstairs, we did our best to protect the lad, but—"

"There's only so much a servant can do without risking their position."

"Precisely, madam." The respect that she read in Mrs. Robson's eyes surprised her. Perhaps Viola really was coming to grips with her role as Countess of Renfrew. "But none of us believed that young Master Toby deserved such severe punishment. The lad was more suited to the outdoors than those dusty books in the library, but there was no harm in him. You'd never meet a kinder, more generous boy. His lordship has a good heart, my lady. But you know that, loving him as you do."

Viola was glad that she wasn't drinking her tea when she heard that. No secrets from the servants indeed.

"Yes, he's a good man." She meant it, despite wanting to cosh him on the head with a fire iron right now.

"The punishments were so cruel, too. The late earl was a clever man, so he knew just how to make his son's life a misery. Young Master Toby couldn't be still, even when he was asleep. So his father would tie him to a wooden chair and keep him there for hours. He'd beat him, until the boy could hardly walk. When that didn't break his spirit, he sold the lad's pony. Desperate fond of his pony was Master Toby. Any chance he got, he was hanging about in the stables. Then when the boy took a fancy to one of the hounds, his father ordered the dog shot. Madam, I'm sorry. I shouldn't have spoken."

*Oh, Toby, Toby, Toby. I knew it was awful, but this is beyond enduring.*

"I'm sorry." Viola dragged the edge of the sheet up to mop her overflowing eyes. "He mentioned some of these things, but to hear it all now is—"

"Unbearable. The number of times I hugged that little boy and promised him life wouldn't always be so bad, I've lost count. He didn't believe me. When he brought you to the house, it was the first time I saw him happy. Not just happy, but proud of who he is. You've performed a miracle, my lady. Everyone downstairs blesses your name." Mrs. Robson pulled a handkerchief from her sleeve and wiped her eyes. It seemed Viola wasn't the only watering pot in the room.

With shaking hands, Viola opened the drawer on her nightstand and tugged out a handkerchief. She blew her nose and regarded the housekeeper through bleary eyes. "You're too kind."

The woman shook her head with an emphasis that bolstered Viola's determination to banish the curse that lay upon Brazey Castle forever. "No, I'm not. There's laughter in this house now. There never was before. A devil in human form crushed all the life out of my mistress and tried to do the same to her son. His father wanted Master Toby to become his mirror image, and he was determined to whip all trace of the Ansteys out of the boy. You've given his lordship a second chance. You've given Brazey Castle a second chance. Now there's a baby coming for the nursery, and I couldn't be more pleased."

"Thank you." Viola managed a misty smile. "The house just needed a good dose of love."

As far back as her wedding night, she'd diagnosed the problem. Right now, she could accept that Toby didn't love her. But she'd be damned before she let another child grow up at Brazey without a loving father.

It was time to find her husband and have everything out.

She flung away the covers. Before her sleep, her maid Jenny had put her into a filmy negligee. "Will you help me to get dressed?"

"Very good, my lady. But Dr. Purcell recommended a few days in bed. His lordship has ordered a tray for your room tonight and says he'll eat in the library."

Did he indeed? He was avoiding her, the rogue. If Toby thought she'd let him get away with that, he underestimated her.

Viola's chin set with resolution. "A little fresh air before dinner will do me good. I'm having a baby, not dying of an incurable illness. I refuse to spend the next six months wrapped in flannel."

Toby slumped on a stool in a corner of the stall furthest from the stable doors. Closing his eyes, he released a heavy sigh that had Belvedere nudging forward. He leaned his face against Bel's noble nose and drank in the scents of hay and dust and horses. During the worst days of his life, that evocative blend had always comforted him.

Not today.

It was getting dark. Half an hour ago, he'd heard the men finish up and leave. O'Toole, the head groom, must have told them not to speak to him, thank God. O'Toole had been a junior groom in his father's time. He'd been one of Toby's few boyhood friends, although the pater would have had a fit if he'd guessed that his heir fraternized with the lower classes.

Toby should go. He really should. The stables had failed to work their magic, and he owed his wife better than hiding here in the shadows. More, he had to make amends for the way that he'd reacted to the news of impending fatherhood. He'd struggled to appear pleased and proud, but Viola had caught him by surprise. For a solitary instant, he hadn't guarded his expression.

A solitary instant was all that it took for her to see his fear and dismay.

Bel shifted close enough to snuffle at Toby's hair. Toby groaned and rested his cheek on the horse's chest. What the devil was he going to do?

When he opened his eyes, Viola watched him from the stall's gate.

"How did you know I'd be here?"

Bel sidled away and started to nose at his oats.

"The stables are your refuge. That first day when you showed me around the castle, you seemed to set aside an intolerable burden, as soon as you stepped in here." He couldn't tell much from her neutral tone. "I assumed that if you were troubled, this was where you'd come."

As a gentleman should, he rose to his feet, despite his aching heart quailing at the sight of her. He wasn't ready for this discussion. He wasn't sure that he'd ever be ready for this discussion. "Are you feeling better?"

"Yes, thank you." A line of lanterns lit the central aisle, but because her back was toward them, her features remained in shadow. "The sleep helped."

She sounded polite, too. Like a stranger he met at a ball. Regret soured his gut, as he recalled the affinity that they'd enjoyed these last months. Times when he'd been so deep inside her that he wasn't sure where he ended and she began. But other occasions, too, when they'd laughed together, or when they'd shared a perfect understanding. For the first time in his life, he hadn't been lonely.

He felt as lonely as Robinson Crusoe right now.

"I'm glad to hear it." Could he sound more artificial? Even though he *was* glad to hear it. Memories of his wife losing consciousness and crumpling toward the floor would give him nightmares.

"I'm sorry for frightening you."

Was she talking about when she fainted? Or when she announced her pregnancy? He didn't feel brave enough to ask. His father was right. He was a coward.

"I suspect I'll be the sort of husband who hovers to make sure that no harm comes to his wife." He tried to ease the atmosphere with their familiar teasing, but the unreliable light revealed no returning smile.

She unlatched the barrier and stepped into the stall. "Toby, we have to talk."

His gut knotted. Did the English language contain any more doom-laden words?

The problem was that Viola was right. He'd been out here alone, steeling himself for what promised to be an agonizing conversation. But he remained as unprepared as he'd been in the library, when she'd turned his world upside down.

"Yes, we do." Reluctance turned his voice leaden. "Shall we go back to the house?"

To his surprise, she stepped closer. "You feel comfortable here, and we have space and privacy."

She was right. Again. There was room. Belvedere, as befitted the earl's favorite mount, had an entire loose box at his disposal. Nor did Bel blab about anything that he overheard. He'd always been the perfect confidant. "It's hardly fitting for the Countess of Renfrew, though, is it?"

"The stables are more welcoming than the castle."

Toby felt her eyes on him, although the dimness made it impossible to read her expression. No doubt it was sharp with disappointment. After his childhood, he should be used to letting people down.

Somehow it was worse to let his wife down. Perhaps because until now, she'd convinced him that she was happy with her choice.

An unamused smile lengthened his lips. "Not anymore. You've turned the house into a home." Those were words that he'd never expected to say in his lifetime.

A short, bristling silence crashed down before she responded. "A home implies a family."

Her tone was uncompromising. Battle was joined.

"Yes, it does," he said, treading warily.

There was no mistaking the irritation in her sigh. "For pity's sake, Toby. You're acting like a fool. I didn't get myself into this predicament on my own. Ever since we got married, you've been on top of me every chance you got. All that marital duty was likely to end up in a child. I knew that, even before Juliet gave me her unhelpful little talk. It's the outside of enough that you're throwing a tantrum over the result of your attentions. You've been aware of the facts of life much longer than I have. If you don't want me to have a baby, plague take you, why didn't you leave me alone?"

He couldn't blame her for being angry. This was all his fault.

"I can't keep my hands off you." His voice was bleak. "You know that."

With another audible exhalation, she curled her hand around the top of the gate. She shut it behind her with a hint of a slam. "Then you should be prepared to accept the consequences."

"I hoped I might have a little longer to come to terms with the idea." Toby didn't bother pretending that her pregnancy hadn't rattled him. What was the point? Most of the time, he loved that she knew him so well. But this was the price of that intimacy. He had no hope of persuading her that fathering a child didn't make him want to run for the hills.

"I doubt more time would help."

"So do I."

Another thorny silence.

"Why do you hate the idea of me bearing your child?" she asked in a small voice.

He emerged from his almighty funk to realize how profoundly his reaction had wounded her. Appalled at the damage he'd done, he stepped closer and reached for her, before he realized that he'd lost the right to hold her in his arms. "Viola...darling, no, no, you misunderstand."

"No, I don't." Her shoulders drooped with defeat. The attitude was so foreign to his brave girl that he felt sick. "I saw your face when I told you. You looked like your best friend had just died."

Viola wiped her eyes, and he loathed that he made her cry. By God, better he'd never met her than that he caused her pain. Although without her, his life would become a barren desert. By God, without her, his life had been a barren desert.

All his naughtiness in London had been a futile attempt to escape thinking too hard about the chasm gaping inside him. Now, damn it all, that inadequacy threatened to destroy the magnificent creature he'd married. Because he didn't underestimate the blow that he'd dealt her today. A blow that she didn't in any way deserve.

He struggled to speak. "Yes, it was a shock – and I know an apology is hellish inadequate, but I apologize nonetheless."

"It is inadequate." Tears thickened her voice.

"I'm sure you'll be a wonderful mother. The problem is me. What sort of father will I make? The only example I have is the devil who sired me. What if I mistreat my son or daughter, the way he mistreated me? Even worse, what if he was right about me all this time? What if I am a complete waste of the air I breathe? A child needs more from its father than a ready quip and a too extensive knowledge of London's trouble spots."

He winced to hear his voice break. He loathed confessing the truth about himself, although Viola was sure to find him out in the end. He was astonished that she hadn't found him out already.

"Oh, Toby," she murmured, and the aching pity in her tone burned his skin like acid. He braced for some meaningless reply, but the silence returned, sharp as knives.

Turning away, she fumbled with the gate. She stumbled out, leaving him alone in the dark. He released a long breath, as he recognized that he'd destroyed an irreplaceable treasure. His weakness and selfishness and cowardice had snatched something precious and smashed it to pieces forever.

And he couldn't bear it.

# CHAPTER TWENTY-FIVE

His heart as heavy as stone, Toby followed Viola into the empty aisle separating two lines of stalls. When she stopped with her back to him, her heaving shoulders and erratic breaths betrayed that she was crying.

Guilt punched him anew. "Viola..."

He raised his hands, before once again letting them drop to his side. The blessed peace that she always gave him was absent. Instead, he was all roiling self-hatred and remorse. Until now, he hadn't realized just how he'd come to rely on that stable center to his whirling world over these last halcyon weeks.

Toby felt lost. Untethered. Insubstantial. The way that he had as a boy, listening to his father conduct another caustic assessment of his character, his intelligence, and his potential.

"Viola, I..." Again, he trailed off. Because what could he say?

Toby detested feeling so helpless. He didn't know where to step without causing her further injury.

She turned to face him. With her eyes red and wet, she looked the picture of misery. Another excruciating stab of guilt. He had reason to regret that she'd stepped into the lamplight.

Especially when her jaw firmed, and her eyes sharpened. He supposed that she was about to say that she was leaving. Dear God above, how on earth would he survive her departure? But after this, how could she stay?

To his knee-weakening relief, she didn't straightaway announce that she meant to order the carriage to carry her back to Afton Park. "I almost wish your father had never been born. Except if he didn't exist, neither would you."

"Better I didn't," he said bitterly.

"Toby, you have to rise above self-pity." Her eyes narrowed. "There's too much at stake."

"Self-pity?" For the first time, his temper spiked. "What the hell gives you the right to say that?"

She didn't back away. She never backed away. This was gallant Viola. She'd face down Satan himself, if he dared to stand in her way.

"I'm your wife. I'm soon to be the mother of your child." Her strident tone softened. "I...care for you."

Before he could say that he cared for her, too, she rushed on. Perhaps for the best. In the circumstances, any declarations from him would sound cheap.

"I'd hoped that these last months had overcome your father's poisonous influence. You've seemed so much happier. You've even shown signs of being settled here at Brazey."

"I have been," he said urgently. "I am."

"I've been a naïve idiot." One hand cut the air to repudiate his response. "I've had you for a season.

Your father had you for most of your life. How on earth can I compete? You hear his voice, don't you?"

"I—"

She didn't wait for the answer. "That voice insists that you'll be a deficient parent, just as you're sure that you make a deficient earl. That voice insists that if our child takes after you, it will be a disaster." Her voice roughened. "That voice is a filthy lie."

He sighed as if his world came to an end. In a very real sense, it did. "My father was considered one of the cleverest men in England."

Her lips thinned. "He was stupid about anything other than the Etruscans. He had no heart. In human terms, he was as dead as that civilization he devoted his life to. If he'd possessed an ounce of generosity, he'd have devoted himself to the motherless boy in his custody instead."

Toby's sweeping gesture discounted her statement. "He tried to create someone just like him. What if he succeeded? If he did, I'm not fit to be a parent."

"Toby, you act as if you have no say in any of this." Viola looked more obstinate. "If you don't want to be a bad parent, don't be."

"That's all very well for you to say. You grew up in a loving home. You have a model for how to nurture a child. The example I have—"

"The example you have is enough to tell you that if you feel the urge to do what your father did, just stop and do the exact opposite. I'd call that a useful example, if a negative one. Just as useful as the example of a loving home that I have." She paused to suck in a breath and wipe her eyes. She wasn't crying now. She was too busy fighting. "Anyway, you're nothing like your father."

"That's true," he said flatly. "He was famous for his brilliance, while I'm as thick as a brick."

The remark sparked a snort of contempt. "No, you're not. You've got a fine mind. More than that, you have a good heart. I haven't been married to you all these months without seeing that. If you listen to your heart, you won't go astray. In life or as a parent. Do you hear me, Toby? Your sire failed to turn you into a self-satisfied prig. Every day, I thank God that he did. You'll be a marvelous father."

He knew that she believed what she said. But to him, it was just words.

Because his father had been right about him. It was bad enough that Viola was bound to such a wretch for life. But making him responsible for an innocent? The thought left him wanting to sink deep underground and never come up again. "What if I'm not? I couldn't bear to inflict a childhood like mine on another living being."

"You speak as if you're alone in this endeavor." Her jaw firmed. "I'll be at your side."

"Will you?" Skepticism edged his question.

"What on earth are you thinking?" Aghast, she regarded him. "That I'm going to give you up as a hopeless case and hare back to Papa? If that's what you want, you'll be disappointed. I intend to fight for our future. I hope you'll fight with me."

"I don't want you to go." He forced the words out past the roaring relief that crammed his throat and threatened to knock him to his knees.

Viola wasn't leaving him. Gratitude crashed through him like a landslide.

"Then I make you a promise. I'll stay with you forever."

"You can't make that promise." His lips felt as stiff as wood. "Not now. Not when you're carrying my baby. You're forgetting that my mother died in childbirth."

The last half hour had been the worst experience of Viola's life. Worse than her humiliation when she'd stepped before an avidly curious crowd to admit to sneaking out of the ballroom to kiss Toby. Worse even than reading unequivocal rejection in her husband's eyes when she told him that she was pregnant.

But this morning, she hadn't understood the titanic problem facing her. By heaven, she did now.

What a lot of sadness Toby had known as a boy. A father who was callous and cold. A mother dead before her son had a chance to know her.

Caution counseled her to step with care. Except that Viola had stepped with care, and the problem between them had only grown. Perhaps it was time to speak out. Which was good, because so far, she'd been brutally frank.

"I'm not going to die," she said, as if the idea was preposterous. When the bleak truth was that it wasn't. She was sickly aware that women died in childbirth all the time. Not just Toby's mother.

"That's wishful thinking." She hated Toby's cynical expression. "What about your mother?"

Viola realized with a shock that she'd never told Toby about her mother. Reminder that for all their closeness over these last glorious days, they had so much more to discover about each other. "She fell off a horse."

He frowned. "She didn't die in childbed?"

"No, she broke her neck during a hunt." Her voice cracked. While Viola had only been five at the time of the accident, the memory retained the power to hurt. She rarely spoke of that tragic day, which was why Toby hadn't heard the story. "She was a punishing rider, and she set her mount at a fence that was too high. From what I can gather, she had three easy deliveries with my sisters and me. She was a Castellaine. They're renowned as excellent breeders. I have no reason to think I'll be the exception to that rule."

Her admission didn't appear to reassure him. "Nonetheless, you can't promise you'll live."

"No, I can't. Nobody can." She sighed with more impatience. "But you and I are mad for each other. We're young and healthy. We're likely to have a horde of children before we're done. You can't fly up into the boughs like a hysterical ninny, every time I get pregnant."

"Like a hysterical ninny?" he repeated on a rising note of resentment.

It seemed that she'd definitely decided against sparing his feelings. "Yes." Her tone firmed. "Anyone with half a brain, even the dullard your father called you, knows that you're not like him. A good father is someone who loves their child and protects it and wants the best for it. Are you saying that you're incapable of loving our baby?"

"I—"

She realized that she'd marched right up to him and her nose was only an inch from his impressive chest. "The fact that you're out here tearing yourself to shreds with worry tells me that you're desperate to be a wonderful father and the idea of failing is too awful to accept. Otherwise you wouldn't give a fig."

She saw that she cut him to the quick. "Of course I bloody well care." A couple of horses poked their heads out of their stalls to see what was going on.

"Then show me that you do by standing up and saying you want our child. Don't make me feel like I have to do this on my own."

"You won't do this on your own, Viola. Don't be an idiot."

"I want you beside me in every way. A physical presence isn't enough." She glared at him. "I want to know that you're with me in spirit, too."

His lips turned down. "You don't ask for much, do you?"

"I deserve your best." She spread her hands in appeal. "Our child deserves that, too."

He looked weary. "I'm not sure I can measure up to what you expect."

An angry growl emerged from her throat. "The man I married is strong. He doesn't run away from a small challenge like having a child." Her tone gentled. "Instead, he'll love that baby, and do everything he can to ensure it thrives and has a happy upbringing."

"Viola, you underestimate the scale of the difficulty. You keep talking about love, but I don't know what love is. I never had any love growing up. Nor have I experienced any love as an adult."

When Toby tunneled one hand through his hair, a lock fell over his high forehead. Viola had spent most of the day wanting to wring her husband's neck. So it seemed odd that now her heart melted at how charming he looked.

But she couldn't weaken yet. She needed his commitment to their family and their future.

"The Robsons love you."

"They're paid to serve me."

"Yes, but they also love you. They did their best to shield you from your father. You know they did. They love you now. That alone should reassure you that you're not like your papa. I'm yet to hear anyone say one affectionate word about him."

"All right," he said grimly. "The Robsons."

"And your mother loved you."

"You don't know that," he snapped.

"Yes, I do," she said with matching heat. Before he could argue, she blurted out the secret that she'd concealed for so long. "And I love you. I love you so much that I'm half-demented with it. More than that, your children will love you. Because you're irresistible and wonderful and...lovable. So lovable. Even if you can't see that."

"You..." He went white and staggered back as if she'd hit him. "Say that again."

"You're lovable."

An emphatic wave of his hand rejected her answer. "Not that bit. The bit where you said you..." His voice trailed away as if putting the thought into words was too much to manage.

She straightened her shoulders. She had to be brave. So did he, even if he was doing his best to avoid the necessity.

In soppy fantasies, she'd imagined Toby declaring his tender regard. Preferably on his knees in a rose garden.

Viola was no sentimentalist. She knew that was never going to happen. But while her husband mightn't love her the way she loved him, she was convinced that he cared for her. Deeply. She had the evidence of the past months to confirm how much he cherished her.

"I love you, Toby. I loved you almost from the first." Her voice was steady. "I defied my father and Juliet to see you because I love you. I agreed to marry you because I love you. Because I love you, I'm beside myself with joy to have your baby."

His shoulders slumped, and his eyes went glassy. "You can't love me."

Despite all her sensible lectures to herself about not asking for the moon, something bright and hopeful in Viola withered and died when she observed his unencouraging expression. "How can I not?"

She shoved away her disappointment. It wasn't as if his response was a surprise. After all, she'd refrained from telling him that she loved him, because she knew he didn't love her back.

Raising her chin, she leveled an uncompromising stare upon him. "That's not the issue today."

"It's not?" He looked lost, as he must have looked lost when he hid in his dead mother's room and tried to sense her presence. "Forgive me, but it seems a devilish important matter."

"Yes, it is. Important, but not something that needs an immediate solution. I'll go on loving you, whatever happens. That won't change."

He frowned. "I never guessed you loved me."

"That's because you're blind to the love that surrounds you. I blame your father. Now that you know, perhaps you'll look around and see how much people love you, almost in spite of yourself."

"You love me." He sounded as if he tried the words out for size. He went on with more conviction. "You love me. You've loved me this whole time, and I didn't know. Why didn't I know? I should have known. I'm such a blockhead. We've been so close. Every time I looked in your eyes, I should have seen the love. Damn it, I see it now."

"You're not a blockhead. At least about most things." Her voice was dull. "Haven't you been listening? But you are a blockhead if you throw away this chance to become part of a family, to give our baby everything you missed out on, to fill Brazey Castle with love and make it a true home."

He looked hunted. "You keep talking about love."

"Because it's the only thing strong enough to break the curse on this house." She paused and spoke with a slow emphasis that she prayed he'd heed. "And the curse on you."

At last, he abandoned the pretense of carelessness that kept the world and its curiosity at bay. Its curiosity, and the cruelty that he'd learned far too much about far too early.

For the first time, he made no attempt to hide the seeping wounds in his soul. The self-doubt. The gnawing fear. The news of her pregnancy preyed on his most profound terrors. "You think I'll make a good father?"

"I'm sure you will." She didn't have to try to sound like she believed it. Because she knew this man, and she knew that he wouldn't let her or her baby down. As she'd told him, if he wasn't so frantic to do the right thing, this awful scene would never have occurred.

She waited, as he worked through everything that she'd said. His expression shifted from heartbreakingly vulnerable to brooding to determination. She could guess how excruciating it was to face up to what he needed to do.

No, she wouldn't soften and take him in her arms. She might long to comfort the lost and lonely little boy that he'd once been, but right now, she needed him to step up to his obligations.

Relief made her head swim, as she watched him stiffen his shoulders. He set his jaw at a purposeful angle. "I've let you down badly, Viola. I promise you now that I'll do my best."

Viola sucked in her first full breath since she'd told Toby about the baby. Despite all the forces ranged against her, she'd succeeded. It was going to be all right. She felt like dancing and shouting hallelujahs.

But she kept a rein on her tumultuous reaction. He remained as skittish as a shying horse.

She had every faith in him coming good in the long run, but she needed to treat him with extreme care until he'd settled to the idea of having a child. He wasn't there yet, though her aching heart told her that he'd get there in the end.

"Your best will be outstanding."

Toby stared at her as if she was a strange mythical being beyond his ken. "You sound so certain."

By now, she felt easy enough to snort with impatience. "Of course I'm certain. The only person who underestimates you, my darling husband, is you yourself."

He frowned, less in displeasure than puzzlement. "I've been acting like an ass, haven't I? Your news put me in a complete spin. I couldn't think past my own dread." He shot her a direct look. "Will you forgive me for being such a deuced selfish brute?"

With each subtle sign that he emerged from his panic, Viola's tension faded. Since she'd told him about the baby, she'd felt like she'd swallowed a hundred cobras. Toby wasn't the only person who had been terrified. The idea of losing everything that she'd created since her marriage left her rigid with fear. Nor did she want to contemplate a future where she was torn between her husband and her child.

Now something taut and frightened deep inside her loosened and settled. Toby would be fine. Thank heaven.

"Of course I forgive you. I love you."

The first time that she'd told Toby she loved him, he'd reacted as if she bit him. But she noticed with growing hope that every time she spoke the words, he verged closer to accepting them. Perhaps by the time he was sixty, he might feel ready to say them back to her.

She refused to dwell on the lack of romantic declarations. As she'd told him, today they needed him to wrap his mind around the idea of a baby. Sweet vows of devotion could wait.

Until now, he'd been too on edge to touch. But after their fraught encounter, she was desperate for some gesture of affection. When she extended her hand, she noticed that it was trembling.

She'd won. Or won as much as she was ever going to win at this stage. But it had been a close-run thing. As reaction set in, she felt ready to collapse in a heap on the tiled floor.

He took her hand, and his lips twisted in what approached a smile. Not quite, but getting there. "There's no 'of course' about it. My father remembered every single one of my infractions and continued to punish me for them until the day he died."

"We've already established that your father was a tyrant and an overweening bully." Viola stepped closer. How she wanted his arms around her, but after what they'd just been through, she wasn't confident enough to ask him to hold her. "I, on the other hand, am a saint, and when I say I forgive you, I do. Utterly and wholeheartedly."

Her nonsense achieved its aim. This time, his smile looked a little more convincing.

He raised her hand to kiss her knuckles. The reverence in the gesture reassured her as nothing else could. "Then shall we share a kiss of peace, my lovely and far too merciful wife?"

She'd spent too much of today crying. His soft question sent more tears rushing to her eyes. Only now that she'd come through did she admit how this rift with the man she loved had ripped at her.

"I'd like that," she said in a choked voice, angling her face up.

To her surprise, he didn't take up her invitation straightaway. "You're crying again."

With a tenderness that she'd feared lost forever, his thumb brushed her wet lashes. A clogged huff of laughter escaped her. "I believe a lady expecting a happy event is inclined to be overemotional. Or so all our neighbors used to say. I've never been with child before, so I can't speak from experience."

He rolled his eyes, and for the first time, he looked like the man she'd married. Her giddy heart skipped a beat. "We've got six soggy months to look forward to?"

Despite his sardonic response, he didn't sound like he minded. The fact that he felt capable of joking about the baby told Viola that he was coming to terms with becoming a father.

"I'll try and keep my feelings in check."

"No need." He shrugged. "I'm sure I'll cope."

Startled, she realized that while she'd always believed that – she'd always had more confidence in Toby than he had in himself – he now believed it, too.

Relief tumbled over into happiness. "You will."

"Now kiss me, Viola."

She rose on her toes and touched her lips to his.

"You can do better than that," he murmured, lashing his arms around her and crushing her against his body for a passionate kiss, unlike any kiss they'd shared before. Perhaps because they'd faced the devastating possibility of losing each other. As she'd told him, she'd never abandon him, but the thought of living together as strangers, hostile or not, turned her blood to ice.

Viola gave herself up to the seeking heat of Toby's lips. Her heart had undergone so many powerful emotions today. Excitement. Despair. Anger. Pity. Love. Devastation. Now it raced, as an unquenchable tide of hunger rose.

Why not? What could be more life-affirming than union with the husband she loved? They celebrated their enduring bond, after so very nearly coming to ruin. Even more, they celebrated the prospect of a new member of their family.

Her knees threatening to fold beneath her, she drew away and stared up at Toby. At least she no longer had to hide her adoration. "We've never made love in the stables."

"I know. Is it safe?"

"The grooms are at dinner in the servants' hall."

"No, I mean is it safe for the baby?"

With that, Viola realized that she was right to predict that he'd be a magnificent father. Because if ever a man looked ready to ignite with desire, it was Toby.

She took his hand to lead him toward an empty stall just down from Belvedere's. "Dr. Purcell says marital relations may continue."

"God bless Dr. Purcell," Toby said fervently, opening the gate and letting her precede him inside. He stepped in and glanced around with a disgusted expression. "I'd pictured seducing you on piles of hay."

Viola surveyed the pristine space and hid a smile. "These stables are far too well-managed."

"I'll have a word with O'Toole."

She backed toward the wall and sent Toby a come-hither look under her lashes. "We can do it standing up."

With a predatory prowl, he trailed her across to the shadowy corner. Even without seeing his face, she sensed his passionate intent. Possessive hands seized her hips. She didn't mind. Because she had a feeling that while he possessed her, she possessed him right back.

She stared up at him, trying to read his expression, but this obscure corner was too dark. "What is it?"

He gave a long-suffering sigh and spoke in a resigned tone. "The Castellaines are known for their fertility?"

She smiled with a hint of smugness. "Yes."

"God help me."

"I should have warned you before we got married."

"At least somebody should." His voice lowered into seriousness. "I'm sorry, Viola. I've been an idiot. I promise not to put you through this drama next time."

"That's good to hear." She cradled his face in both hands. "My constitution won't support it."

"Mine either."

Her heart flipped over, as he hitched her up off the floor. With unconcealed eagerness, she wrapped her legs around his hips and arched forward. "Please, Toby, take me to heaven."

He leaned in until her back hit the wall behind her. She felt him settling between her thighs. Through his breeches, his member was hard against her stomach. "That would be my pleasure, sweetheart."

"And mine," she whispered, tipping her face up for another kiss. "Always mine."

# CHAPTER TWENTY-SIX

*Brazey Castle, March 1818*

"He's the finest boy ever born in the history of the world," Toby murmured, as his newborn son nestled in his arms.

His wife responded with a weary laugh. "Perhaps a slight exaggeration."

He glanced up from the rosy face of the sleeping child to study Viola, propped up against a stack of pillows in the earl's massive bed. She wore a rose-pink velvet peignoir, and her thick dark gold hair was confined in a single plait that draped over one shoulder.

It was late, near midnight, and the candlelight lent her a soft radiance. Or perhaps it wasn't candlelight at all, but happiness. Outside, a snowstorm raged, but in this chamber, all was warmth and contentment.

"Not at all, Lady Renfrew. And I'll add that his mother is the cleverest, loveliest, bravest, best girl in England."

She smiled at him. "Only in England?"

He smiled back. "In the world."

"Better."

He went back to staring entranced at his son. The baby had been born with a thick swatch of tawny hair. More Anstey than Sutton, although Toby hoped that one day soon those blue eyes might deepen into Viola's silvery gray.

His father would loathe that the child lacked the Sutton coloring. Toby waited for the usual resentment to sour his gut at the thought of the late earl. But his world overflowed with too many marvelous gifts. His father's toxic influence couldn't find anywhere to perch.

Toby sucked in a breath and realized with astonishment, that the bitterness was gone. Herbert Sutton was dead to him at last. All his life, he'd carried the burden of his father's contempt. Odd that the burden had lifted without him noticing.

The baby had been born a couple of hours ago, after a short labor that Dr. Purcell had called very easy. Toby, who had felt every minute of Viola's ordeal as if it was a year of torture, wouldn't have described it like that.

With the onset of his wife's labor, Toby had been banished to the library downstairs. In a life too full of agonizing situations, the delay before Mrs. Robson had come downstairs to tell him that all was well counted as the worst.

It turned out that his countess had stayed true to her Castellaine bloodlines. The baby was born healthy and squalling, and Viola had sailed through the whole experience. When Toby was allowed into the bedchamber to see her and his son at last, she'd remarked that he looked worse for wear than she did.

Toby had responded with a dutiful laugh, but only when he'd kissed her did he truly believe that she was in no danger. For six long months, the thought of losing her had tormented him, although he'd done his best to hide his fears. This was despite Viola being the picture of health throughout her pregnancy.

"Have you thought about names?" Viola asked after a harmonious silence.

He glanced up. "Have you?"

She looked thoughtful. "We could call him after Papa. Or Leighton."

Leighton and Kate had become regular visitors to Brazey, as had Viola's family. Lord Portdown had soon overcome his doubts about the match, when he saw how happy his daughter was. These days, Toby was proud to welcome his friends and kin to the old house that had once felt like such a prison.

He went back to gazing at the infant. He'd never found babies very interesting before, but this one was utterly fascinating. The tiny features scrunched up then smoothed, as if a dream disturbed his peace. Did newborns dream? Toby had no idea.

"Two Leightons in the family might be asking for trouble," he said absently. While his cousin had become an exemplary family man, in his time he'd been called the worst lord in London. Whereas it was already obvious to Toby that this little one was going to fill a catalog with his perfections. "All the Sutton names are rather daunting. Herbert. Horace. Vavasour."

"Vavasour?" Viola asked on a splutter of amusement.

"Yes, the fellow with the piggy eyes and the big collar in the gallery."

"Then we definitely won't call him Vavasour. What about following Frain tradition and calling him something Shakespearean? Papa would like that."

Toby wandered over to sit on the edge of the bed beside his wife. He wasn't a man prone to dynastic thoughts, but there was something profoundly satisfying about sharing this quiet warm room with his cherished helpmeet and his firstborn. "Bottom?"

"No, you lunatic." Viola punched him gently on the arm, careful not to disturb the baby. "What about Julius or Antony?"

"A little too grim and Roman."

"What about someone from a comedy? Orsino? Orlando?"

Toby stared down at the child. "Orsino Sutton? Orlando Sutton?"

The baby's lips pursed as if he considered each option in turn before discounting them.

"Benedict?"

"Benedict Sutton?"

The baby frowned, then sighed and settled back to slumber. Toby glanced up and smiled at Viola. "He seems to like that."

"Then Benedict he is." She glanced down at her son in her husband's arms. "Do you want me to take him?"

"He's happy where he is. You'll get your turn."

Viola smiled with unabashed approval. "I didn't think you'd be so smitten."

"Damn right I'm smitten. Didn't I tell you what a splendid little lad he is?"

Viola rolled her eyes in the way that always made him want to laugh. "Only about a hundred times."

Toby leaned in, moving gingerly so as not to disturb Benedict. He kissed Viola with all the poignant gratitude that welled up in his soul. "He's almost as splendid as his mother."

She raised one hand to cup his jaw and bring him back for another kiss so sweet that it dissolved his bones to molten sugar. "I can't tell you how touching it is to see how much you love Benedict."

Love? Was that what this piercing feeling was? This aching weight in his chest? This invincible need to protect and nurture and encourage?

Toby had always said that he didn't know what love was. But what else could he call his all-encompassing wonder as he looked at his baby son, but love? A feeling that needed a million words to do it justice.

Or just one. Love. Love. *Love.*

As he lifted his head to meet his wife's warm gaze, he realized what a blind fool he'd been. Because he loved Benedict. Of course he did. But the emotion wasn't unfamiliar. The emotion had swept into his life the day he met Viola.

Viola, who had given him a purpose and promised him that she was on his side forever. Viola, who thrilled him as no other woman ever had. Viola, who was so smart and funny. And valiant and loyal. Viola, who had made his life complete in ways that he hadn't even known were lacking.

Viola, who gave him the priceless gift of this beautiful child.

And another priceless gift. An unconditional love that demanded nothing in return.

Or at least so she'd once told him, when they'd been at odds and he'd been paralyzed with terror at the thought of losing her.

He should have recognized then that he loved her. But he'd been too stupid and too caught up in old suffering to recognize the radiant truth right in front of him.

Toby swallowed to shift the jagged mass blocking his throat. His voice emerged as a low rasp. "You once told me you loved me."

She frowned, as if she didn't remember, and his newly awakened heart cramped in denial. She wasn't a shallow woman. He prayed that she hadn't changed. Although he remained painfully aware that since that day in the stables, she'd never spoken the words again. Even if when he looked back over the last months, he could discern her love in every moment they'd shared.

He'd been wrong about so much. By Jericho, he couldn't be wrong about that.

"I did."

"Have you stopped?" The question emerged stark and vulnerable.

"Don't be a dolt, Toby. I haven't stopped." A self-derisive smile turned down her lips. "I love you more now than I did when we got married. And I loved you so much then, I thought I'd die of it."

Thank God. He blinked away the unfamiliar mist that formed in front of his eyes. "I'm so glad."

She made a helpless gesture. "I wasn't sure you liked me loving you when you don't love me back. But my feelings haven't changed. For all my quietness, I'm stubborn. Juliet always said so."

He'd come to value his wife's strength of character. She'd make an outstanding mother. And he, he was now sure, was going to be a good father. He swore it on his son's downy head. "Juliet got it right."

"Juliet is always right," Viola said in a long-suffering tone.

"But, my darling, you aren't."

"Oh?" A curious gray gaze fastened on him. Not for the first time, he felt like she penetrated all the way to his soul.

"You said I don't love you."

"But—"

He rushed on. He'd never declared his love to anyone before. It turned out to be devilish nerve-racking, even now that he knew that his wife returned his feelings. "When I love you more with every breath I take. When you transformed my life. When I hold you in my heart always."

Her eyes widened, and her lips parted in astonishment. "Toby, I—"

Again, he cut her off. "I love you, Viola." He sucked in a shuddering breath, and the next time he spoke, the words emerged more naturally. "I love you, my darling."

He watched a beatific smile illuminate her features. She was always beautiful to him, but she'd never looked lovelier. Tears brightened her eyes, and emotion thickened her voice. "And I love you. So much."

She curled her arms around him and kissed him with a clumsy enthusiasm that reminded him of the entrancing innocent he'd wed. Without thinking, he surged forward to embrace her.

A mewl from Benedict reminded Toby to be careful. But it was too late. The baby was awake and crying.

With a choked laugh, Viola shifted back to take the baby. "Our son objects to our excess of emotion."

Content with the world, Toby arranged himself on the bed beside Viola and curved his arm around her shoulder, as she fumbled with one hand to open the peignoir.

"He'll get used to it," Toby said in a comfortable tone that would have been foreign to the flibbertigibbet she'd married all those months ago.

"He'll have to," Viola agreed, settling the baby to her nipple.

A tranquil silence fell. Toby cuddled his wife to his side and stared down at this small miracle that they'd created together. Created out of love, despite him being a little slow to recognize that was the case.

Life had blessed him with so much. A wonderful wife. A gorgeous son. And a love that would inspire and sustain him to the end of his days.

What a very lucky man he was.

# EPILOGUE

*Brazey Castle, April 1841*

"What do you think?" When Viola stepped back, she felt her husband's arms curl around her waist from behind.

"It's fit for a queen." Toby dropped a kiss on her shoulder, bare under the wide collar of her blue silk dress.

"It had better be." Viola surveyed the east tower's main bedchamber. It looked magnificent, draped in gold brocade and furnished in the latest fashion.

When the young Queen Victoria and her new husband Prince Albert had announced their intentions of visiting historic Brazey Castle and staying the night, everyone on the estate had dived into a flurry of activity. The staff had spent the last fortnight dashing around as if the world was coming to an end. The grooms in particular had a reputation to maintain. In the stables waited a perfect white pony as a gift for Her Majesty. Throughout England, the riding horses produced on the Brazey estate were renowned as the best in the land.

Now it was the afternoon of the day before the royal party's arrival. Everything was ready.

Toby turned Viola in his arms and stared down at her with the glow in his eyes that she'd long ago recognized as invincible love. "You've done a marvelous job. Would it be disloyal to say that I wish all the fuss was over and I had you to myself again?"

Viola studied her handsome husband. The years had been kind to him. He had the sort of chiseled features that became more distinguished with age. He told her that she didn't look a day older than the girl he'd married, but she thought he needed glasses.

She wasn't as slim as she'd once been. Bearing six children saw to that, and her thick hair had darkened from honey to a rich mink brown. But when she looked in the mirror, she saw a happy woman. Her face showed the marks of years of love and laughter, so she didn't mind a bit that maturity had left its traces on her.

"If they heard you, they'd rush you away to the Tower and chop off your head." She leaned forward, cursing the new, fuller skirts that placed so much fabric between her and her husband's body. The dresses of her youth hadn't been as bulky. "Which would be a pity when it's such a pretty head."

His grip on her waist firmed. "You're biased."

"I am," she agreed, as he brought her close for a tender kiss. A tender kiss that had warmed into heat by the time he raised his head to inspect her with green eyes that retained a hint of the rascal.

"How is it that I still go weak at the knees when you kiss me?" she asked in a shaky voice.

His laugh was affectionate. "Magic."

He kissed her again with more intent, so Viola was breathless when he pulled away.

"Even after the Queen moves on, the house will be full," she said. "All the children will be here for Easter."

"We don't stand on ceremony with the children." Toby's lips curved in a smile. "I can whisk you away for a tryst, without worrying about committing high treason."

Viola rested her head on his chest. "I'm so looking forward to seeing them."

"So am I. Although I'm also looking forward to our trip to Paris next month." Two years into their marriage, Toby had taken her to Paris as promised. It had been wonderful, and they'd become frequent visitors since.

But it was also wonderful to come back to Brazey and their rambunctious brood of offspring. Toby and Viola had brought up their three sons and three daughters to be free spirits, which had made for many interesting times but few tedious ones. Viola was sure that the antics of his son and grandchildren kept the late earl turning in his grave.

*Good.*

Tonight Benedict arrived back from touring Italy. Tomorrow, they'd see their daughter Jessica, who had spent the last year studying painting with the famous Marina Mackinnon in the Highlands of Scotland. Nineteen-year-old Orlando was home from his studies at Cambridge, where he excelled in the new science. Right now, the twins Lysander and Rosalind were in the schoolroom with their tutor, while Viola and Toby's youngest, five-year-old Hermia, was out in the grounds with her beloved nanny Miss Compton.

Hermia had arrived as a surprise. With the twins, who were now sixteen, Viola had imagined the family was complete. She'd imagined wrongly. Now everyone at Brazey was under the spell of an exquisite little sprite, who promised to grow up to become the image of Toby's mother.

Life was good. Brazey was no longer cold and unwelcoming, but a beloved family home. She and Toby had only grown closer with time, and their happiness spread its influence through the whole house. The children were all busy and thriving. When Viola thought back to the scandalous beginnings of her marriage, she still had trouble believing that so much good had flowed out of their hurried wedding all those years ago.

"We can have plenty of trysts in Paris," she said.

Toby cast a meaningful glance toward the pristine silk covering the huge bed that they'd ordered from London.

Viola gave a horrified giggle. "No, we couldn't. That really would be treason. The palace informed us that everything must be brand-new for Her Majesty."

Toby shrugged and stepped toward the bed. "Don't you fancy a romp in the royal sheets, my lady?"

She narrowed her eyes, even as she thrilled to the idea. "You remain a scoundrel at heart, don't you?"

His smile took on a familiar hint of devilry. He sat on the bed and drew Viola between his spread thighs. With no hint of reluctance, she cooperated. "You like me that way."

"I love you that way." She kissed him with all the adoration in her heart. So much adoration that she took her time to do the feeling justice.

Toby swung her around, until she lay under him on the bed. She reveled in the way his muscled weight pressed her into the mattress.

"I love you, Viola," he said, his voice serious. "I hallow the day you came into my life."

How silly that after near a quarter century of marriage, he could stir her emotions to the point of tears. She blinked away the moisture in front of her eyes and placed her hands on his powerful shoulders. "I didn't come into your life. You crashed into mine, and nothing has been the same since, beloved."

"Thank heaven for broken branches," he murmured, reaching down for the hem of her voluminous skirts.

"Thank heaven for you, my darling," she whispered and gave herself up to her husband's passionate kiss.

# ABOUT THE AUTHOR

Australian Anna Campbell has written 11 multi award-winning historical romances for Avon HarperCollins and Grand Central Publishing. As an independently published author, she's released more than 30 bestselling stories. Right now, she is working on a new series called Scoundrels of Mayfair, set amidst the glamour and sensuality of Regency London. Anna has won numerous awards for her stories, including RT Book Reviews Reviewers Choice, the Booksellers Best, the Golden Quill (three times), the Heart of Excellence (twice), the Write Touch, the Aspen Gold (twice), and the Australian Romance Readers' favorite historical romance (five times).

Anna loves to hear from her readers. You can find her at:

Website: www.annacampbell.com

facebook.com/AnnaCampbellFans

twitter.comAnnaCampbellOz

bookbub.com/authors/anna-campbell

# The Worst Lord in London: Scoundrels of Mayfair Book 1

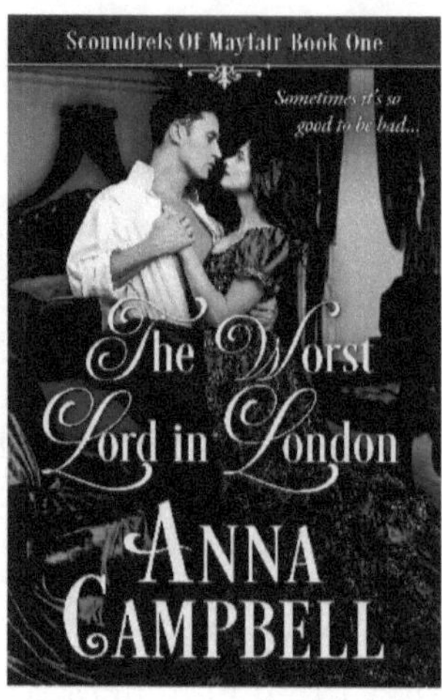



## *Headlong into the unknown...*

Independent, willful Kate Starr has cherished a penchant for handsome Lord Shelburn since she was sixteen years old, but as a mill-owning industrialist, she moves in a different world from the libertine earl. Then one fateful day, Shelburn invites her to accompany him in a scandalous race, and immediate physical attraction swiftly turns into blazing passion.

## *The hunter caught...*

Leighton Anstey, Earl of Shelburn, glories in his reputation as the worst lord in London. His fame as an irresistible seducer is unrivaled, although his amours are notable for their explosive heat, not their longevity. The dashing lord has never met a woman who can hold his wandering attention, until he tumbles into a liaison with a mysterious woman who enthrals him, body and soul.

## *A brief encounter or a forever love?*

Neither Kate nor Shelburn views their torrid affair as more than a shooting star, flaring red-hot for a brilliant instant, then destined to fade to nothing. But does the fiery desire raging between them blind them to the chance of finding lifelong happiness together?

# The Trouble with Earls: Scoundrels of Mayfair Book 2

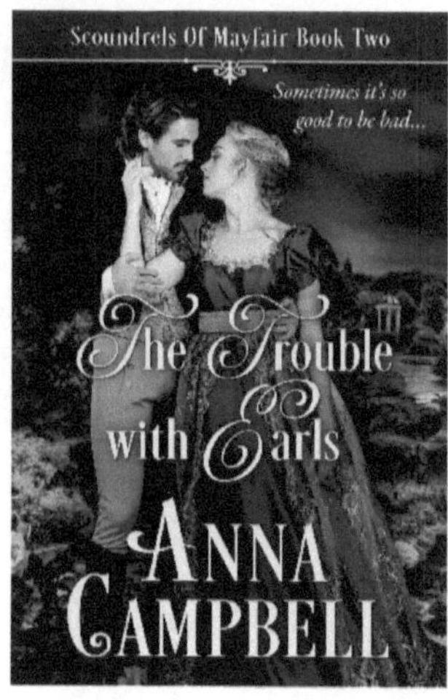

## *The wild rogue and the wallflower!*

Toby Sutton, Earl of Renfrew, is a notorious libertine with no interest in marrying a wellbred young miss and making her his countess. But when he meets lovely Lady Viola Frain, irresistible desire creates an explosive mix with his native recklessness. Within a matter of days, he and Viola are joined in a hurried marriage of convenience, patched together to scotch an almighty scandal.

## *Marry in haste, repent at leisure?*

With two spectacular older sisters, shy Viola Frain is used to being the overlooked member of the family. When handsome Lord Renfrew literally falls at her feet, Viola finally meets a man who thinks she's special. But before the fragile bloom of

attraction can flower, she finds herself wed to
Renfrew and whisked away to brooding Brazey
Castle, where shadows of old tragedy threaten her
frail hope of happiness.

### *The trouble with earls...*

Society watches avidly, forecasting disaster for an
alliance between two people so mismatched. Can
passion unite the rake and the recluse? Or is the
truth just as Viola fears? That the trouble with earls
is that they're bound to break your heart.

# The Last Duke She'd Marry: Scoundrels of Mayfair Book 3

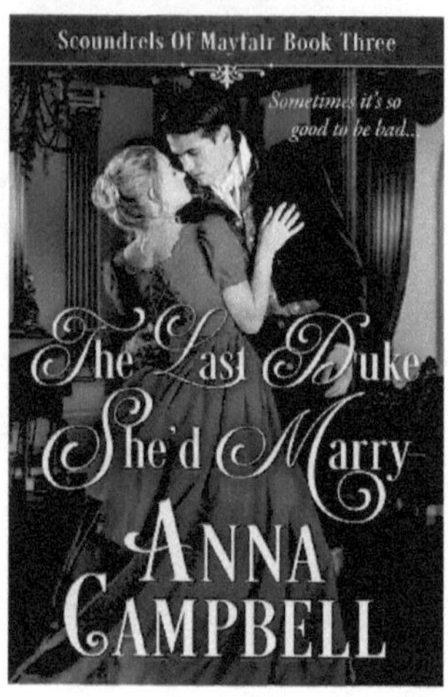



*She wants to be a duchess. Just not HIS duchess!*

Pure and proper Lady Juliet Frain was born to be a duchess. Everyone says so. Now society awaits the announcement of the elegant beauty's engagement to the dignified and honorable Duke of Granville. However all Juliet's plans go awry when she meets the scandalous but sinfully attractive Duke of Evesham. The wild libertine is the last man Juliet wants to find irresistible, yet somehow she can't keep her hands off him. And suddenly to her chagrin, nobody is calling Juliet either pure or proper!

*He's no Romeo...*

After ten riotous years on the Continent, Lucas Hebden, Duke of Evesham, has returned to London, trailing a well-earned reputation as a rake and a reprobate. But an unexpected loss in a card game finds him far from London's fleshpots and playing at amateur dramatics in the country. Even worse, he's starting to confuse the poetic passion in *Romeo and Juliet* with the real-life passion that has him pursuing his disapproving but breathtakingly lovely leading lady. It's clear that Lady Juliet Frain has no time for bad boys, and any sensible man would give up – but then nobody ever called Evesham sensible!

**When Juliet's suitor Granville arrives to propose, it's the battle of the dukes! Once the curtain falls, which duke will emerge victorious and take the starring role in Juliet's heart?**

Coming in 2023!

# The Duke Says I Do:
## Scoundrels of Mayfair Book 4

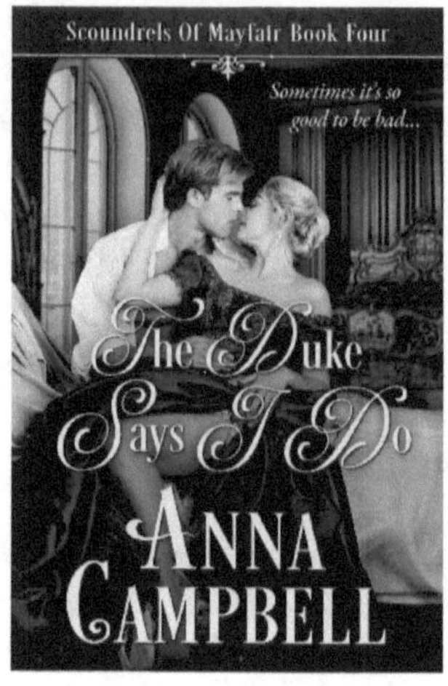

Portia's story! Coming early 2024.